I've travelled the world twice over,
Met the famous: saints and sinners,
Poets and artists, kings and queens,
Old stars and hopeful beginners,
I've been where no-one's been before,
Learned secrets from writers and cooks
All with one library ticket
To the wonderful world of books.

© Janice James.

The wisdom of the ages
Is there for you and me,
The wisdom of the ages,
In your local library.

There's large print books
And talking books,
For those who cannot see,
The wisdom of the ages,
It's fantastic, and it's free.

Written by Sam Wood, aged 92

THE RELIC MURDERS

In 1523, Roger Shallot, self-proclaimed doctor and physician, rogue, charlatan and secret emissary of King Henry VIII and Cardinal Wolsey, is commissioned to steal back for the crown the Orb of Charlemagne, now under close guard at the priory at Clerkenwell before being taken to the Hapsburg Emperor Charles V. Roger and his master, Benjamin Daunbey, have no choice but to agree. They enter the house by stealth, only to discover that a massacre has taken place and the Orb has been stolen. Drawn into murder, mayhem and blackmail, they race against time to find the Orb and save their necks.

Books by Michael Clynes
Published by The House of Ulverscroft:

THE WHITE ROSE MURDERS
THE POISONED CHALICE
THE GRAIL MURDERS
THE GALLOWS MURDERS

MICHAEL CLYNES

◆

THE RELIC MURDERS

Being the sixth journal of Sir Roger Shallot
concerning certain wicked conspiracies
and horrible murders perpetrated
in the reign of King Henry VIII

Complete and Unabridged

ULVERSCROFT
Leicester

First published in Great Britain in 1988 by
Headline Book Publishing
London

First Large Print Edition
published 1998
by arrangement with
Headline Book Publishing
a division of
Hodder Headline Plc
London

The right of Michael Clynes to be identified as
the author of this work has been asserted by him
in accordance with the
Copyright, Designs and Patents Act, 1988

British Library CIP Data

Clynes, Michael
The relic murders.—Large print ed.—
Ulverscroft large print series: mystery
1. Shallot, Roger (Fictitious character)—Fiction
2. London (England)—History—16th century
—Fiction 3. Detective and mystery stories
4. Large type books
I. Title
823.9′14 [F]

ISBN 0–7089–3948–1

Published by
F. A. Thorpe (Publishing) Ltd.
Anstey, Leicestershire
Set by Words & Graphics Ltd.
Anstey, Leicestershire
Printed and bound in Great Britain by
T. J. International Ltd., Padstow, Cornwall

This book is printed on acid-free paper

For Joseph on the occasion of his 70th birthday remembering the excitement after the lecture at St Emunds's. With much love — M

Some historical personages mentioned in this text:

Henry VIII, King of England 1509 – 1547: The Great Beast or Mouldwarp

Cardinal Thomas Wolsey: Archbishop and Chancellor: Henry VIII's First Minister

Catherine of Aragon: Henry VIII's first wife, Spanish princess, aunt to Charles V

Charles V: Hapsburg ruler: Holy Roman Emperor. His empire included Spain, the Low Countries, parts of Italy and most of modern Germany. He was also 'Beloved nephew' of Catherine of Aragon.

Anne Boleyn: Second wife of Henry VIII and mother of Elizabeth I, Queen of England

Christopher Marlowe]
                     ] Elizabethan
                     ] playwrights
William Shakespeare]

Sir William Cecil; first Minister of Elizabeth I

Francis Walsingham: Elizabeth I's spy master

Thomas Cromwell: Henry VIII's principal minister after the fall of Wolsey

Alfred the Great: Anglo-Saxon king of the 9th century, regarded as founder of the British monarchy. A great war leader and ruler.

Charlemagne: Frankish ruler of the 9th century. First emperor in the West after the fall of Rome. Ruler of France and what is now the Low countries as well as most of Western Germany

Prologue

Oh, the bloody terrors of the night! Oh, Grim Death's dark shadow! How many times have I, Roger Shallot, Lord of Burpham Manor, risen from between my silken sheets, forsaking the warmth of those marvellous twins, Phoebe and Margot, leaving their luscious, marble-white limbs sprawled out in wine-soaked sleep? Lovely girls! My satin-skinned bedpans! How many times have I trotted across to my chamber, pulled back the drapes and stared out over a garden bathed in the light of a weeping moon? Oh, phantasm! Oh, horrors! Oh, the effect of too much claret! I have seen the demons dance in the moonbeams as motes in a shaft of sunlight! Oh, the night is the Devil's black book when I retreat to my cushioned chair and let my memories tumble out!

In my soul's eye I sink down into the Valley of Death where eye-pecking ravens hover above rain-sodden, evil-smelling huts in which witches, beldames of Satan, sit mumping their knees against fires of pure ice. I travel on. In the midnight of that valley I meet the Lord Satan raking over

1

the bones of long-dead men as a gardener gathers in the rotting leaves of autumn. Oh, believe me, I have seen the horrors and heard the chilling chimes at midnight! Corpses piled high like maggots caught cold in mouldy cheese! Rivers of blood splashing in torrents! Cities wrapped in the flames of hell which roar up to an implacable sky!

It's always the same at night. I awaken as if some sanctus bell in my soul tolls away the hours, the minutes, and stirs me from my sleep. Oh, I fable not! I have seen visions which would curl your hair and turn you into Medusa. They come at night when my pillows become hard and sharp, as if stuffed with thistles. Like Hamlet or Macbeth, (oh, by the way, I had my hand in both those plays) I am forced to sit until Satan sweeps into my chamber.

"Shallot!" he roars. "A man should roast away, not wither up! Look at you, past your ninetieth year and stuffed by the physicians with oils and herbs like a cook would stuff a pudding!"

The devil casts out his net of silver hooks, and dangles it before my eyes. On each hook hangs a memory of my life. And what a life! In my prime I was of medium stature and comely, with a clean-shaven face and curly, black hair and slight squint in one eye. A

2

laughing face: a bubbling-hearted boy, full of pranks and subtle mischief! Sharp wits, faster legs and the most cowardly of hearts! I have been in all the great fights (well to the back!); in all the great pursuits (firmly in the centre!); and in many valiant retreats (at least ten good horse lengths in front of anyone else!). I have diced with kings, especially fat, blubbering Henry Tudor, that Prince of Darkness! The Mouldwarp prophesied by Merlin! The Great Beast! The blood-thirsty bastard! Henry the Horrible! Henry the Eighth and, if God is good, Henry the last! Mind you, he wasn't too bad. Well, once he was in his old age and his legs turned purple with ulcers and his mind became loose as a leaf in October. I could control him then. I used to push him, in his specially constructed chair, around the galleries of Whitehall. Sometimes, just for the fun of it, I'd take him to the top of some stairs and threaten to throw him down. Oh, he'd blubber! Oh, he'd plead with a wicked, devilish glare in those piggy eyes of his! So I'd change my mind and take him back to his chamber for comforts and a glass of wine. Afterwards he'd paw at my arm.

"Roger," he'd hiss, "Roger, my soul mate."

He would kiss me on the cheek and,

3

when he'd fallen asleep, I'd wash the spot till the skin bleached. Within the hour, the fat turd would wake, screaming and yelling like a baby.

"Light the candles! Light the candles, Roger!" he'd bawl. "Look! Look in the corner! Can't you see them? The ghosts have come to plague my soul."

Corner! You'd need all of St Paul's Cathedral to harbour the ghosts waiting for Henry's soul. Gentle Thomas More, saintly Fisher, the monks of Charterhouse, the hundreds that old Jack of Norfolk hung along the Great North Road when he put down Aske's rebellion. And then my pretty ones. Anne Boleyn. Blackeyed Anne! Brave, wanton, as full of courage as a lion! Young Catherine Howard, plump and comely; soft of skin with a will of steel. Catherine of Aragon, dusky-faced, holy of mind and pure of heart. I talk of her soul rather than her physical organ — when they opened her body, her heart had shrivelled to black ash, Henry's doctors had pumped so much arsenic into her blood.

Ah well, enough of Henry. I've also diced with other princes. Francis I, rotting away with every known love disease under the sun — when he died the palace stank for weeks even though they scrubbed every ceiling, wall and floor. Catherine de Medici:

wicked and wanton, the Queen of the Poison. Charles IX, who never made up his mind whether he was a man or a woman. Selim the sot: drunk on hashish, surrounded by his houris and, in the shadows, the stranglers ready to snuff out your life as easily as you would a candle flame. And what about Philip of Spain in his dark, gold-encrusted chambers of the Escorial? And we mustn't forget that mad bugger in Moscow, must we? Oh, I have seen the times and Satan knows it. But I am not afeared! Not me! Not Sir Roger Shallot, Lord of Burpham Manor, Knight of the Garter, Justice of the Peace. I give Satan as good as I get! I call him a bag pudding, an ice-brained, splay-footed gull. I make the sign of the fig with my little finger. I climb back into my bed and cuddle down between my two lovelies. So, you young men, remember, this: whatever nocturnal terrors come, there's nothing that a prayer, a spark of courage, a cup of wine and a lovely girl can't cure. I can't vouch for the first two but I certainly can for the last!

In the morning, as now, when Phoebus rolls his chariot across the ancient sky . . . Lord, what a silly phrase! My little chaplain and secretary, that decayed dotard, wants me to use words like that! He sits squirming on his little cushions waiting for me to continue my memoirs. Every so often he interrupts to comment on my diction. Why? Because he's seen too many bloody plays, that's why! He tries to keep out of range of my ash cane — little does he know I have bought a longer one. I have seen his fat shoulders shake with mirth at some of my tales — he's soon recovered from his own tragedy, hasn't he? He was betrothed to a sweet girl, ready to become handfast at the church door. Oh yes, Shakespeare said love is blind and it must be when it comes to him. There, there now, he protests.

"You are always name dropping," he blurts out maliciously, envious of my friendship with sweet Will.

Well, look who's talking! He's always on about God — indeed, listening to his sermons, you'd think that the good Lord had breakfast with him every day. But back to his beloved. Oh, what a tragedy! Oh, the heartbreak! Oh, I laughed till my sides hurt! You see his beloved lived some miles away: she was the daughter of a prosperous yeoman. My little chaplain asked me to write love letters to her and so I did. I admit, I helped myself to some of Shakespeare's sonnets but who really cares? Will often comes here to see me and, if you can't lend a friend a phrase or two, then what's the use of friendship? Anyway, these love notes were given to a young farmer to deliver at her door. But the strangest thing happened — she never wrote back! So my little chaplain plucks up courage and goes down to see her and — guess what? Oh, the perfidy! — his betrothed had married the farmer who delivered the messages. Mind you, his heart soon healed. When he met two sisters, one tall, the other short, he asked me to which one he should pay court. Keeping my face straight, I told him that he should go for the shorter girl.

"Remember your philosophy," I declared sonorously. "When confronted with two evils, always choose the lesser."

Mind you, the girl was as innocent as a dove. Of tender years and sweet demeanour. Her mother, a prosperous tenant of mine, came all afeared to me because my chaplain had taken her daughter out for a stroll on a balmy summer's evening. The poor woman knows my chaplain. He doesn't get the straw on his clothing from helping out at harvest time! Indeed, he spends more time in my hay loft than he does in the parish church.

"Oh, please, Sir Roger," the poor woman pleaded. "Find out what your chaplain did to my daughter last night?"

I had the girl brought by the captain of

my guard to where I sit at the centre of my maze, protected by my two great wolf hounds.

(Oh yes, I may well be past my ninety-fifth year but it is surprising how few people forgive and forget. The secret agents of every crowned head of Europe, and a few beyond its borders, would pay good gold to have my old head on the tip of a pike. But enough of that for the time being. Soon I'll come to my story: about the orb of Charlemagne, about the Noctales, the Men of the Night, and old Shallot's desperate fight to stay alive in the blood-chilling days of Henry VIII.)

Anyway, pleasant things first. The young girl was as sweet and brown as a nut. I sat her on a chair and gave her a silver piece. "Tell me, my doucette," I began. "What did my chaplain teach you last night? Where did he take you?"

"Oh, he bought me some sweetmeats," the little joy replied. "And took me by the river bank."

Oh dear, I thought. "And what did you do there?" I asked.

"He took me by the hand."

"And what did you do?"

"I laughed."

"And then what?"

"He touched me on the breast."

"And what did you do?"

"I laughed," she replied, eyelids all a flutter.

"And then?"

"He touched me on the knee."

"And what did you do?" I asked.

"I laughed!"

Now the conversation went on like this for a few minutes until I stopped and said, "Sweet one, why did you laugh every time my chaplain touched you?"

"Because the sweetmeats were hidden in the pocket of my cloak all the time."

Innocent she was and simple so I gave my chaplain strict instructions to keep her that way. He should be cautious of marriage. Lust and love go hand in hand and both can wither like apples on a branch. Only the other day I was riding down a lane behind a funeral cortège: some poor woman's coffin being carried to the parish grave. The procession passed a tavern where a man sat drinking cheerfully from his tankard. As the coffin passed, I saw him put down his blackjack of ale, doff his cap and go down on his knees. Much touched by this, I rode up.

"Kind sir," I said, leaning down from my horse. "You show great respect for the dead?"

The fellow, bleary-eyed, red-faced, his nose burning like a coal in hell, just smiled back.

"Why, Lord Roger," he slurred. "It's the least I can do after forty years of marriage to her!"

Oh, I see my chaplain shake with laughter. The little noddle! The little sweet bag! My little marmoset!

"Come on. Come on." He turns in his chair, quill poised. "Sir Roger," he expostulates. "The Queen waits for the next extract of your memoirs."

He is referring, of course, to Elizabeth — lovely girl, beauteous queen, my lover, my helpmate, mother of my son, apple of my heart.

Ah well, I suppose he's right. Here, as I sit in my chamber, perched on my gold stuffed cushions, at my ease, in the centre of my manor, I can revel in its wealth. A veritable palace with its bright red bricks, its master joints picked out in black and white; its galleries of flint chequer work. Within, the rooms are decorated with cloth of gold and ermine hangings, the works of great master painters, tapestries of silk, chests stuffed full of silver and gold pots. My shelves are lined with Italian Majolica, Delft from the Low Countries, Spanish lustre ware. No rushes cover my floor but polished Flemish

10

tiles, and my windows are filled with green leaded mullioned glass. Warm stoves heat my kitchens and butteries whilst water is brought in along pure elm pipes. Oh, I lead a life of luxury, but it wasn't always like that. Time's hand draws back the curtain of the past. I sneak a look down the gloomy, vaulted passageway of history, lined with skulls and laced with the blood of those I ate and drank and, God forgive me, sometimes slept with. I must speak clearly so my words do not come out like some tangled chain: in doing so, I'll exorcise the ghosts of my salad days when I was green in judgement yet had such horrors to face.

I do not have to walk far down the long, dusty passageway of time before I meet Murder squatting there, his silver skin laced with scarlet blood, his body riven by gashed stabs, face black and full of gore, eyeballs protruding further out than they should in a living man. He has that basilisk stare, ghastly, gasping like a strangled man. His hair is upstanding, his nostrils flared with struggling, his hands stretched out like someone tugging for life. That's Murder! I met him many a time in those turbulent days of Henry VIII when I and my great friend, tall, dark, angel-faced Benjamin Daunbey, nephew of Cardinal Thomas Wolsey, were hired to hunt subtle murderers and crafty assassins. Let time be my witness, none of these was more cunning, more artful, more deceitful than those who planned to steal the Orb of Charlemagne and nearly sent old Roger to a watery grave. I cannot remain silent. Murder, though it has no tongue, will speak and I am duty bound to recall it. At Michaelmas the queen will come again. She will hear Mass secretly in my hidden chamber and, afterwards, sit at my table to drink claret and pluck at golden capon. Great Elizabeth will lean across and tweak my cheek.

"Come, Roger," she'll whisper. "Bring me the next chapter of your memoirs. Let me see those times again!"

And she will! Murder beckons me down time's sombre gallery, back into the golden, sun-filled, bloody autumn days of 1523 when King Henry, that murderous imp, still ruled England and Cardinal Wolsey, his brain teeming more than a boxful of vipers, tried to rule the king.

1

After that bloody business at the Tower in the summer of 1523, Benjamin Daunbey and I, now released from the services of Cardinal Wolsey, returned to our manor outside Ipswich. Benjamin took over the management of the estate and the running of the school he had set up for the ungrateful, snotty-nosed imps from the nearby village. I, of course, true to my nature, returned to villainy as smoothly as a duck takes to water. I was bred for villainy. I was reared on it. People shouldn't really object. I am not an evil man. I just like mischief as a cat does cream. "Ill met by moonlight!" You could wager your last farthing that I was. When Benjamin slept, I'd quietly slip out to meet young Lucy Witherspoon. She was a comely wench who worked some time in the White Harte tavern and, at others, as a chamber maid for the Poppleton household across the valley. I have mentioned these Poppletons before: spawns of Satan! The family was dominated by a woman I called the Great Mouth, Isabella Poppleton, and her cantankerous, flint-faced sons led by

Edmund. She hated me and I reciprocated in kind. May her lips rot off!

Now Lucy and I would spend those early, balmy autumn nights lying in the cool grass beside the river. Lucy was a lovely lass who, when I cradled her in my arms, would whisper, "My cup overflows with happiness!" It was a quotation she'd learnt from the wall of the parish church. She said it always tickled her fancy and, I suppose, I did the same. When she left, with my sweet words ringing in her ears and a silver piece in her purse, I'd stay to pick mushrooms, herbs and plants. I still had a deep, abiding desire to be a great physician and make my fortune with miraculous cures. I'd always be back by dawn, sleeping like an angel in my bed, and would awake later in the day to wash, shave, dress and plot fresh mischief.

Benjamin. Well, I loved Benjamin deeply — a scholar, a swordsman and a gentle soul — but a slight coldness had grown up between us. The cause (isn't it always?) was a woman: the marvellous Miranda, daughter of Under-sheriff Pelleter in the city of London. Oh, what a tangled web, the eternal triangle! Benjamin loved Miranda: Miranda loved Benjamin: Roger loved Miranda: Roger loved Benjamin: Benjamin loved Roger. However, here's the rub! Here's the soreness! Here's the canker in my soul, the hatred in my heart! Miranda did not love Roger!

My little secretary sniggers. The scurvy knave says love's not a triangle. If he's not careful I'll take my sword, prick his bum and take him down to the crossroads to my triangular gallows. What does he know of love? The little tick brain! The want wit! Monsieur Muckwater! Triangles, squares, rectangles? Love knows no shape. Whatever, I loved Miranda. I loved her hair, her eyes, her mouth, her body, her soul, her spirit. Oh, she was kind: "Good Roger," she called me. "My dear friend." But Miranda's eyes hungered only for Benjamin. And here's the second rub. Old Roger Shallot, by some nimble footwork, by playing the counterfeit-man, by devious trickery and subtle wit, had arranged for 'dear' Benjamin to be sent on an embassy to Italy, whilst I, poor Roger, was to stay at home looking after the farm. However, when the time was ripe, I'd foray into London to lay siege to Miranda's heart. Oh villainy! But can you blame me for loving? I, whom few people loved, had a heart bursting with that sweet fragrance and all of it was centred upon Miranda.

Now Benjamin may have been a scholar but he was no dullard. He spent his days preparing to leave, drawing up instructions, yet I would catch him watching me with his dark, soulful eyes.

"You'll not go to London?" Benjamin declared one afternoon when I was helping him place clothing in a chest.

Now I am a born liar but I couldn't lie to Benjamin. "Sometimes, master," I replied, turning away.

"And you'll not see Miranda?"

"Master, master!" I knelt down to buckle up some saddlebags, deciding to make light of it. "You've heard, master, the story about Lord Hudson?"

"No."

"Our good king sent him on an embassy to Spain. The old lord did not trust his young, fresh-faced wife so he locked a chastity belt about her and gave the key to his best friend. Well — " I threaded the strap through the buckle. "Lord Hudson was at Dover, about to climb into a wherry boat to take him out to the waiting ship, when a messenger arrived from his best friend." I got to my feet, keeping my back to Benjamin. "He delivered a note," I continued. "Lord Hudson opened it. Inside was the key with a message: 'WRONG KEY'."

My laughter was cut short by a prick of steel just beneath my left ear.

16

"Turn round, Roger."

I did so. My master was standing, his duelling sword only a few inches away from my eyes, but it wasn't the sharp point which frightened me. (There are some things more terrifying to even old Shallot than cold steel.) Benjamin's face was white with fury. No gentle eyes now or kind, smiling mouth but a mask, fierce and hard.

"Master!" I stepped back.

Benjamin followed me.

"Master!" I protested.

"Roger, you are my brother and my soul mate. I am your man in peace and war. Yet, I will not, I shall not share Miranda with you!" He laid the point on my chest. "If I return, Roger, and find you have, if I suspect that you have crept where I would not dream of creeping, I shall kill you because if you do you are no friend of mine and I am no friend of yours!"

This was no jest. Benjamin's eyes brimmed with tears. He was a man of his word. He'd once loved a woman whom another had seduced and sent insane. Poor Johanna was in the care of the kind nuns at their convent at Syon on the Thames. Benjamin had killed Cavendish, the young nobleman responsible.

"I have loved once and lost, Roger,"

Benjamin continued as if reading my mind. "I shall not love and lose again. Give me your word."

I lifted my right hand. "On the sacrament," I swore.

"And on your mother's soul!"

Benjamin knew me well. Mother had died young but all my memories of her were sweet. God knows I dreamt of her every night in some form or other. To me, her memory was sacred.

"On my mother's soul!" I declared.

Benjamin sighed but the sword point didn't fall.

"Oh no, master," I joked. "Don't say I have to take an oath not to drink wine or kiss any girl?"

Benjamin smiled thinly. "While I am gone, Roger, I will worry. You are back to your medicines, aren't you? Cures for catarrh; to make hair grow where it doesn't; to make the fat lean and the lean plump."

I swallowed hard.

"Roger, you know such trickery will take you to the gallows. I want you, now, to bring all your medicines down here. Go on!"

I hastened to obey. I suspected what was coming. I could have wept as I filled my bag with dried cowpate (Shallot's cure for baldness); lambs' testicles (Shallot's cure for impotence); dried newt (Shallot's veritable cure for catarrh); juice of valerian (for those who couldn't sleep); and my latest discovery, dried sunflower seed mixed with pig's urine and ground dates to make a man more virile. Into an old leather bag I piled the phials and potions, saying goodbye to each of them as if they were close and bosom friends. I returned downstairs. I looked fearfully at the spade Benjamin held in his hands though, thankfully, his sword was now sheathed. He took me out across the meadow to an old and ancient hill that overlooked the mill. I gazed tearfully down at the rush-filled riverside, savouring the memory of my sweet nights with Lucy Witherspoon.

"What are we going to do, master?" I asked.

Benjamin started digging. I watched with curiosity, hope once again flaring in my wicked heart. Benjamin was interested in antiquities: we had dug here before, looking for ruins of an ancient Roman fort, collecting the artifacts left by that ancient people.

"You are searching for something, master?" I asked expectantly.

"No, Roger. Just digging a very deep pit."

He dug on. I stood woebegone; my sack of miraculous cures in my hand, and then I noticed it. Isn't it strange, how simple things can be a pointer to events yet to come? Benjamin unearthed a spearhead, an ancient one, covered in rust but still good and hard; beneath the rust and clay, I saw an emblem: the Roman eagle with wings outstretched.

"You can keep it, Roger." Benjamin wiped the sweat from his face and handed the spear to me. "A relic from the past."

Relic! Relic! I tell you this, before I was much older I would come to dread the very mention of relics. That spearhead was a pointer, a dark omen of the terrors to come: the prospect of the gallows, the cart and the axe! Of hearts steeped in black wickedness and bloody, mysterious murder. Threats from the Great Beast, the parry and thrust of dagger and sword fights, brutal, sordid assault and, above all, poor old Shallot in danger of his life. My sweat poured down to soak the earth, my bowels turned to water, which they always do when I think even a hair on my precious head is in jeopardy. Oh, believe me, gentle reader, if I had known what was coming I would have jumped into that hole and buried myself, taking refuge in the bowels of the earth. As it was, I slipped the spearhead into my wallet and watched my master dig. At last he stopped and held his hand out.

"Give me the sack, Roger."

I smiled wanly but handed it over. I even thought of brushing a tear from my eyes but I am glad I didn't. I have studied Richard Burbage's players and, as I have written to the man, some of them do cry overmuch and it spoils the effect. Benjamin took the sack and knelt down. He took a small phial of oil from his pocket, poured it over the sack and struck a tinder: the rough, dry cloth was soon alight. Benjamin climbed out of the hole and we both watched as the flames roared, turning the sack to blackened ash. I must say I was fascinated. Only the good Lord knows what was in those cures. I mean, it's not often you see blue fire! Benjamin took me by the shoulder.

"It's the best way, Roger. It will keep you out of villainy. I don't want you going into London. I don't want you seeing Miranda. And I don't want you selling medicines. Do you understand?"

I blinked innocently. Benjamin smiled, shaking his head and, taking his spade, began to fill the hole. I stood and watched, fingering that old spearhead in my wallet; already a vague idea was beginning to form but silence is the best counsel to follow in such matters.

We returned to the manor. Benjamin

now seemed light-hearted, and the tension between us had dissipated. I decided to relax and enjoy the golden autumn sun. The next day I was supposed to be helping with the early harvest. I forget the precise details. Anyway, whilst everyone else was working, I and young Lucy Witherspoon found ourselves on top of a haystack. I was teaching her the principles of mathematics and counting, using the laces across her ample bodice as an exemplar. I had just reached the last lace when I heard Benjamin call my name. I looked over the haystack, whispering at Lucy to stay there with the wine I had brought. Benjamin was staring up at me.

"Roger, come down. You look tired. You've been too long under the sun!"

I just ignored him, my flesh already turning cold at the sight of the visitor standing next to him: Doctor Agrippa! I have talked about this creature many a time. Of medium height and cherubic face, Agrippa had twinkling eyes which could, at a drop of a coin, turn iron hard. As usual he was dressed in sepulchral black from head to toe, his jovial face almost hidden by the broad-brimmed hat. Whatever the weather, he always wore a cloak and black leather gloves on his hands so people couldn't see the strange emblems, bloody crosses on each palm. Warlock? Wizard? I don't know. He was Wolsey's familiar. Agrippa claimed to have lived when the legions still strutted across Europe and the Barbarians hadn't yet poured across the great northern rivers. A man who had been in Palestine when Christ our Lord was crucified. Agrippa claimed to have seen the Golden Horde led by Genghis Khan and been present at Constantinople when the gates were breached and the Turks poured in. A man doomed to live for ever! Agrippa had come to England to stop, as he once told me in hushed tones, the river of blood that Henry the Great Beast was about to unleash. Agrippa was very worried by Henry. He called him the Mouldwarp, the Dark Prince prophesied by Merlin who would turn England from the path of righteousness and unleash horrors for which the kingdom would pay for centuries. He was fascinated by me, was our good Doctor, always sidling up to me. I can still recall his strange odour when he was pleased, the most fragrant of perfumes, cloying and rich. When he was angry or sad, the smell changed to that of an empty skillet left over a roaring fire.

Did he live for ever? Ten summers ago I commissioned my good ship *The*

Witherspoon to go a-pirating on the Spanish Main. My captain put in at a port in Virginia, and was sitting in a bottle shop, when in strolled Agrippa. According to my man's description he wasn't a day older. He was accompanied by tribesmen with shaven heads and painted faces. Agrippa explained he had been out west across the great mountain range but he still remembered Old Shallot and asked the captain give me his most tender regards. Only a summer ago, when I was in the Mermaid tavern joking with Ben Jonson and lying fit to burst, I saw a man standing in the doorway looking across at me. He smiled, raised a hand and was gone. I recognised that face immediately. Doctor Agrippa had returned.

Ah well, the passage of time! The crumbling of the flesh! These things were yet to come. On that golden autumn day, with the sweat like silver pearls on my young body, I just stared at Agrippa and groaned. Dearest Uncle, Cardinal Thomas Wolsey, clad in his purple silk, was about to summon us in to the lair of the Great Beast.

Agrippa must have read my thoughts. He came to the foot of the ladder and stared up at me.

"No, no, Roger," he whispered in that

gentle parson's voice of his. "You are not for court, my lad. I come to say goodbye to Benjamin. I've brought tender messages from his sweet uncle as well as the King's good wishes for both him and you."

"Bugger off!" I snarled. "There's mischief afoot, isn't there?"

Agrippa just shook his head. "Come down, Roger. I've also brought a bottle of red wine from Italy; Falernian to wash the mouth and clear the stomach. And my boys, my retinue, would love to shake the dice."

His boys! The nicest group of cutthroats you'd ever hope to meet. Villains born and bred. Old Agrippa knew I felt completely at home in their company.

I came down that ladder as quickly as a rat along a pipe. Little Lucy would have to wait a while before I finished my lesson in numbers.

Agrippa's rascals were waiting for me in the yard and fell about my neck like long-lost brothers. I drew my dagger and told them to stay away from my purse. They all laughed, slapped me on the back and said what a fine fellow I was and wouldn't I like to play dice? I told them to keep their hands to themselves and that I knew how many chickens we had in the yard. I then joined my master and Agrippa in the solar.

At first we listened to his chatter about the court and who was in favour and who was not. Later, as we feasted on beef roasted in mustard, our silver plates piled high with vegetables served in a mushroom sauce, Agrippa ordered the servants to be dismissed and the door closed. For a while he just sat and discussed Benjamin's forthcoming visit to Venice.

"You won't be there long," he declared. "Deliver some letters, give His Majesty's felicitations to the Doge and the Council and then . . . back to England."

"Then why should I go at all?" Benjamin asked.

Agrippa pulled a face. He doffed his hat and hung it on the back of his chair but he still kept his gloves on. He glanced up; his eyes had changed to that fathomless black.

"You have to go, Master Daunbey. You are the Cardinal's good nephew. The Doge would see it as a great honour."

"Yes," Benjamin replied caustically. "I suppose the King needs Venetian galleys to watch the coast of France?"

"Aye, and to seal the straits of Hercules," Agrippa replied.

He fell silent, staring down at the white tablecloth, humming softly, rocking himself gently backwards and forwards. Darkness had fallen. The candlelight and the flame of the torches suddenly flared as a cold breeze swept through the room. The silence turned eerie. There was no sound except Agrippa's humming. A shiver ran up my spine. I felt we weren't alone: as if Agrippa was calling upon some dark force, beings who live on the edge of our existence. I glanced into the corner expecting to see some sombre shape lurking there. Benjamin too was caught by the spell so he grasped the good doctor's gloved hand.

"Master Agrippa!"

Our visitor kept his eyes closed.

"Master Agrippa!" Benjamin shook his hand.

Agrippa opened his eyes. In the candlelight his face had changed: it was younger, the skin smoother, taking on a more olive Italianate look. I had seen such a face upon a Roman fresco that my master had unearthed in a villa outside Norwich.

"I am sorry." Agrippa shook himself free of his reverie. "But it's beginning . . . "

"For God's sake!" Benjamin snapped. "What is beginning?"

"The Mouldwarp, the Prince of Darkness, the Devil's Dance. The King is determined . . . "

"To do what?" I asked.

"Win back English lands in France.

27

Outdo the feats of Henry V. Create an English empire in Europe." He paused. "And something else, secret, that even the Lord Cardinal doesn't know."

I suppose we should have questioned him on that but Agrippa talked on hurriedly about Fat Henry's military ambitions. When he finished Benjamin groaned, and even I could see the folly of it all. The Great Beast hated Francis I: our King also saw himself as a second Alexander, a warrior more puissant than Edward III, The Black Prince or Henry V. Only Calais remained in English hands but Fat Henry wanted to change that: annexe Gascony, Normandy, Maine and Anjou. A war which would turn Europe into a living hell. Agrippa glanced at Benjamin.

"That's why you are off to Venice, Master Benjamin. The King will need galleys to transport his troops." He grinned at me. "The King doesn't want you to go, Master Shallot. He's frightened that you'll start a war with Venice."

"Tell him — " I started hotly but bit my tongue.

Agrippa filled his wine glass, which in the flickering light looked like a goblet full of blood. For all I know it probably was!

"There's more as well," Agrippa continued.

28

"The King wants a great alliance with Emperor Charles V of Germany. In return the Emperor has asked for the return of the Orb of Charlemagne."

"The what?" I asked.

"The Orb of Charlemagne," Agrippa explained. "It's hidden away, kept in a locked coffer in a secret chamber in the Tower. It's a gold ball studded with gems and surmounted by a silver cross and a large amethyst. Now, according to legend, this Orb was sent by Charlemagne to Alfred the Great, not as a gift, but as a symbol of friendship."

"And the English never returned it?"

"Precisely. Now Charles V claims it back. Henry has conceded that the Orb is in England and, in return for Hapsburg gold and troops, the Orb will be returned."

(I could just imagine that. Long-jawed Charles Hapsburg constantly worried about his soul. He was the ruler of Spain, the Netherlands and most of Germany, and had no difficulty in thinking he was God's Vice-Regent on earth, the reincarnation of the great Emperor Charlemagne. At times, old Charley-boy with his big jaw was like an old woman. Once he wanted something, it was nag, nag, nag until he got it. Catherine of Aragon was his aunt and Charles knew how to apply pressure on Henry. The English treasury was bankrupt. Henry loved his feasts and banquets but they all cost money.)

"The Orb," Agrippa continued, "is precious not only to the House of Hapsburg but also to France and the Papacy. Inside this orb are said to be miraculous relics of great power: some of the Virgin Mary's hair and a phial of Mary Magdalene's blood." He glanced at Benjamin. "You've heard the story?"

"Some of it," Benjamin replied.

"Well, according to legend," Agrippa continued, addressing me, "Mary Magdalene, after the Resurrection of Christ, allegedly fled Palestine and took ship to Marseilles. She was accompanied by Lazarus and others who had known Christ during his lifetime.

"Well, to cut a long story short, the legend says that Mary Magdalene married and from her line sprang the Merovingians, the sacred, long-haired kings of France who fashioned the Orb." Agrippa sipped from his goblet. "So we now have a pretty little potage. The Emperor's men are in London led by their ambassador the Count of Egremont. He is assisted by those they call the Men of the Night, the Noctales."

"And the French?" I asked.

"They're here too, not to mention the Pope's envoys, all vying to buy the Orb."

"And the King?"

"Oh, he's loving every minute of it, like a young maid being courted. First he favours one side, and then another, simpering and pouting."

(I could just imagine it. Henry liked to see himself as the warrior, the huntsman, the great lover. Well, if the truth be known, as a warrior he could just about swing a sword. And as a lover? Alas, let's put it this way, he wasn't well endowed. Rather small like a little pig. You don't believe me? Well, I'm a man who has slept with Anne Boleyn and what she told me, between giggles, is not worth repeating, particularly if there are ladies about. My little clerk shakes his head in disbelief. I rap him across the wrist with my ash cane. Go down to the muniment room in the Tower, says I, and search out the last letter poor Anne sent to Henry whilst she lay in the Tower. She makes no bones about it then. What I really want to say is that I sometimes suspect Henry would have loved to have been a woman. He certainly liked to be pursued. He liked to simper and be coy and — no, don't think it's the time to tell you about the occasion I found him dressed in one of Anne of Cleve's gowns!)

"But Henry will give it to the Germans?" Benjamin asked.

"Yes, yes, I think he will. He's just baiting France and the Papacy."

"But it doesn't concern us, does it?" I asked.

"No, I don't think it will," Agrippa replied slowly. "The Orb will be removed from the Tower — it needs re-burnishing — and then passed over to Egremont to verify that it's no forgery."

(A wise man, Egremont, I wouldn't have trusted Henry as far as I could spit.)

"But it doesn't concern us?" I repeated, fearful lest the Great Beast invited us into his lair.

"I've told you I don't think it will," Agrippa replied. He drummed gloved fingers on the table. "Yet the King is a fool, he is playing with fire. The orb is no bigger than a tennis ball. It could be replicated, it could be stolen. Every footpad and counterfeit-man in London will hear of it. They'll smack their lips, narrow their eyes and speculate on what a fortune they could make." Agrippa tapped his knife against the wine glass, the sound tinkling through the room like a fairy bell. "There'll be trouble," he declared. "The Orb of Charlemagne is unlucky. Harold insisted on carrying it, and he was killed at Hastings. Rufus treated it like a bauble and he was mysteriously shot by an arrow in the New Forest. Edward II gave it to his catamite Piers Gaveston as a present and both were murdered." He scratched his chin, a faraway look in his eyes. "And I remember Richard II, that golden-haired boy. You have seen the Wilton diptych showing Richard between two white harts? In his hand he carries the Orb of Charlemagne. He was deposed and murdered."

"In which case," I retorted, "Henry must be glad to see the back of it!"

"Ah, no." Agrippa sipped from the goblet. "If the Orb falls into the wrong hands, which so the legend goes are those who do not have a pure heart — " he winked at me — "and if it is not treated with respect, then its power is unleashed. But for those who treat it with awe and reverence, it brings its own rewards. Anyway — " He scraped back his chair. "Time for sleep. Tomorrow, Benjamin, we're for Harwich: the King's ship will take us down to London."

"Don't say you are tired, Doctor Agrippa," I teased.

"No, Roger." He got up, shifting back the chair. "I just want to sleep, perchance to dream."

(Yes, that's where Will Shakespeare's Hamlet got it from!)

"Of what?" I asked.

"Of golden sands by blue seas. Of galleys laden with exotic perfumes. Well away from this cold Island and its vengeful King."

In retrospect Agrippa was a prophet. Sometimes I wished I'd sailed to Italy and stayed there but, ah, the foolishness of youth! The next morning we woke well before dawn. Benjamin's bags were loaded on to sumpter ponies. He drew up letters, left me money and gave me hurried snippets of advice. And then we left in a cloud of dust, Agrippa's retainers fanning out before us, making fair speed to the port of Harwich. I won't describe the scene to you and make your gentle eyes weep. I embraced Benjamin and told him not to tarry long. I clasped Agrippa's hand, gave the most obscene gestures to the good doctor's retainers, and headed like an arrow to the nearest tavern to drown my sorrows.

Now I am not a hypocrite. I sat drinking and soon recovered my good spirits. Benjamin was an able, young man, well protected. He'd travel to Venice and then return, so whilst the cat's away . . . Nevertheless, I hadn't forgotten my master's look when he forced me to take that oath. No London! No Miranda!

A group of sailors came in, lusty men, everyone a charlatan or swaggerer, so I spent the rest of the day carousing and quaffing with the best of them. I remember a young tavern wench, golden and ripe as an apple, and us bouncing like fleas on her bed at the back of the tavern. Golden times! We giggled and we kissed all night long. The next morning I rose, bent on mischief and of course I found it. Yet, on reflection, life is strange and full of the most deadly coincidences. If I hadn't stayed at that particular tavern, and if I hadn't left it at that hour . . . but, isn't that the mystery of life? Out of the frying pan and into the fire!

I'd collected my horse and was halfway across the market square when I glimpsed the relic-seller, dressed in a colourful motley of rags, laying out his wares on the steps of the market cross. He was tall, and singular looking; his skin burnt brown by the sun, with clear blue eyes and lank, black, greasy hair. Now, one thing about being a rogue (and it's old Shallot's rule) is that you can recognise a good man when you meet one, whilst you can sniff a kindred spirit half a mile away. He introduced himself as Nathaniel Ludgate, and his villainy was as thick as clotted cream. I told him to hold my horse's reins, then walked backwards into the tavern to get us each a pot of ale. I kept my eye on the rogue, a grand idea forming in my mind. He stood grinning at me and, when I returned with the ale, toasted me, his eyes dancing with mischief.

"You are interested in relics?"

"Oh yes," I replied airily. "I've even seen the Orb of Charlemagne."

Well, you should have seen the fellow's face. Eyes popping, jaw slack.

"The Orb of Charlemagne!" he whispered. "Men would kill for that. Indeed they have." He scratched his black, pointed heard. "But, there again, it can bring ill fortune."

"Are they your work?" I taunted, pointing to the relics he had laid out.

"No, no, sir." His voice rose to a chant as he recognised a prospective customer. "Genuine relics, sir, every one!" He described each one.

And what a bag of tipple!

Ringlets from Samson's head, before Delilah shaved it. A thorn from the crown which the Romans put on our Saviour's head. One of Mary Magdalene's perfume clasps. A feather from the wing of the Angel Gabriel. A wooden hammer once owned by St Joseph. A piece of iron, supposedly from the griddle on which St Lawrence had been burnt. Two pieces of the true cross. A napkin used by Our Lady. Pontius Pilate's wife's earring. A portion of Herod the Great's foreskin. Five pieces of the good thief's loincloth. A battered cup once owned by St Ursula. Strands of hair from each of the ten thousand virgins executed by the Romans in Germany.

"All collected by me," Ludgate declared. "I have travelled, sir, beyond the Golden Horn. I have seen the devil's wings over Arabia and faced many dangers collecting these. A priceless fortune blessed by the Holy Father!" He clapped me on the shoulder, all manly and honest, and looked me straight in the eye. "Take these to London," he urged. "Go to the tavern, the Flickering Lamp near White-friars. Boscombe, the taverner, will let you sell them in the surrounding alleys and streets. A good site, where the faithful stream by to the London churches."

(Now you young people, children of the reformed faith, don't realise that in the days of relic-selling, a trader had to have a domicile before he could sell relics: taverners, in return for a fee, often provided this.)

I gestured at the collection. "How much is it all worth?"

"Fifteen pounds sterling, good silver."

"Twelve," I replied.

"Thirteen," he countered.

We spat and clasped hands and I returned home, one of the great relic-sellers of Europe.

2

I found it strange to be back at the manor by myself. However, the stewards and bailiffs were honest hard-working fellows, and the school had been closed down, so I spent all my time and energy preparing my great relics. London was forbidden to me so I took out our old vellum map and gazed greedily at Ely, Norwich and the other prosperous wool towns where people might be parted easily from their money. I searched amongst Benjamin's library, found a treatise on relics and avidly studied every word. The jewel in my collection was the spearhead I'd found so fortuitously when Benjamin had burnt my medicines. The steel was still good and, with a special polish of herbs, I began to clean it carefully. Finally, it lay on the table, glowing grey steel, the eagle of Rome and the letters 'S.P.Q.R.' firmly etched upon it. God knows where it came from! It probably wasn't a fighting spear but some ceremonial shaft carried by the soldiers in their religious ceremonies.

I went out to the forest and found a suitable piece of ash, which I stripped, dried and rubbed with charcoal to make it look more ancient than it was. A few dabs of blood and I had the spear with which the centurions pierced our Saviour's side. The blood, I reasoned, wasn't the Lord's but that of some martyr who had hidden it until I, Roger Shallot, relic-seller and buyer to His Holiness in Rome, found it through my own intuition and Divine favour. So, I was ready for the market, but was the market ready for me?

After five days' hard work, I strolled down to the White Harte tavern in the village, the miraculous spear and a few other relics in my bag. I took a seat in the taproom near the window where I could watch the door. (I trust that you young men will act on my advice. If you go into a tavern or ale-house, you never know when you will have to leave, sometimes it's quicker than you imagine, so, always sit near the window or door. If trouble breaks out, you can flee like the wind.) The place was full. I noticed Edmund Poppleton, the Great Mouth's son, holding forth on the price of corn. As I stared at his greasy face, with its scrawny moustache and beard, and his beer gut like a barrel, I wondered why men such as he have to collect riches they don't really need whilst the poor go hungry to bed? I sat sneering at him over my ale:

like a coney he rose to the lure.

"Master Shallot, Master Shallot!" His face creased into a smile. "You are being rather discreet, sitting there so doleful, cradling a tankard."

"I have no choice," I replied. "I always do this when listening to someone speak. It's so fascinating . . ."

He narrowed his eyes, too shrewd to ask why I found it so fascinating.

"Your master," he cooed, "is off to Italy?"

"Yes," I lied. "Gone to see the Holy Father on the business of his dear uncle, His Eminence Cardinal Wolsey, as well as to make a report on other matters that might disturb His Holiness."

Poppleton flinched and I knew the rumours were correct. The Great Mouth and her sons had been flirting with the new doctrines of Luther. Now the Poppletons hated me and I hated them. You may recall from my previous memoirs how I tricked them when they dared to call my master a catamite. They hadn't forgotten and, full of malice, could never resist baiting me.

"And you saw your dear master leave?"

I saw my chance. "No, no." I shook my head. "Not just that, something much more important."

The noise in the taproom stilled.

"I went to Harwich with my master to receive special gifts: artifacts and relics that my master and I discovered when we visited Florence." I shrugged. "Well, not really discovered. They were more gifts from His Eminence Cardinal de Medici."

"Piddle poo!" Poppleton scoffed. "Master Shallot, you are well known for your tales and your trickery. What relics are these? Goliath's foreskin?"

I sat back. I hadn't thought of that one and mentally added it to my list. Poppleton now had the attention of all the customers. I looked round and saw that young Lucy Witherspoon was not present. I was sad as I'd hoped to impress her.

"Relics!" Poppleton scoffed. "You have no relics, Master Shallot!"

That was my signal. I undid the neck of the sack and took out the spear shaft.

"Look," I said, standing up, deliberately turning so the polished steel caught the sunlight; this gave it a spiritual aura as it shimmered and reflected the light. The appearance of the spear brought 'oohs' and 'aahs' from everyone. Turning sideways I pointed the spear at Poppleton, every inch the Roman soldier.

"This is the spear," I intoned, "the centurion used on Calvary when he pierced the Lord's side. This is the blood of a martyr who buried it until Roger Shallot was given it as a gift in Florence!"

"Pig's trotters!" Poppleton taunted.

Giggling broke out. I stared round and saw old Doctor Littlejohn sitting there, tankard grasped in his hand, staring blearily at me. The old fool styled himself an antiquarian. He had been a schoolmaster and knew some Latin. I thrust the spear under his nose.

"Master Littlejohn, what do you think?"

The old fellow put on his spectacles. He took the spear shaft and held it gingerly in his hands. He examined the steel and even he, who looked as if he lived half-asleep, became visibly excited as he glimpsed the eagle and the letters S.P.Q.R. He touched the steel reverentially.

"I cannot say," he declared, "whether this is the actual spear used on Calvary but it is definitely very ancient and was once used in the armies of Rome."

Well, that shut old Poppleton up for a start. Everyone crowded round. Offers were made but I just shook my head. Like the coy young maid, you show your customer your garters but that's as far as you go. Time was on my side: rumour and greed would grow and the gold would come pouring in once this spear, this most holy relic, was accepted.

It would only be a matter of time before I got round to Goliath's foreskin.

"If it's a relic," Poppleton declared, shouldering his way through the crowd, his lips coated with a white foam of ale. "If it's so holy, it should be able to perform miracles."

"That's right!" another cried. "Miracles! We want a miracle, Shallot!"

My stomach curdled: I hadn't thought of that.

"A cure!" another cried. "Perhaps it can cure my leg!"

"The only thing that cure your leg," someone cried out, "is to stop drinking ale and work a little harder!"

I tried to hide my apprehension. With all my subtle planning, I hadn't thought of such a challenge. Poppleton was sneering at me.

"Come, come, Master Shallot," he taunted. "A little miracle is not too much to ask."

"There's Lucy," Tom the taverner shouted from where he stood beside the barrels.

"Lucy?" I shouted as a diversion. "What's wrong with her?"

"She's upstairs in a chamber, sick with a fever," Tom replied, coming forward.

"Oh yes, that's right." Poppleton planted himself squarely in front of me. "The wench hasn't been to clean for days."

His greasy smile widened. "I believe Lucy has given you her favour?" He was cooing like a stupid wood pigeon. "Surely, Master Shallot, it's not too much to ask that you use this great relic to cure the love of your life?"

"Let me see her," I declared.

I put the spear back in the sack and followed Tom up the rickety, wooden stairs to a small garret at the top of the tavern built just under the eaves. Oh, Lord help me, but Lucy looked dreadful. She lay asleep on the soiled sheets but her face and hair were soaked with sweat. She tossed and turned, murmuring to herself and my heart skipped a beat as she muttered my name. I felt her brow, it was hot as a steaming pot.

"Out late she was," Tom declared. "Out late then came back with a chill, coughing and sneezing fit to burst," he told the rest crowding the stairwell behind him.

"Cure her," Poppleton whispered. "Lay the sacred spear upon her!"

I wetted dry lips, my mind racing like a rat down a hole. I wished I had my medicines then I remembered something.

"Listen," I said. "I will lay the relic upon her but not yet."

Poppleton lowered his head and began to

snigger. There were groans and moans from the stairwell.

"Tonight," I continued, "I shall return. This room is to be cleaned. Vicar Doggerel should bless and make it ready for this great relic. At seven o'clock tonight I shall return."

Poppleton's head came up. "No trickery, Shallot!"

"Of course not," I whispered back. "Only divine intervention."

"We'll see," he snarled.

I was glad to be out of that tavern. I rode swiftly back to the manor house, went upstairs and, from a secret casement in my chamber, pulled out a locked coffer. I opened it and stared at all the things truly precious to me; a lock of my mother's hair; a ring Benjamin had given me: a love letter which I never had the courage to despatch. Above all, a small phial, the real diamond amongst all my cures; a powerful potion I won at hazard from a Turkish physician in a tavern off the Ropery. God knows what was in it. The Turk had told me it was the scrapings of dried milk fermented in a soup of moss, a veritable elixir for any fever. I opened the phial, shook the white, chalky substance into my hand. I then locked the coffer, recited an Ave Maria, and fortified myself with two cups of malmsey.

Once dusk fell I returned to the White Harte. Now the whole village had turned out. Poppleton and his younger brother were waiting for me in the taproom. They looked the same, two cheeks of the same hairy arse. Tom the taverner took me upstairs. Lucy still lay tossing and turning, angry spots of fever high in her cheeks. However, the chamber had been swept and cleaned and the poor girl now lay between crisp, clean linen sheets. Vicar Doggerel the village parson, (to whom I'd sold cow dung as a cure for his baldness) was also present. He had a stole around his neck and an Asperges bucket and rod in his hands.

"I've blessed the room," he announced. "But, Roger," he whispered, "what knavery is this?"

"God works in wondrous ways, Father."

"If he's working through you then he certainly does!" Doggerel replied.

"Well come on!" Tom shouted.

"God does not act because we click our fingers," I snarled back. "Does he, Father?"

The vicar nodded. I took the spear from my sack and laid it on the bed.

"It may take all night," I replied.

A murmur of disapproval came from the group, led by the Poppletons, who thronged in the doorway.

"Come, come," I replied. "Surely you are not going to add the sin of heresy to that of doubt?"

(I would have made a fine preacher!)

I laid the spear next to Lucy. "I wish to be alone," I declared, "for an hour. I will then leave and the chamber will be locked, but I shall sleep here tonight. Now, all of you, go!"

Vicar Doggerel supported me so the crowd, led by the Poppletons, scowling and muttering under their breath, went back downstairs. Tom, who could now see a great profit in the evening's procedures, fairly leapt from foot to foot.

"Master taverner," I said. "A small jug of ale." I smacked my lips. "Nothing more."

The taverner agreed. He withdrew and I could hear the gossip and the shouts of laughter from the taproom below. A slattern came up to find me kneeling by the bed, eyes closed, hands joined, with that oh-so-sanctimonious look on my face which the pious believe they must wear whenever they address the Almighty. She put the tankard down and tiptoed out. Up I leapt like a jack rabbit. I drank most of the ale but left enough in the bottom. Lucy was stirring on the bed, her eyes still closed. God knows how much I should have poured in but I mixed some of the powder with what was left of the ale, and made her drink. I waited an hour and gave her some more. Then I left the spear beside her and went down to rejoin the other revellers in the taproom.

I didn't drink that night. I stayed in the taproom for a time and then slept in a chamber just beneath Lucy's.

The next morning I was woken by a pounding on the door and, before I could answer, it was flung open and Tom, followed by a heavy-eyed Lucy, walked into the room. I must admit the girl looked rather pale, with black shadows under her eyes, and her hair still unkempt.

"Roger!" She flung her arms round my neck and kissed me. "My cup," she smiled, "truly overflows."

I gently pushed her away. "Where is the spear?" I asked. "Some bastard hasn't stolen it?"

"Roger, a miracle." Lucy's eyes were bright.

If Tom hadn't been there, we'd have ended up romping on the bed. However, old Shallot is not ruled by his codpiece.

"Has anyone else seen her?" I asked.

"No, no, the Poppletons left. They said they would be back at ten." Tom rubbed his hands together. "The rest are all sleeping

48

like hogs in the taproom below, farting and belching fit to burst!"

"Then let's hasten, sweet Lucy," I said. "Tom, a bowl of water and a towel."

I took Lucy back to the chamber, where the spear still lay on the sweat-soaked bed. I was elated. My mind was full of dreams of riches pouring in. Anyway, to cut a long story short, I stripped Lucy off and washed her myself. She said she felt well and energetic so we had a romp upon the bed, bouncing and kissing. She kept murmuring how her cup truly overflowed. Afterwards I combed her hair, she painted her face and put her best gown on. When she had finished she looked as pretty as any queen, the picture of health. She kissed the spear. I tightened the buckle of my purse, lest anyone glimpsed the phial. Thankfully Lucy could remember nothing except the spear and me kneeling beside her. (Oh, she was a grand lass, such a pity she died such a terrible death!) She claimed to have had visions of a spear burning brightly before her and a power emanating from it which enveloped her body. I couldn't have asked for better. I heard horses' hooves on the cobbles below and, like a king and his queen, we swept down to the taproom. I held up the spear like some silly Lancelot of the Lake escorting his Guinevere. The

Poppleton brothers, Edmund and Robert, just stared open-mouthed, and the rest of the taproom broke into loud cheers and clapping. I was hailed as Lucy's great saviour with many an envious glance at the spear. I didn't want some accident happening to me as I travelled home half-drunk so I left immediately. Naturally, I threw triumphant glances at the Great Mouth's sons who stood, cups in hand, muttering and glowering back.

Once I was back in the manor it was days of wine and roses. The news spread and soon I had a constant stream of visitors to the hall: some came just to touch the spear, others to receive a cure. Now, as any doctor will tell you, believe that you are going to be cured and you are well over halfway to good health. I did a roaring trade! (Oh yes, Goliath's foreskin, hairs from Balaam's ass and a cracked mirror once used by Delilah.) My little chest of coins grew. I basked in the approval of my neighbours. But ah, foolish man. Just when my greatness was ripening it was nipped in the bud by a savage cold frost. Late one afternoon the Poppleton brothers arrived at my door, with a group of their henchmen, servile as worms, bowing and scraping, friendly eyed, their mouths stuffed with flattery. We took sweetmeats and white wine in the parlour. They complimented me on my growing fame and then Edmund, the elder weasel, leaned forward, a bag of silver clinking in his hand.

"Dearest Roger." Tears brimmed in his eyes. "Mother is unwell, a fever; would you, for love of us, bring the spear to cure her?"

I should have sensed a trap but the clinking of silver was music to my ears. Moreover, you can fake a relic but very rarely a real fever so I agreed. We journeyed back across the valley to the house of the Great Mouth. For once she was silent, lying like some great bloated toad against the bolsters, her black hair damp with sweat, her fat, pasty face shimmering like a lump of lard under the sun. She had a fever. Now I had brought the phial with me and asked the Poppletons for a cup of watered white wine. Edmund and Robert hurried off together and they brought it back in a heavily embossed pewter cup with a broad bowl, thick-stemmed on a heavily bejewelled base. I sought a diversion asking for a napkin and poured the powder in. Edmund then took the cup and gave it to his mother. At my insistence she sipped and sipped, then I laid the spear by her side.

Now, I certainly didn't want to shelter in the house of my enemies all night. I declared I would stay until dusk when they would see a change in their mother's complexion. The brothers left and I wandered round the chamber. There were a few little gee-gaws, a ring, a cross, which all disappeared into my sack. I had sensed a change in the Poppletons' attitudes: their veneer of politeness was now punctuated by sneers and malicious looks. I doubted if I would get my silver so I also took the cup. Lying sprawled on the bed, the Great Mouth was becoming calmer, her breathing light, her skin cool to the touch so, when I heard the village bells chiming across the fields for Vespers, I took my spear and made to leave. The Poppletons, still servile, surprisingly paid me my silver. I passed Lucy in the gallery, winked and blew her a silent kiss. I collected my horse and rode like the wind back to the manor.

In retrospect, I admit, I was a little-brain. I should not have been deceived by those glass-faced flatterers, those vipers, those malt worms, those diseases in human form.

I was awoken just before dawn by a pounding on the door. I woke thick-headed, my mouth still sweet with the taste of wine. Lucy, accompanied by my bailiff John Appleyard, a good, honest man, stood in the gallery.

"In heaven's name!" I exclaimed.

"Roger, you must flee!" Lucy pushed me

back into the room. "Roger, you must flee or you'll hang!"

"In heaven's name, woman!"

"Mistress Poppleton is dead! Her sons are now claiming you poisoned her!"

"She had a fever!"

"Aye, and you made it worse!" she exclaimed. "No one but you gave her anything to eat or drink. A physician was called and has already shrieked poison." She grasped my shoulders and shook me. "Roger, they'll take and hang you!"

"She speaks the truth," Appleyard declared. "They'll know Lucy is gone by now and they'll not wait for the sheriff. Master Roger, you know the Poppletons! An axe in your head or an arrow in your back and they all take the oath that you were trying to flee."

"But I hardly touched the woman!" I cried.

"They say you are a thief, that you stole objects as well as the cup in which you put the poison."

I closed my eyes. Oh, what a terrible pit I had fallen into. I had stolen and, in my heart, I knew Appleyard was correct. I dressed quickly. I took my war-belt and stuffed my panniers with whatever coins I could lay my hands on. I filled another saddlebag with my relics, a change of clothing and all that I had borrowed from the Poppleton household. I took the fastest horse from my stable, told Appleyard to look after the manor and gave Lucy a juicy kiss. I then fled, even as Appleyard cried that he could see dust along the trackway as the Poppletons approached.

I rode like some bat spat out of hell. I stopped at night to rest my horse and ease the ache in my bones. On the following morning, despite my master's strictures, I entered London. Oh, it was good to be back in the melting pot, in that great cauldron which bubbles all day and every night with excitement and knavery. I kept well away from the beaten path and, in those early hours, I crossed the city into the stinking alleyways and maze of warrens around Whitefriars.

Now, I am not going to give you a treatise on coincidences. In the end, I suppose, everything is woven together. During my flight into London, I'd recalled the advice of Ludgate the relic-seller so I searched out the tavern he'd mentioned. The Flickering Lamp was a shabby, two-storeyed place, though the taproom was spacious with a small garden beyond. Boscombe was not the usual greasy, fat-gutted taverner. He was tall, wiry as a whippet, his face tanned and weather-beaten. He must have been well past his fortieth year but his smiling eyes and mouth made him look younger. When I met him he was dressed as an arch-deacon and, seeing my surprise, he explained how he often entertained the customers by dressing up in various disguises. I told him about Ludgate, explaining that I had relics to sell and needed to hire a chamber so I might sell them in the streets around. He shook his head.

"I've three chambers upstairs," he replied, his voice rather guttural. "But I don't let them out: not even the scullions and tapsters sleep here." He studied me closely. "Anyway, what do you know about relics? I mean real ones?"

"I have heard of the Orb of Charlemagne," I replied.

He narrowed his eyes. "Aye, and I've heard about the true cross. Who told you about the Orb?"

"My master," I retorted, deciding to name drop. "Benjamin Daunbey, nephew to Cardinal Wolsey."

"I couldn't care if he was nephew to the Great Cham!" He raised one hand in mock benediction, a sign of dismissal.

I picked up my saddlebags and walked to the door.

"Shallot?"

I turned. Boscombe was smiling.

"On second thoughts, I'll rent you the chamber. But keep it clean and no fighting!"

I spent that first day at the Flickering Lamp lying on my back staring up at the rafters, trying to discover what had happened: going back to that chamber where the Great Mouth had lain sweating on her bed. Had she been poisoned before I arrived? I shook my head. NO, her two brats would be very careful. They'd have all the servants and cooks ready to take the oath that the only thing to have passed Mistress Poppleton's lips was the cup of watered wine I gave her. The woman had been poisoned, I was sure of that. But how? By her sons? But for what reason? I wished Benjamin was back but, there again, crying over spilt milk is not one of my failings. My busy mind turned like a ferret in a rabbit warren as to how I could sell my relics.

Now, I had been down on my luck in London before. The last time was when the sweating sickness had raged like some storm around the streets, but now all was quiet. Of course I could have gone to court but the Poppletons would be searching for me there so, the next morning, I took my bag of relics, bought a tray off a journeyman and began

56

to wander the streets selling my wares. Now, you young people, don't misunderstand me. I enjoyed what I did and I loved London. Oh, it was good to be back with the foists and the naps, the prigs and the dummerers, the counterfeitmen, the cranks, the roaring lads and bully boys; the swaggering thieves, the bucks in buckram, the punks in taffeta, the whores in their garish wigs and colourful dresses. I tell you this, such rogues do not live long but they live well and I rarely got to bed before dawn. I have a silver tongue and, provided I keep my face shaved and clean, I can look as honest as a nun at prayer. Soon I began to make a profit but then things turned sour like milk left out in the sun.

The London underworld is full of flotsam and jetsam. You live your life and pick up the cards Mistress Fortune deals out. Like the rest of the scum I floated on a dirty pool. I'd forgotten about the pikes that swim deep in the darkness. One afternoon I returned to the Flickering Lamp, where Boscombe stood behind his barrels, peering across at me as if I was a sheriff's tipstaff come to arrest him. The taproom was half full, men squatted quietly around the tables.

"What have we here?" I swaggered in, a silver piece between my fingers. "Master taverner, a leg of chicken and a capon. Ale by the quart!"

A figure came out of the shadows. He was dressed in white from head to toe: white hose, white boots, white doublet, white coat, a band of white silk around his neck. However, if his clothes were strange, his face could only be described as hideous. One eye was missing, and a small glass ball took its place: the other contained as much malice and evil as you'd ever see in a thousand eyes. The skin of his long face was tawny, his bloodless lips were pitted with a strange blue dye whilst, instead of a nose, he had a silver cone held on by straps tied at the back of his head. His black hair, receding on his scalp which was also pitted with blue, hung in coils to his shoulders. He carried no weapons, only a silver topstick which he tapped on the wooden floorboards as he walked. I abruptly realised that many of the strangers at the tables around me were part of his retinue. I had not seen any of them before. These weren't cranks and counterfeit-men but killers; mean-eyed, narrow-mouthed and armed to the teeth with swords and daggers, some even had large horse pistols in their belts. They fanned out around me. I realised this was not a social visit. A dagger pricked the nape of my neck.

"On your knees before the Lord Charon."

"Who in hell's name is he?" I snarled.

"He is Lord of the Underworld."

I turned. "And you?"

"I," a red-haired, dog-faced man replied, "am his faithful Cerberus."

"Oh yes," I sneered. "And I'm Lucrezia Borgia."

A kick to my legs sent me on my knees. My head was yanked back and I was forced to stare up into Charon's hideous face. Memories stirred, stories about a vagabond king, a Prince of Thieves who controlled the rogues and riffraff of London. He took his name from the Greek ferryman of the underworld who had a snarling dog called Cerberus. Charon had supposedly been a gunsmith, a master of the King's ordnance, until, at some siege on the Scottish March, powder had blown up in his face. Such a man now stared down at me. I couldn't decide which was the more horrible: the good eye glittering with malice or the ball of glass that gave him the look of a living corpse.

"Welcome to my court." Charon's lips hardly moved. "Who gave you licence to trade in the city? To harvest the fields of my manor? To reap where you have not sown?"

"Piss off!" I shouted back. "Boscombe allowed me!"

(I am a born coward but one with a hot temper. I don't like being threatened. I wish I had just given my true nature full rein, grasped the ruffian's ankles, kissed his feet and slobbered for mercy. I might have been spared that knock on the head which sent me unconscious and the horrible nightmare which followed.)

I returned to consciousness in a cavern lit by cresset torches and rushlights. The smell was strange, savoury roasting meat mixed with the more pungent, iron smell of dirty water. I picked myself up and saw that Charon was sitting on a throne-like chair, his feet resting on a gold-fringed, velvet footstool. On either side of the cavern his companions lounged at trestle tables covered with silver and pewter plates. Rugs of pure wool, at least three inches thick, covered parts of the floor. Tapestries of different colours and bearing various insignia, especially the letters 'I.M.', covered the walls. Behind Charon's chair I glimpsed chests, locked and padlocked, but one was open, a small moneybox filled to the brim with silver coins. Cerberus swaggered over. He pushed a cup of wine into my hands.

"Drink!" he growled. "All of the Lord Charon's guests drink."

"Where am I?"

Cerberus pulled a bodkin from his belt and jabbed it in my arm. I screamed with pain.

"Drink!" he ordered.

I did so: it was the best claret I had supped since I had left Ipswich.

"Do you know where you are?" Charon leaned forward. "Master Shallot, do you know where you are?"

"Judging by the company, somewhere in hell."

Charon snapped his fingers and the bodkin went in my arm again. I tried to grasp Cerberus but he danced away, then came back and stung me again. I crouched back on my heels, nursing my arm.

"Please," I pleaded, "I have done no wrong."

Immediately all the ruffians grasped their own arms, swaying backwards and forwards.

"Please," they mimicked, "I have done no wrong."

I kept a still tongue. My belly was beginning to bubble and cold sweat made itself felt.

"You are in the sewers of London," Charon spoke up. He gestured airily at the vaulted roof. "The Romans built these." He got to his feet again, clapping his hands gently. "I want to show you something, Shallot." He tapped me on the nose. "I should really cut your throat or place you face down in some filthy sewer. Or, even better, show you what happens to those who cross me. But you are Shallot, aren't you? Friend of Benjamin Daunbey, nephew to the great cardinal. What are you doing in London?"

"Selling relics."

"The Orb of Charlemagne?"

I smiled ingratiatingly. "Not that," I replied. "At least not yet."

"Do you know about the Orb?"

"A little."

Charon's glass eye bored down at me. "I should kill you," he whispered. "But you've powerful friends and I have bigger game to hunt. You may prove useful." He drew himself up. "So, this time a warning, as well as confiscation of all your goods."

He pointed to a pile of my possessions in the corner. I glimpsed my saddlebags, shirts, relics, even the small bag of coins I had hidden under the floorboard in my chamber at the Flickering Lamp.

"I want to show you something. Bring him forward."

Hustled by two ruffians I followed Charon out. We entered a long gallery lit by torches with caverns off the walkway. To my right was the sewer water, black, glinting in the torchlight.

62

"The stench is not so bad," Charon said over his shoulder. "Hardly any offal comes this way." He shrugged. "My sense of smell I lost with my nose but cleanliness is next to Godliness, Shallot! My ruffians here have directed the offal elsewhere."

We walked further down the causeway then Charon stopped. He took a torch from the wall and held it out over the black, slopping water. Something was floating in the water, lazily, like an otter in a stream.

"Throw some food," Charon ordered.

One of his henchmen cast some bread into the water as well as on to the opposite ledge. The water swirled. I moaned in terror at the black, slimy rat which crept out of the sewer and on to the far side. Now, you gentle readers know what I think of rats! I have been pursued by leopards, wolves, and savage hunting dogs but nothing terrifies me more than a rat. This was not one of your little brown gentlemen but a long, black, slimy bastard, at least a yard in length from the tip of its tail to that quivering snout. He grasped the scraps and gnawed at them. Looking up, the rodent stared across at me, as coolly as a man would inspect some juicy meat pie. Charon led us on. The air grew colder. We turned into a cavern. A corpse lay in an iron gibbet on the floor. It was beginning to decay and the air was rich with the stench. Rats were already moving amongst the iron bars. There's only so much my poor mind can take. I closed my eyes and, God forgive me, swooned like a maid.

3

I awoke in an alleyway. At first I didn't know who, or indeed where, I was. My hands and feet were tied. I struggled to my knees. My head throbbed and my side ached where someone had kicked me. A beggar came out of a doorway and stared pityingly.

"Faugh!" His hand went to his nose.

I looked down. I was naked and covered in thick, clammy mud from head to toe: I had been rolled in the contents of a midden heap.

"Help me!" I wailed.

"Piss off!" the beggar grated.

I crawled along the alley. I felt so miserable I started to pray: desperately, I swore great oaths that I would never touch another drop of wine or even think of lifting a girl's petticoat.

(You can see how low I must have fallen!)

Even the beggars stayed away from me whilst a drunk kicked me with his boot. The ropes around my ankles and wrists were tied tightly, the cord biting into the skin. At last I crawled to the steps of a church. I fainted and, when I regained consciousness, my hands and feet were freed and I was staring into the kind eyes of a friar, his weather-beaten face, greasy, straggly moustache and beard framed by his cowl.

"Help me!" I begged.

"I can do no more," the friar replied. "I've cut your cords." He lifted a battered, tin cup to my lips. The wine was watered but it tasted like nectar. He pointed to some sacking on the ground beside me. "Put this on." He got me to my feet, helped me put the sacking over my head, and fastened it round my middle with a piece of cord. He then gave me a staff and thrust a piece of bread into my other hand. "God have mercy on you, Brother!"

And he was gone. Ever since I have always had affection for the little brothers of St Francis. Even now, in my secret chamber, I have that piece of sacking. Moreover, on the walls of my chapel, despite the fact that my chaplain is of the reformed faith, I have had the words of St Francis boldly painted: 'GO OUT AND PREACH THE GOSPEL. PREACH! PREACH! PREACH! SOMETIMES YOU CAN EVEN USE WORDS!'

After the friar left me, I realised I was in Grubb Street to the north of Cripplegate. The sky was already scored with the red gashes of sunrise. I slipped through a postern gate into the city and made my way along an alleyway near Mugwell Street. As I walked my confidence returned. My throat was parched, the bread had long disappeared, and my belly ached for food. I thought how splendid it would be to stretch out between crisp sheets with young Lucy.

"Penny for a beggar!" I cried outside a church. "Penny for a poor man!"

The early morning worshippers ignored me. I moved to the church of St Ursula and tried again.

"Penny for a poor Christian!" I wailed. "On pilgrimage to the Holy Land, I was taken prisoner by the Turks, and ransomed by the Holy Father himself."

Within an hour I had collected a shilling and, after a beef pie and two cups of wine at an alehouse, I was striding back along the alleyways towards the Flickering Lamp. Boscombe greeted me as if I was the prodigal son.

"Master Shallot." He put his arm round me and brought me into the taproom. "Roger, my dear." Boscombe wrinkled his nose. "What's that smell?"

I looked down and realised that though the kindly friar had removed some of the mud, most of it still remained. I immediately stripped and went to the pump in the yard and had the most thorough bath I've had for many a day. Boscombe provided me with new clothes, loaned me a shilling as well as half a roast chicken, some bread and a bottle of ale. Boscombe watched me eat. When I had finished, he beamed across the table.

"No more trickery for you, Roger my boy," he declared. "The Lord Charon has paid visits before to deliver an invitation to his underworld. No one has ever returned. If he sees you begging on the streets again, your torso will be found in the Fleet and your head in the Thames."

"Master Boscombe." I leaned back and patted my stomach. "Your kindness I won't forget. As for Charon, the Lord be my witness, I will repay him in kind."

"Shush!" Boscombe waved his hand, begging me to lower my voice.

"However," I continued, "discretion is the better part of valour and revenge is a dish best served cold."

Boscombe nodded.

"So, what do you suggest?"

Boscombe shrugged. "You are personable, Master Shallot, you have friends in high places. Why not go to them?"

I shook my head.

"I just couldn't do that. I've told you

68

about the Poppletons and I'm convinced they would follow me. Although I am lower than a worm, I couldn't crawl to great Tom Wolsey to beg for his protection."

(Of course that was not true: I can beg with the best of them but the problem was that the sly bastard might not favour me. But years later, when old Tom Wolsey was in disgrace, dying in his bed at Leicester and the servants had fled, taking everything that could move with them, old Tom grasped my hand.

"You should have come to me, Roger," he whined, tears streaming down his face. "All those times you were in danger, you should have come to old Tom Wolsey. I would have helped!"

"If you'd served me," I retorted, "as I have served you, you wouldn't have to say that!"

Wolsey let go of my hand and turned his face to the wall.

"If I had served my God," he murmured, "as well as I have served my King, he would not leave me to die like this." And die he did.)

However, on that autumn day so long ago, Wolsey was my last refuge. Boscombe was staring at me, picking at his teeth.

"You owe me money," he grated. "And I've a few possessions of yours." He was referring to the few items I'd given him as surety. "But you need money," he continued. "You should go to St Paul's and hire yourself out."

Boscombe was right, or so I thought at the time; I couldn't beg, my relics were all gone and I daren't go back to Ipswich. So I took his advice and decided to try my chances with the rest of the masterless men walking up and down the main aisle of St Paul's Cathedral, waiting to be hired near the *Si Quis* door. But who would want to hire me? I had no letters or accreditation, no references from a previous employer. And what could I do? Bawl out that I had done special work for his Eminence Cardinal Wolsey? I walked round and round that bloody church till I was exhausted, before Fortune intervened.

I was sitting with my back to Duke Humphrey's tomb when I saw a pair of laced shoes and, just above them, a cream satin petticoat under a blue satin dress. I looked up and smiled. The woman who was standing over me was plump and comely but, I could tell from one glance at those hot eyes and wet lips, she was a lecher born and bred. She had a false, sweet smile and looked me up and down as hungrily as a fox would a chicken.

"I need a porter," she simpered, "to

carry goods up and down the stairs." She touched her back. "I've had a touch of the rheums."

Well, I was hired. Her name was Beatrice Frumpleton, wife to some notable in the city with a fine house, all plaster and black timber on a red brick base, in Chancery Lane near Grays Inn. It was a busy household with scullions, maids, servants and retainers, all with one duty under God — to keep Mistress Beatrice Frumpleton in a good mood and to satisfy her every whim. The house was beautiful, with polished wainscoting, galleries, broad staircases, heavy oaken furniture with Bruges cloths and drapes hanging on the walls and cupboards stuffed full of fine pewter plate and silver.

Now, you know these great mansions, they are a law unto themselves: a strict hierarchy rules amongst the servants and strangers are distrusted. I learnt that Beatrice's husband was someone important in the courts but, for the rest, I was left alone although I received the odd pitying glance from some of the male servants. I soon discovered why! Mistress Frumpleton made her husband a cuckold a thousand times over. He was out at the crack of dawn and only returned well after dusk. During the day, certain 'kinsmen' came to visit; they were always entertained in the private chambers, and when they had left Mistress Frumpleton's face was always pinker than before.

To be honest, I don't think even a stallion could have satisfied her. And, yes, you've guessed, my time came! It was during the afternoon, about a week after I had arrived. There was a fair outside St Bartholomew's and the servants had been allowed to attend, all except me. This latter-day Messalina, this Cleopatra of the Thames, not satisfied with me moving provisions and other stuffs around the house, now invited me to her chamber.

I found the room darkened, the windows shuttered and the drapes pulled. A single lamp burned at the side of the fourposter bed upon which Mistress Frumpleton lay as naked as the day she was born. Well, you've heard the expression, 'in for a penny, in for a pound' and I had to do my devoir. Soon we were bouncing about, she squealing, legs and arms flailing, when suddenly the door opened and one of her young kinsmen came into the room. Beatrice sprang from the bed as speedily as a roebuck startled from a thicket. She pushed the young kinsman out of the room, locked the door and turned to me.

"Get dressed!" she hissed.

And, while I did, so did she.

Outside, the 'young kinsman', Oliver or whatever his name was, was hammering and banging. Beatrice threw open the door. The young man, probably aping some Spanish masque he had seen, came in dramatically, with sword and dagger drawn. I picked up a bedpan and waited to defend my virtue. The young man, his spotty face full of hauteur, danced towards me but he was even more lily-livered than I. I lifted the bedpan and he danced back. Beatrice loved every minute of it, wailing and crying, clasping her hands — you'd think she was the fair Lucretia waiting to be raped by an entire legion of perfidious Tarquins. I was getting tired of this, and was looking eagerly towards one of the windows when the door was pushed open again. Oh dear! Oh Lord! In strode Beatrice's husband, home early for the first time ever.

In retrospect, I believe that our Messalina intended that! She wanted to show her husband what a cuckold he was and I was to be the sacrificial lamb: her subtle story was to save 'young kinsman'.

Oh, the perfidy of women! Oh, their duplicity! Oh, their wanton fickleness! Oh, tigresses' hearts wrapped in a human hide! Oh, how I love each and every one of them!

"What is this?" Old Greybeard intoned. "Wife, what goes on here?"

The young man quickly sheathed sword and dagger. I lowered the bedpan. Beatrice winked at me, then threw herself on her knees before her husband, clasping his legs.

"Oh, husband!" she wailed.

Now, you young people, listen — for even I, with all my skill in lying, couldn't better this.

"Oh, husband!" she wailed, eyes rolling heavenwards, "Oh, light of my life!"

"Yes, yes, yes," Old Greybeard replied testily. "Who are these young men?"

I breathed a sigh of relief: at least the silly, old dodderer hadn't recognised me as one of his household.

Burning Beatrice realised this as well.

"Oh, husband," she intoned again, stretching one hand out to me. "This young man came here seeking sanctuary from this one," she pointed to the 'young kinsman', "who followed in hot pursuit intent on his blood." She breathed in. "I was at my orisons when this young man," again, pointing to me, "burst in and sought my protection from this young blood bent on vengeance."

Well, I couldn't believe it! For sheer brevity of wit, for skilful subtleness of mind, she could not be bettered! Both I and the

74

'young kinsman' just looked at each other open-mouthed.

"Is that true?" Old Greybeard demanded.

We both nodded.

"Then get you gone!" he declared, pointing dramatically to the door. "Go different ways or I'll call the watch. Settle your quarrels elsewhere."

We fled like two rabbits freed from a trap and, by late afternoon, I was back, leaning against Duke Humphrey's tomb in St Paul's, waiting to be hired.

I had no luck that day and Boscombe's generosity was wearing thin when, late the following morning, Dame Fortune gave her wheel another twirl. (Although, in retrospect, she was given some assistance this time.) I was leaning against a tomb making lascivious eyes at a young serving maid when I felt a tap on my shoulder. I glanced up: the man standing over me was tall, noble-faced, strong-jawed with an aquiline nose; his grey eyes were gentle, the brow under the balding head furrowed and concerned. He was dressed soberly but his fur robe was of good-quality cloth whilst the gold rings on his fingers were not gewgaws from some tinker's tray.

"Master Shallot." He extended a hand,

I scrambled to my feet and shook it. He introduced himself. "Sir Hubert Berkeley, goldsmith. I've a shop in Goldsmith Row between Bread Street and Friday Street."

"My congratulations," I replied.

He smiled, took his gold-topped cane, which had been resting against a pillar, and leaned on it.

"I know you, sir: you're servant and equerry to Benjamin Daunbey, nephew of the great cardinal. I'm his banker."

My face split into a broad smile.

"Sir Hubert, of course!"

In fact I hardly knew the fellow though my nimble mind was turning like a Catherine wheel. I kept my money banked with the goldsmiths in Ipswich and it didn't stay there for very long, but Benjamin was a cautious soul. I also remembered that Berkeley was a royal goldsmith, a powerful man.

"I heard you were here, what is the matter?" he asked, head cocked slightly to one side.

(Do you know, I liked the man: he had nobility of character. In my secret chapel, because I am still of the Catholic faith, I have his name listed in my Book of the Dead because, in the end, I failed him, or I think I did, and brought about his dreadful death . . . but that was all in the future. After all, if hindsight was wisdom, we'd all be Masters of Philosophy.)

"You are not in trouble, are you?" he insisted.

"Well!" I jumped from foot to foot and stared round at the other men and women waiting to be hired. "A little dispute in Ipswich whilst my master's abroad in Italy . . . !"

"And you are too proud to beg?"

"Yes, Sir Hubert, I am too proud to beg."

"You are a rascal, Shallot." Berkeley came closer: he pressed a silver piece into my hand. "You are a rascal born and bred but, so Master Daunbey has told me, a good man in a fight and you are of the court. I've been searching for an honest bullyboy like you!"

I swallowed hard. I wished my master wouldn't boast about me. (You know old Shallot! Oh, I'll fight all right but so will a mouse when it's cornered!)

"I'm a bachelor," Berkeley continued. "I live with my maids and servants, apprentices and journeymen."

"Why do you need a bullyboy?"

Berkeley's eyes slid away. I felt a faint tingle along my spine.

"Secret business." His voice dropped to a whisper. "King's business, Shallot: that's why

I'm hiring you." He pointed to my hand. "You can keep that coin for friendship's sake. I'll need you for a month. You'll receive two of those every week."

An hour later, having sent a message to Boscombe, I was in Sir Hubert Berkeley's house. There is nothing like silver to calm the fears in my cowardly soul. I've never been one to look a gift horse in the mouth and, at the time, I thought Berkeley was the nearest thing to divine intervention. (I only wish I had listened to him more carefully when he hired me.) The goldsmith had a truly spacious house and shop which stood in its own grounds. The base was of red brick, the other three storeys a mixture of white-and-red plaster and black-oaked timbers with a tiled roof and new-fangled chimney pots. Every window had paned, mullioned glass. The floor of each room was covered in red tiles whilst dark wooden wainscoting, the panels carved in the linen fashion, covered two-thirds of every wall. Soft carpets deadened the sound, and gaily coloured tapestries from the looms of the Low Countries gladdened the eye. Window sills and ledges were filled with baskets of flowers whilst the furniture had obviously been fashioned by the best carpenters in London.

Berkeley was a scholar, a collector of books and the lord of a very harmonious household. There was no distinction between those who served and the master. We all sat at the same table in Sir Hubert's long hall and ate the same appetising food and drank the same good wines. Every man, woman and child had their own bed and chest. I was given a clean-swept garret at the top of the house, and was as happy as a little pig in its sty as I became immersed in the routine of the household. Up before dawn, morning prayers, Mass at a nearby church and then work right through to sunset. Of course we were allowed to break our fast and we dined at noon on a light collation. Once dusk fell the shop was closed and we all gathered round the table for the evening meal.

My duties were light. I was given a war-belt, sword and dagger and I had to look brave, supervising the apprentices and journeymen as they set out the stalls in the two great rooms in front of the house that served as the shop. Now, looking brave, walking with a swagger and glaring fiercely at some ragged-arsed urchin, was easy for old Shallot. I'll be honest, when I saw Will Shakespeare's Henry IV and watched old Nym and Bardolph tread the boards, I laughed till the tears ran down my cheeks as I recognised myself.

Nevertheless, I am quick of wit. I wondered why Sir Hubert should hire me now? A young serving wench, with breasts like plums and a kiss as sweet as sugar, whispered that I was the first such bullyboy to be taken into the household, though Sir Hubert had been looking for someone trustworthy for weeks.

"So why now?" I asked, unlacing her bodice and wistfully thinking of Lucy Witherspoon.

"I don't know," she simpered back. "But the master has something hidden away in his secret chamber down in the cellars."

"What?" I asked.

"I don't know," she repeated, putting soft arms round my neck. "But it was brought here by — " she closed her eyes " — a foreign man, dark-faced with strange orange hair."

"Orange?"

"That's how it appeared to me. I forget his name. There was an Englishman with him. Sir Thomas Kempe."

A chill caught my spine. I knew Kempe. One of the Great Beast's *Agentes in Rebus*. I had met this collection of lovelies before: a gang of assassins, spies, secret agents whose motto was: 'THE WILL OF THE PRINCE HAS FORCE OF LAW'. If the

80

Great Beast wanted something — anything — they'd oblige!

I finished my tryst with the young lady but, I'll be honest, my mind was elsewhere. If Kempe was around I intended to stay in the shadows. Two days later, he and the stranger, Theodosius Lord of Egremont, imperial envoy to London, slipped into the shop just before dusk. I stayed at the back of the house because Sir Hubert insisted on dealing with them alone. I heard the clink of steel outside and knew Kempe had brought some of his braves along. I stared through the poor light and caught Egremont's features. He was swarthy-faced, cruel-eyed and narrow-mouthed, lean of visage and his wolf-like face was not helped by his hair, which was dyed a disgusting colour. Sir Hubert took them downstairs to the fortified chambers in the cellars where he kept his most valuable commodities. An hour later they returned, and then Kempe and Egremont disappeared into the night.

Later on, after supper, Sir Hubert asked me to stay behind. Whilst the hall emptied, he chatted about everyday matters before he grasped my wrist.

"Roger, if something happens to me . . . "

I looked up in alarm.

"If something happens to me," he repeated

hoarsely, "go upstairs to my chamber, where there's a tapestry on the wall depicting Daniel come to judgement. Take that down and behind it you'll find a small door. The handle is intricate: you can only open it if you press it down twice, then up three times. It's the work of London's best locksmith. No keys but, remember," he pointed at me, "two down, three up, gentle pressure. Anything else and the door will not open."

"Master," I whispered, drawing closer. "What nonsense is this?"

"No, no, listen."

And I had to, even though my stomach was beginning to curdle.

"In the little recess," Berkeley continued, "there are valuables: my will, and certain manuscripts. More importantly, there's a velvet pouch containing two keys: one is to the middle door in my cellars. When you open this you'll find nothing there except a steel box with three locks. The second key will open all three but only in sequence. The middle one first, followed by the one on the right, then the lock on the left."

"Master," I asked. "Why trust me?"

"I have to." Berkeley smiled. "You may be a villain, Roger, but I've watched you. Since you arrived here, not one piece of silver or gold has disappeared."

"Master!" I stared in mock anger. "As if I would!"

"You are a rogue, Shallot," he quipped back. "But an honourable one, not a dog that bites the hand that feeds it." He drummed his fingers on the samite tablecloth. "On second thoughts," he declared. "Stay here." He walked out of the hall.

A few minutes later he returned, a velvet pouch in his hand, and beckoned me to follow him. We went along the gallery and he opened the door leading down to the cellar. He paused to light a lamp and then I followed him down the steps into the dank, cold passageway. Berkeley stopped again to light other lamps that were placed on hooks against the brick wall. The gloomy passageway flared into light. I noticed three cells or storerooms, The door to each was reinforced with steel bands and metal studs. Berkeley opened the centre door and went in. The room was a perfect square, no windows, no other opening whatsoever, just a stone floor with brick walls.

In the centre of the room stood an oaken table and, on it, the metal chest Berkeley had described. He locked the strong room door behind us and showed me how to open the chest. He lifted the lid and carefully took out a brown, velvet bag. He loosened the cord at the top and, with both hands, held up the Orb of Charlemagne. If I had known what that bloody thing meant for me, what danger it would place my tender life in, I would have run screaming from the house. At the time I just stood and stared at this gold ball ringed with bars of silver in which precious jewels glinted and gleamed. At the top of the orb was an amethyst, so pure it caught the light and gave off its own fire. Fixed to the top of the amethyst was a pure gold cross with a ruby in the centre.

"Hold it, Shallot," Berkeley whispered. "Take into your hands the Orb of Charlemagne, held by Europe's greatest Emperor!"

I did so: it wasn't heavy. "Why is it here?" I asked, giving it back.

"Because the King has decided to hand it over to Emperor Charles V. My task is to clean it, ensure it is in perfect condition and then, at the appointed time, deliver it to Charles' envoy, Theodosius Lord of Egremont."

"Clean it!" I exclaimed.

"Make sure it's in good order," Berkeley stammered. "That there's no damage, nothing missing." He refused to meet my eye and I wondered what he was concealing.

"And this is what I am really guarding?" I asked.

"Yes, it is." Berkeley placed the orb back in the velvet pouch, returned it to the chest, patted me on the shoulder and led me out of the strongroom.

"Very few people know the Orb has been moved. Soon, however, the tittle-tattle will begin. And you know what happens if you light a torch and put it above a carp pond?"

I smiled back. "All the fish rise to the top."

"Precisely," Berkeley declared. "It's not the fish which frighten me, Roger. It's the pike and the other dark things that live in the muck and slime at the bottom." He locked the strong-room door and grinned at me. "And, before you say it, Roger, you can recognise pikes!"

"You fear for your life?" I asked.

"The love of wealth is the root of all evil, Roger."

He led me up out of the cellar. He sighed and rubbed his stomach.

"The Orb is a precious relic as well as an object of rare beauty. There are men who would give their right hand just to see what you have seen." He blew out the lantern and put it back on its hook near the cellar door.

"Remember what I've told you."

I did and was to thank God that he had warned me. Two nights later I was carousing in a tavern at the top of Goldsmith Row, the Silver Lion, a spacious place where I could sit in the shadows and enjoy my ale. On that particular evening, feeling good and wondering when Benjamin would return, I was about to leave. Indeed, I was just through the door leading into the lane, when two cowled, hooded figures stepped out of the darkness. My hand immediately went to my dagger.

"Don't draw!"

I recognised the voice, soft as the hissing of a snake. Charon, Lord of the London underworld, pulled back his cowl. In the light from the tavern window his face looked more liverish and ghastly than ever.

"Well, well, Roger." He looked me up and down from head to toe. "Like a cat, aren't you? Landed on your feet!"

"I have employment," I replied.

"Yes, yes, so you have, with Sir Hubert Berkeley the royal goldsmith."

I felt behind me for the latch to the door.

"Don't go yet." Charon stepped closer, his breath stank of fish. "Have you noticed anything, Roger?"

"Yes, you smell."

86

"Now, come, come!" Charon declared. "You don't want to visit my halls again, do you, Shallot? I asked you a question, have you noticed anything untoward in Master Goldsmith's house?"

"There's a comely wench." I replied. "She has breasts like plums . . . "

My words were cut off as Charon drew his knife, and the tip caught me under the chin. "Ever the wit, eh, Shallot? But listen," he continued. "If you notice anything out of the ordinary arriving you'll come and tell us, won't you? Where it is and how to get it." He nodded to his masked companion. "Cerberus, my good dog and your friend, will be drinking here every night after Vespers. He'll also be waiting, Roger, for any little tidbit you can offer."

They disappeared as quietly as they came. I went back into the tavern and stood by the beer barrels drinking a large goblet of wine to stop my stomach pitching and my legs trembling like twigs in the breeze. Yet the horrors of the night were not yet over. I was about to have the goblet refilled when a voice behind me shouted, "There he is! There's my poor mother's assassin!"

I turned. In the doorway, with members of the Watch thronging about them, stood the Poppletons.

4

Oh, what a fall! Like Lucifer! Like lightning from heaven! It only shows how fickle Fortune is — just when you think things are all right, some bastard comes along and pricks your good fortune like a child does a bladder. I didn't even have time to finish my wine, before the Poppletons and the Watch were upon me. I was buffeted and shoved, both Edmund and Robert managed to get in blows to my cheeks whilst the rest of the rogues helped themselves to whatever valuables I had: my coins, my cloak, my hat all disappeared in the twinkling of an eye. I didn't even have time to seek help from Sir Hubert before I was hauled off to the horrors of Newgate prison.

Oh, Lord save us, don't ever go there! The gloomy, cavernous gatehouse; the stench of human misery; the middens piled high in the cobbled yard. A Stygian darkness lit by flickering cresset torches. Burly, evil-faced men stripped me of all my clothes. All I received in return was a piece of rough sacking. Barefoot, I was pushed down a dank passageway and into a filthy cell, where the

Poppletons, grinning and sneering, bade me a fond farewell. I saw the bastards pay the gaoler a silver coin — not for my sustenance but to make my life as hellish as possible. He did: a bulbous-faced toad, a hog of a man, he showed me the warrants which the Poppletons had sworn out from a local justice.

"You are for the assizes at Guildhall," he added gloatingly. "And then it'll be a cart and the gallows for you."

"I know people at court," I stammered back. "Cardinal Thomas Wolsey."

"Aye," the fellow replied. "And I'm related to the queen."

"Will you not at least take a message to Sir Hubert Berkeley?" I pleaded.

The fellow stretched out his hand.

"Payment, sir."

"He'll pay you."

The keeper brought back his hand and smacked me across the face.

Two mornings later I appeared before the Justices in the Guildhall. The corner of my mouth was a bloody mess and both my eyes were beginning to close. I was unshaven, smelling of gaol and vermin: I could tell from the supercilious look of the clerk that His Majesty's Justices would not spend long on me.

The Poppletons were there with some sprig of a lawyer. I stood chained to the bar. The Justices came in, and sat down and all three stared across at me. My heart sank. Oh, most cruel of coincidences! Oh, weep for poor Shallot! The bugger in the middle, dressed in a scarlet gown lined with ermine, was no less a person than that Frumpleton who had caught me in his bed chamber with his wife. Ah well, such is the way of the world. The trial was a farce. The Poppletons presented their evidence depicting me, poor little Shallot, as a rogue and a charlatan who had settled grievances by poisoning their mother. They described how they had tracked me to London and how an informant outside St Paul's had directed them to a tavern in Whitefriars. After that it had been easy. They had called at Berkeley's household and been told I was drinking at the Silver Lion.

"Do you have anything to say in answer to these charges?" Frumpleton bellowed, glaring hatefully at me.

"I'm innocent!" I bleated.

His cruel mouth twisted into a sneer. "Aye, as innocent as Herod: a fine teller of tales."

The Justice on his right, a liverish-faced sprat, spoke up.

"A teller of tales! Well, well, Shallot, tell us a tale, and perhaps you won't hang."

I saw him nudge Frumpleton, and knew they were only mocking me. The Poppletons, now full of themselves, smiled maliciously. They rubbed their hands, hardly able to wait before sentence was passed.

"Yes," Frumpleton bellowed, wrinkling his nose. "Tell us a funny tale, Shallot, and you probably won't hang." He glanced sneeringly sideways. "Well, at least, not immediately."

(Now, you know Shallot. When I am down, it's bad enough but to be baited as well!)

"I'll tell you a funny story," I shouted back, rattling my chains. "One day there was a dispute between God and the Devil."

"Yes!" Frumpleton nodded. "But no blasphemy, Master Shallot!"

"Oh no, sir, the truth. Well, the dispute couldn't be settled so God went back to Heaven and Satan back to Hell. A short while later God sent an emissary to Satan, saying he was unable to get legal advice."

"Why?" Frumpleton asked.

"Oh, you see, my lord," I smiled coolly, "there aren't any lawyers in Heaven!"

Well, that was it! On went the black cap and I, Roger Shallot, was sentenced to be taken to a place of lawful execution, namely

Tyburn, as soon as possible, which meant the following morning, and hanged by the neck until dead.

I was hustled from the court, the bailiffs beating and shoving me, and was returned to the condemned cell at Newgate where I spent the night fighting off the rats. The only consolation offered was that just after midnight, when I was sitting blubbering in a corner bemoaning my fate, the Bellman arrived outside. I could hear his voice as he rang the bell for the condemned felons.

"You who in the condemned cell do lie,
Pray on your knees for tomorrow you die!"

"Piss off," I screamed.

I mean, it's bad enough being hanged without having someone ringing a bloody bell and telling you to pray. When dawn came I was really frightened. In my life I've always been plucked from danger just in time but who would do that now? Benjamin was away. Berkeley probably didn't know where I was and how could I get a message to the court?

When I was dragged out of the cell the next morning I was beginning to shake.

Thank God, the friar who climbed into the cart to accompany me to Tyburn had a wineskin and he let me drink liberally from it. By the time the executioner joined us I could hardly sit straight. He glowered at me through his red mask.

"No trouble from you, my boy. Up the ladder you'll go, fast as a monkey, then jump, as hard as you can. It will snap your neck: they say it's better than strangling."

"Do you want to show me how it's done?" I asked.

The executioner grinned. His assistant climbed on to the seat, gathered the reins in his hands and the cart trundled towards the main iron gates. They swung open. The crowds were massed outside, gathering to watch another human being die. I could hardly believe it: I, Roger Shallot, was about to get my just deserts — but for a crime I had never committed! I thought of jumping from the cart but my feet were shackled. I saw the door to the gaoler's office open, and the fat toad waddled out, followed by two other figures. The keeper held up his hand for the horse to stop.

"Oh, let me die!" I moaned. I didn't want another punch in the face as a fond farewell.

"Stop!" the keeper cried.

"Release that man!" another voice shouted.

I narrowed my eyes: the other two figures were my master and Doctor Agrippa.

"Release him!" Agrippa repeated, coming up towards the cart. "I bear a pardon from the King himself."

Well, that was too much for old Shallot. I fell into a dead swoon. I awoke lying on clean sheets in the Fleur de Lys tavern, just opposite St Sepulchre's. Agrippa sat on one side of the bed, my master, looking more swarthy than ever, sat on the other smiling down at me.

"Welcome home," I murmured. "I am sorry."

Benjamin just leaned over and pushed a cup of wine between my lips.

"Drink, Roger," he urged. "Drink and rest."

I did so. I remember the sunlight coming through the window. I fell asleep again and when I awoke it was dark but I felt refreshed and as hungry as a wolf. Agrippa was standing by the window, and my master was asleep in the chair with a rug thrown over him. I sat up. Benjamin shook himself awake. He wouldn't hear any explanation but went and ordered the taverner to bring up food.

We sat round the table for my feast. I didn't

talk but ate as if it was my last meal. My two companions simply sipped at the wine and watched me intently. Benjamin seemed no worse for his travelling. He remarked, with a humorous smile, that because I hadn't been with him, his journey to Venice had been speedy and uneventful. On his return, the King's cog had docked at one of the eastern ports and he'd travelled swiftly to our manor where he had found out what had happened with the Poppletons.

"After that," he concluded, "I came into London. The King and the court are at Eltham. Doctor Agrippa and I combed the city but, thankfully, it didn't take long to find you. Berkeley the goldsmith told me how the Poppletons and the Watch had called to find you and how he had heard that you had been taken by the constables but could not find out where."

"I did." Agrippa broke in. He put a black-gloved hand over mine. "Always in trouble, Roger." He sighed. "I knew it must be the Fleet, the Marshalsea or Newgate. A few hours more and we would have been collecting your corpse from Tyburn." He peered into my face. "When you were asleep I shaved you!"

My hand flew to my chin.

"And a tavern wench washed you." He

grinned widely. "Don't worry. She was delicate in all her movements."

"Which is more than I can say for that bloody keeper!" I retorted.

Agrippa stroked my hand soothingly. "Don't worry," he murmured. "You are my friend, Shallot. The keeper will know the King's wrath soon enough."

"And the Poppletons?" I asked.

"Gone back to Ipswich like beaten curs," Benjamin replied. "Their tails between their legs." He pointed a finger at me. "But, Roger, I told you — no medicines."

"It was relics I was selling," I protested.

"Trickery and knavery." Benjamin's eyes remained smiling.

"What happens now?" I asked.

"You have been granted a pardon."

"But, to the people of our village," I retorted, "I am an assassin, a slayer of an old woman. I never killed her, master."

"The Poppletons claim you did."

"I found out you had stayed at the Flickering Lamp," Agrippa spoke up. "The landlord, Boscombe, said the Poppletons had been there, not only looking for you but demanding their property, the return of a cup stolen from their mother's room. Boscombe seems a good fellow. He refused to help them and says the cup is still in his possession."

I sat back and looked at a spider weaving a web in the far corner of the room. I hadn't forgotten Newgate and, whatever happened, I was determined to settle with the Poppletons.

"You work for Sir Hubert?" Benjamin broke into my reverie. "You know what he has been doing?"

"Yes, master." I sighed. "He has the Orb of Charlemagne in his care."

"The day after tomorrow," Agrippa remarked, "the Orb is to be removed to a small fortified manor house in the fields to the east of the Priory of St John of Jerusalem. You, Roger, and Master Daunbey are to be its keepers."

I groaned and put my face into my hands.

"Oh no, master, not again: not one of Dear Uncle's subtle plots."

"It's worse than that," Agrippa continued remorselessly. "I think the King's wily brain has other schemes. He wants you and Benjamin to steal the Orb back."

"What?" I jumped to my feet, the chair crashing to the floor, stilling the clamour from the taproom below. "Master, are you party to this?"

He shrugged. "I have to be, Roger. I have listened to the King's arguments. The Orb

97

has been in the hands of the English Crown for the last seven hundred years."

"In which case," I cried, "why doesn't the King keep the bloody thing? And what's the use of offering it if he's going to steal it back? I have seen the Imperial envoy, Theodosius Earl of Egremont. He's no lamb or little mouse."

"No, he isn't," Agrippa agreed. "And, if you think Theodosius is bad, wait until you meet Cornelius. He's Master of the Noctales, the Night Men: the Emperor's secret agents."

"The King had a plan," Benjamin intervened. "Sir Hubert Berkeley is party to the plot. There are now two Orbs of Charlemagne. The genuine article and a replica fashioned by Sir Hubert himself. Egremont, unbeknown to himself, has been shown both the real Orb and the fake, and so far he has not been able to tell the difference."

"Then why not give him the false one from the start?"

"Theodosius was cleverer than we thought. You have seen Sir Hubert's strongbox, which contains the real Orb?"

I nodded.

"Well, last night, Theodosius sealed it with the Imperial seal. He outfoxed the

King. If that box is opened again, and the seal broken, Egremont will know that a transfer has been made. The box will not be re-opened again: it is to be transported to Maleval Manor house near the Priory of St John."

I sat down and laughed. I just could imagine Henry's anger: that mad, fertile brain turning like a water wheel devising schemes and stratagems! If only the Great Beast had managed to have the replica in the metal box when Theodosius had fixed the seals, all would have been well.

"You can laugh, Shallot," Agrippa declared. "But the King is beside himself with fury. You see, he was wrong-footed and so was Berkeley. Berkeley had the replica in certain chemicals to take away any sheen and make it look older than it was."

"But the replica is now ready?"

"Yes, it's ready," Benjamin replied. "Tomorrow, Roger, we visit the King: he will give us our final instructions."

I groaned and patted my stomach. "Master, why did you agree?"

Benjamin gripped my hand. "It was the only way, Roger. If I hadn't, you would have hanged!"

★ ★ ★

"My dear, dear Roger! My beloved servant!"

The Great Beast stood glowering down at me in his private chamber at Eltham Palace. He extended puffy fingers for me to kiss. I did so warily. Fat Henry loved to wear jewelled rings, and he was not above scoring a lip or knocking a tooth out of someone's mouth. Nevertheless, on that autumn morning, he seemed in fine fettle. He was dressed in a white brocaded jacket, stiffened and covered with jewels, and piped with ermine. He wore white hose and soft leather boots. Around his growing girth was a jewelled belt with a dagger hanging in a brocaded pouch. A quilted jacket of dark blue hung over his shoulders and a bejewelled bonnet of the same colour was on his dark red hair. Yet it was the face you watched.

You are getting fatter, I thought, and more pig-like by the day! Henry's face was square and slightly swollen, the puffy red cheeks jutted up to high slanted eyes which could glare with all the hatred of a frenzied soul; he was strong jawed but with a woman's prim, pursed lips. I watched his eyes which were full of mockery. I think he would have liked to have taken my head and squashed it in his great fat paws.

"I am Your Grace's most faithful servant," I stammered.

Henry crouched down so he could stare into my eyes. "Faithful Shallot, what were you doing in the cart on the way to Tyburn?"

"A misunderstanding, Your Grace."

"A misunderstanding!"

Henry got to his feet, smacking me playfully on the cheek. He turned to where Wolsey was sitting in a box chair next to the throne. Wolsey looked haggard, dressed in purple silk from head to toe: his black hair oiled and pulled to the back of his head. His face was lined with care, and there were deep pouches under those gleaming black eyes.

The Cardinal lifted one gloved hand and quickly pressed a finger against his lips, a sign that I should be careful. You see, things had changed at court. Wolsey no longer regarded me as a fool. Indeed, in the last few months, the seeds of a deep friendship had been sown and I would stand by the great Cardinal when, like Lucifer, he fell from grace, never to rise again. The King, however, had forgotten me and had turned to Benjamin. This time his voice was free of sarcasm. He asked a series of short barbed questions about Venice: when my master gave him assurances that the Venetians would put galleys at his disposal, Henry smacked his hands and returned to sit on his throne.

I stared across to where Agrippa stood in

the shadows but the good doctor had his face turned away. I glanced round the chamber, which was fashioned in the Italian style: black and white tiles on the floor, light-coloured wainscoting against the wall. Above hung tapestries, and cloths of the same colour had been wound around the rafters. My knees were beginning to ache. I prayed the bastard would let us sit on the bench provided behind us. The Beast, however, was in one of his great statesmanlike moods, pondering strategy and subtle schemes. My gaze was caught by a spider which scuttled across the floor. I caught the Cardinal's faint smile and recalled the tale that, where he went, spiders followed.

(I don't joke — at Hampton Court, at least when it was owned by Wolsey, the place crawled with them.)

"You may sit," Henry murmured.

Benjamin and I sighed with pleasure, got off the hard floor and sat like two schoolboys facing their master. Henry watched me, eyes screwed up as he scratched at his chin.

"You've seen the Orb, Shallot?"

"Yes, your Grace."

"Charles V wants it back," the King snapped petulantly.

"What the Emperor wants," I replied emboldened, "and what he gets, are two

102

different things, your Grace."

The Beast, flattered, wagged a finger at me.

"Good boy, Roger. It's a pity — " all good humour drained from his face, " — that you and Berkeley were not able to place the replica in the chest."

"Your Grace, Your Grace!" Wolsey soothingly intervened. "You cannot blame Sir Hubert. Lord Theodosius moved quickly whilst poor Shallot here was facing false allegations."

Henry made a rude sound with his lips.

"I want that Orb," he declared. "It's mine, it's been in the line of England since the days of Alfred. Let the Emperor keep the replica and, one day when I no longer need him, I'll tell him the truth. I want that Orb. I want to bequeath it to my . . . " The King paused. "To my . . . "

"To your son?"

Oh Lord save us, I don't know why I intervened. Benjamin nearly fell off the bench. Wolsey's hand went to cover his face. Agrippa sunk deeper into the shadows. Even the spider headed for the wainscoting. This was one thing you never mentioned at Henry's court. Big-boned Henry, with no son to follow him and already sixteen years on the throne: his mind was constantly turning to what would come after. This time, however, instead of losing his temper, Henry smiled beatifically at me, the tears rolling down his cheeks.

"Yes, Shallot, a son." He was almost sobbing. "A little Henry to follow Daddy. Why, Shallot? Why doesn't God give me a son? Have I not served him well?"

I nodded wisely. Now was not the time to mention his drinking and his lechery.

"If you hold the Orb of Charlemagne," I volunteered rashly, "perhaps God will grant your request."

The Beast's mood changed abruptly. He wiped the tears from his face, got up and strode towards me. He grasped me by the hair, pulling back my head, his face only a few inches from mine, so that I could smell the rottenness of his blackening teeth.

Henry always drenched himself in perfume. If his mouth didn't smell, that suppurating ulcer on his leg invariably did.

"The Orb of Charlemagne!" Henry hissed. "The Orb of Charlemagne! You'll get it back for me, won't you, Roger boy?" He breathed in deeply. "You've received a pardon but that's not the end of the matter," he hissed. "In a few weeks' time Captain Buncel is taking my ship the *Peppercorn* down the west coast of Africa. He's looking for officers. If you don't re-take the Orb, it's the *Peppercorn* for you, my lad!"

Henry returned to his chair and sat there moodily.

"Lord Egremont is waiting outside," Wolsey smoothly intervened. "With Sir Thomas Kempe."

"Let him wait!" the King snarled.

Suddenly, behind us we heard a crash and a bark which sounded as deep as a bell. The hair on the nape of my neck curled in fear; Henry sensed this and smiled.

"Gifts, Roger, from his Excellency the Emperor. There are two of them: massive dogs used to hunt bears. I call them Castor and Pollux."

I nodded but my stomach was already beginning to clench. Wolsey, too, stiffened: he knew the King's sick mind and the way he loved to play evil games with me.

"They are both males," Henry continued. "The Emperor made a mistake." He sniggered behind his hand. "I'd like to give one away. Now tell me, Roger, shall we play a game with them?"

I stared back in horror. I knew the Great Beast's games. The last one had me running for my life through Windsor forest pursued by Henry, his courtiers and a pack of hunting dogs. On another occasion I'd nearly been drowned in mud and had my genitals knocked off.

"I have to leave now," Henry said. "Matters of state."

Oh aye, I thought — plunging amongst silken petticoats, more like it! We had arrived at Eltham the previous evening and been given a chamber. Dearest Uncle had informed us that the Queen and her ladies were not present as the King was intent on a week of pleasure. I had seen some of his pleasures! Young, dainty ladies, Henry's whores — so much for his affairs of state!

The King rose to his feet and stretched his great frame until the muscles cracked.

"I was given a riddle, Shallot. A riddle to solve but I don't have the time! Affairs of state."

"Yes, your Grace?" I asked tremblingly.

Henry closed his eyes.

Oh, the bastard loved to bait me!

"A man has to take a fox, a chicken and a bowl of grain across the Thames. His boat can only take the man and the fox or the man and the chicken or the man and the bowl of grain at any one time. If he takes the grain, the fox will eat the chicken. If he takes the fox, the chicken will eat the grain. How does he get all three across?"

Henry took a sweetmeat from a bowl on

the table beside him then wandered across to wipe his fingers on my hair.

"Now, if you can't solve it, Roger," he declared, "you'll have to be punished. But if you can — " he pushed my head back and glared down at me " — you'll win a prize. Now, let that be a warning." His voice fell to a whisper. "Never, never, mention my son again!"

The King swept out of the room. We sat in silence. From the door behind me I could hear those bloody dogs still scrabbling and growling.

"The King is vexed," Wolsey declared. He breathed in noisily through his fleshy nose and glanced pityingly at me. "Shallot, if you have a brain in your head, I would advise you to solve that riddle." He clapped his hands. "But enough is enough, we have business in hand. Doctor Agrippa, bring in Theodosius, Lord of Egremont."

I was about to ask my master if he had any possible solution to the riddle when Egremont strode into the room. The light of day did nothing to improve my judgement of him. He was the same lean-visaged, cruel-eyed man I had glimpsed in Berkeley's house. A wolf in looks and a wolf in nature: he stood, legs apart, surveying us all. A quick curl of the lip left us in no illusion as to what he thought of Benjamin and myself. Beside him Sir Thomas Kempe looked like a stick next to an oak: a small, jovial-faced man with sandy, thinning hair. He was dressed in a dark-green doublet and hose with a cloak of dark murrey, a broad leather sword-belt clasped around his waist. He kissed the Cardinal's ring and made his own blunt introductions to Benjamin and myself. Of course, we had met before but I was not taken in. A native of Yorkshire, Kempe prided himself on his directness and honesty, but only a fool believed this. Kempe's eyes betrayed his soul; dark, black and cold as marble.

Three other men had followed them in. At first I thought they were friars: their heads were shaved and they were dressed in brown gowns which fell just below the knee, with leggings of the same colour pushed into black, high-heeled riding boots. Yet they were not friars. Oh no, not these three lovelies! Leather baldrics hung from their shoulders, each had at least three dagger pouches containing throwing knives. Around their waists were thick black belts with dagger and sword pushed through loops. They didn't swagger, they moved with menace, hands pushed up the voluminous sleeves of their gowns. They bowed very low towards Wolsey, gazed curiously at Agrippa and, with a nod of their heads, acknowledged us. Egremont deliberately allowed us to study them carefully. It was the leader who fascinated me. He was broad and square-faced, with hooded eyes, a sharp, thin nose slightly broken, lips fleshy and full, slightly open as if ready to challenge whatever we said or did.

"This is Cornelius." Egremont's voice was soft, his English was good, only the slight roll on the 'r' betrayed his foreign origin.

"He is a member of my entourage. A special envoy from the Emperor."

"And leader of the Noctales?" Agrippa broke in. "The Men of the Night."

"Ah yes." Egremont's face broke into a lopsided grin. "There are so many legends about these."

"And they are all true." Cornelius spoke up, his gaze fastened on me as if inviting contradiction. I just swallowed hard and hoped I didn't start belching, a sign that I was highly nervous. Cornelius took a hand from his gown. I glimpsed the black diamond fixed into the ring that he wore on his little finger.

"Everything they say about us," he declared, has voice soft, almost dreamlike, "is true!"

(By the way, have you noticed, as I have in my long and varied life, how foreigners speak better English than we do? I blame our teachers: they all need a damn good thrashing!)

"There's no need to bring your guards to England." Wolsey's voice was a harsh rebuke.

"I'm not here because the Lord Egremont asked me to be here," Cornelius retorted.

A flicker of annoyance crossed Theodosius's face. Oh dear, dear, I thought, so there's division in the visitors' camp.

"I am here," Cornelius continued, "because His Imperial Majesty, the Emperor wants me to be here."

I caught the German intonation. Cornelius gestured at me.

"You have your agents, my Lord Cardinal: the Emperor has his."

And this was certainly true. Old Charles, locked away in a monastery watching his clocks, whilst his Noctales, the Men of the Night, watched his subjects. Brown-coated gnats, the Noctales swarmed over the empire listening at keyholes, collecting scraps of information. That pious fool Philip II inherited them: not a donkey farts in Spain that they don't know about. Later in my life, I had the pleasure of meeting the Noctales in the dungeons of the Escorial palace. They had an original way of making you talk; not for them the clumsy, red-hot pincers of the Inquisition. How would you like to spend a night in a pitch-black room, knowing that, somewhere in the darkness, two poisonous snakes waited to pounce?

"Now, now." Kempe walked towards Wolsey. "My Lord Cardinal."

I caught a hint of arrogance in Kempe's voice and, from that moment, I knew his Satanic eminence was beginning to slip down the greasy pole of preferment.

"My Lord Cardinal," Kempe declared. "Matters have now moved apace. Lord Egremont wishes to talk about the transfer of the Orb of Charlemagne and view once more Malevel Manor."

"Agreed, agreed," Wolsey murmured, fingering the silver pectoral cross. "Lord Egremont, my nephew Master Benjamin Daunbey and his servant Roger Shallot will accompany you. They are my personal guarantee, as well as the King's, that the Orb will be transferred safely into your hands."

"In which case," Egremont replied icily, "I shall remember that. On your lives — " he pointed at Benjamin and me " — lies the security of my master's precious relic."

"Aye," Benjamin replied. "And on yours too, Lord Egremont."

5

Ah well, on that pleasant note we all left Eltham: Egremont, Kempe, the Noctales, Doctor Agrippa and his lovely group of cutthroats who served as guards and outriders. We forded the Thames and made our way across the fields past the Priory of St John of Jerusalem. We kept well away from the crowds, though we had to stop at a crossroads near Leather Lane, where they were burying two suicides beneath the gibbet, small stakes having been driven through their hearts. Because of the carts, wheelbarrows and crowds thronging about, we had to wait a while and entertained ourselves by watching the mummers, fire-eaters and sword-swallowers: all those golden boys and girls from the twilight of the city who used such occasions to earn a pretty penny as well as pick a purse. Uneasy, still wracked by anger over what had happened to me in Newgate, I was alarmed at Henry's implied threats, not to mention that bloody riddle. I sat fidgeting. Now and again I would look at the faces around me and it was then I glimpsed him. Someone was stalking us through the crowd!

A man dressed like a tinker, with a leather apron about his waist and a battered hat pulled well over his face. He turned and I glimpsed the dog-like features of Cerberus, Lord Charon's henchman. My hand dropped to my dagger but the crowd swirled and, when I looked again, the villain had vanished.

We rode on. Cornelius pushed his horse alongside mine.

"You seem lost in thought, Master Shallot?"

Despite his appearance the tone was friendly.

"I've been set a riddle by the King," I retorted, glaring over my shoulder at Agrippa. "And I have to resolve it!"

"What riddle?" Cornelius asked.

I told him about the bloody fox, the damn chicken and the pathetic bowl of grain, not to mention getting them across the sodding Thames.

"I am a student from Innsbruck," Cornelius offered. "In my days as a clerk I was a master riddler." He scratched his chin.

"Thank you for your offer of help," I replied, glancing maliciously at Agrippa.

"I cannot help you, Master Shallot," the good Doctor declared. "Oh, and before I forget, the King left a message: you are to have resolved the riddle before we return to Eltham."

If I hadn't had my feet firmly in the stirrups, I would have fallen off my horse. Benjamin leaned over, his long face creased in concern.

"I'm trying to help as well, Roger," he declared. "It's really a mathematical problem. There's a very easy solution but, for the life of me, I can't think of it."

With such supportive words ringing in my ears, we left the highway and followed a rutted track leading to the manor of Malevel. Oh, it was a glorious day! The harvesters were busy working under a warm sun, blue skies and fleecy clouds. It was a perfect day to be in England with a tinge of autumn faint in the air and the fields rich with the promise of a golden harvest. Except for me, poor Shallot: guarding relics, being pursued by Lord Charon and his ilk and riding through the lanes surrounded by some of the most sinister men in Europe. Oh, pity me!

We reached Malevel early in the afternoon. I must give you a careful description of that sombre place. Malevel was built like a square, three storeys high, not from wood and plaster, but of dark-grey ragstone: there were windows on each storey but these were narrow and shuttered. The roof was of red slate, and two chimneys at either end twisted like snakes up into the sky. I could see why it had been chosen: it was a fortified house, probably used by the Crown to detain prisoners well away from the eyes of the city or as a place for the king to meet one of his whores or someone else's wife. Behind the manor was a cobbled yard with stables and out-houses. On either side of it was a narrow garden and, in front, two broad patches of grass divided by a pebble path which swept up to the main entrance. The back door, or postern gate, was small and narrow. The front door, however, was huge: thick blackened timber hung on steel hinges and was reinforced with iron studs. The manor itself was guarded by a high curtain wall built of the same sombre ragstone, at least twelve feet high with spikes on the top. There were no other entrances except under a dark, cavernous gatehouse.

Kempe informed Benjamin and me that the Orb would be moved here. We sat on our horses beneath the gatehouse staring at the manor.

"It was owned by Isabella Malevel," Kempe explained. "Then, one night, about three years ago, the manor was attacked and all its precious objects stolen."

"And Isabella Malevel?" Benjamin asked.

"Oh, she just disappeared. One of life's great mysteries!"

"It's ideal," Egremont broke in. "The best place to keep the Orb. I chose it from the list Kempe gave me."

"It's easy to guard," Sir Thomas added. "Master Daunbey, you and Shallot will stay in the gatehouse."

We left our horses grazing on the grass. Kempe had the keys, and he undid the three locks on the front door and took us in. Now, I have been in many a house of ill repute. I have sheltered in lonely, haunted dwellings on the Scottish March, in ghost-ridden palaces on the banks of the Loire and at gloomy castles along the Rhine. All of them were terrible, blood-soaked places where, as soon as you walked in, the ghosts thronged about you. Malevel was one of the worst.

"It has an air of menace," Benjamin whispered as Kempe led us along a passageway then stopped at a staircase which swept up to the other two floors. I could only agree. Perhaps it was the flagstone floor or the empty walls which caught every sound and made it echo. Or, there again, the narrow windows which only let in slivers of light so each room and gallery had a gloomy appearance with corners full of shadows.

Oh, it was clean all right, it had been swept and washed and there was furniture in every room but I noticed that, because there were no rushes on the floor or hangings on the wall, every sound reverberated. Egremont was proud he'd chosen such a place. He brushed aside Kempe's objections and insisted that we search the house from the tiles on the roof and then down to the dark, eerie cellar.

"Not even a mouse could break in here," I announced.

My master, who had fallen strangely silent, just nodded.

We eventually gathered around the kitchen table, Kempe and Egremont sitting at either end.

"So all is ready," Egremont began. "Now about guards: the Noctales will stay here."

"And provisions?" Kempe asked.

"I shall obtain them," Egremont replied quietly. "We always buy our own food and drink."

"And what about the English guards?" Sir Thomas declared. "The King has promised six of his best archers from the Tower."

"The Orb of Charlemagne will be brought here tomorrow?" Egremont asked.

Kempe nodded. "It will arrive here just after noon."

Egremont scratched his cheek, one finger

playing along a scar from a swordthrust on the side of his jaw.

"The Orb will be brought here," he said, fingers jabbing at the kitchen table. "There will be nine Noctales, the rest will not be needed."

His henchman was about to protest but Egremont made a sweeping movement with his hand.

"I require them, Cornelius," he said softly, "to guard the guards. Now!" Egremont sniffed, narrowing his eyes. "The Orb will arrive here tomorrow and it will remain in its sealed coffer. The house will be shuttered and all doors locked and barred. No one can leave or enter, no matter what happens. This will last for five days until the Imperial caravel has docked in the Thames and all preparations carried out. The Orb will then be transferred to the ship. Until then, my master's relic will be left under the guard of fifteen men: nine Noctales and six of your archers. Do you agree, Sir Thomas?"

Kempe nodded.

"Outside," Egremont continued, "I want dogs to patrol, both night and day. The gatehouse will be guarded by archers, and Cornelius will stay in the gatehouse along with Master Daunbey and his servant. I am satisfied," Egremont declared, "that there are no secret entrances and that my master's relic — " he emphasized each word " — will be safe."

"How do we know nothing will happen in the house?" Benjamin asked.

"We have planned for that," Cornelius broke in. "As the bells of St John's Clerkenwell chime for Matins in the morning, and again at Vespers in the evening, I will bring a shuttered lantern to a window on the first floor of the gatehouse. I shall show it three times. If no lamp is shone in reply, we will know something is wrong."

"How long will this go on for?" Benjamin asked.

"For about five days," Egremont replied. "Until I am ready to sail."

I stared across the table at my master. He had his head down, one hand covering the lower half of his face. He had been listening carefully and I could see he was worried and so was I. If the Great Beast wanted the relic back and replaced with the fake, how could we do it? More importantly, how could I solve that vexatious riddle? My own fear deepened. The Great Beast would be hopping with rage at the way the Imperial Envoy had so cleverly tricked him, so woe betide poor Shallot!

The conversation became more desultory as

Kempe and Egremont hammered out the last details. Even then, before all the horrible and bloody murders began, a thought occurred to me. Why was the Orb being moved here, requiring such secrecy and all these guards? However, when your mind is concentrating on how to get a bloody fox, a chicken and a bowl of grain across the Thames, such Byzantine plans are not worthy of your attention. The meeting ended. As we left Malevel Manor, once again that feeling of unease deepened within me. I thought it was a Hall of Ghosts, a place of misery and sin. I wondered what had really happened to its former owner, the ancient Isabelle Malevel? My master was also quiet. I questioned him closely and found another reason for his misery.

"It's Miranda," he replied dolefully.

My heart skipped a beat.

"She's not unwell?"

"No, worse. She has travelled north to stay with relatives in York. She went shortly after I went to Venice."

(Ah well, the affairs of the heart are always troublesome and, in this story, the beautiful Miranda does not figure but later on, oh yes, she plays a part!)

Benjamin and I went out to the gatehouse and Cornelius joined us. We inspected our

120

chambers: the gatehouse was quite extensive with two chambers on the top floor and two on the bottom, as well as a small buttery or kitchen. Cornelius took one of the top chambers and my master and I the lower two chambers. They were nothing more than narrow cells but they were comfortable. Cornelius inspected the window through which he would show the lantern and pronounced himself satisfied. We heard Kempe calling to us from below. My master went down but Cornelius caught at my sleeve as I prepared to follow.

"I like you, Shallot." His hooded eyes held mine.

"Oh, thank you very much," I replied but grew uneasy. I wondered if Cornelius was one of those bum boys. I know I am not very pretty but, with some people, it's any port in a storm!

"I have to go," I declared.

"I like you, Shallot."

"Yes, of course you do," I said. "And I am a great admirer of your good self."

"I had a brother just like you, who had a cast in one eye. He was as full of roguery as a vat is full of ale: he died of the plague in Innsbruck."

Those hooded eyes still gazed unblinkingly at me.

"You should be very careful," Cornelius continued. "Your king is as mad — how do you say — as a March hare?"

"Nonsense!" I replied. "He's one of the wisest men in Christendom."

Cornelius smirked. "Read that on the way back." He handed across a scrap of parchment.

I walked to the door.

"Oh, and Shallot, take this." Cornelius came over and dropped a small sack into my hands. I felt it carefully, it was some form of powder.

"When you win your prize, use that!"

I gazed quizzically back.

"You'd better go."

I went down the stairs to where Kempe and the others were waiting. I paused halfway down and undid the scrap of parchment. The writing was small and neat, the letters perfectly formed. I read it once, twice, then grinned and put it back in my wallet: I knew the solution to the Great Beast's riddle!

We arrived back at court just before sunset. The Great Bastard was in one of his moods of revelry. He had spent the afternoon flying his falcons out above the marshes so he was in fine fettle, still playing the role of the great statesman relaxing at his pleasures. We met in the same room though, this time,

122

tables had been laid out, covered in silken cloths and decorated with the most beautiful silverware. Henry sat in the middle of a small horseshoe of tables. He was dressed in velvet buckram, his bonnet rakishly pulled to one side of his head. His other cronies were there: Norreys, Brandon the Earl of Suffolk, and their ladies. One beauty caught my eye: tall, elegant, dark-haired and sallow-faced, she was strikingly attractive, dressed in dark-green. She reminded me of some beautiful phantasm, some goddess who appears to huntsmen in the depths of dark woods. Raven brows over eyes full of sensuality. Anne Boleyn! I tell you this — she's been in her grave more than sixty years, buried deep beneath the cold flagstones of St Peter's ad Vincula in the Tower, nevertheless, I can remember every detail about her from that evening. Modest yet saucy, retiring yet alluring, soft spoken and unobtrusive, she drew your eyes and made your heart beat a little faster. I tell the Great Elizabeth whenever she visits: her mother was every inch a woman. Beautiful beyond compare! Like Helen of Troy, mortal sin in clothes. Henry was infatuated with her. You could tell that. He was showing off, seeking her approval for everything he did. She, eyes lowered, would laugh soft and deep in her throat. I envied Henry. I really did. One other thing I noticed: Anne kept the cuffs of her dress well over her hands to cover her extra finger. Years later when I was closeted with her she allowed me to examine this closely. It was nothing much — a slight malformation of her right hand — but her enemies said it was the devil's teat on which she suckled her familiars. Anne didn't need such witchcraft. One kiss was enough!

Anyway, back to the Great Beast's banquet. Cardinal Wolsey was present but he was quiet, rather withdrawn. He was the only man apparently unimpressed by Boleyn and he was intent on showing it. We ate well, roast pheasant, swan, duck, lampreys, eels, the tenderest beef and the most succulent capon, all served in tangy sauces. The wine cups were deep bowled and were constantly replenished. We ate and drank while, in a far corner, boy choristers entertained us with a song composed by Abelard. Henry, like the pig he was, drank deeply until his fat cheeks glowed, his eyes glittered and, in his malice, he turned on old Shallot.

"Tell us now, Roger," he bawled. "Tell us the solution to the riddle!"

"What riddle?" Norreys cried, as if the lying bastard didn't know.

"A man has to take a fox, a chicken and

a bowl of grain across the Thames," the great pig bellowed. "His rowing boat can take only the man and the fox, or the man and the chicken or the man and the grain at any one time." Henry sighed at the knowing looks of his cabal. "If he takes the grain, the fox will eat the chicken. If he takes the fox, the chicken will eat the grain. So, Roger, how does he get the three across?" The fat turd licked his fingers. "If you can't solve it, you must pay the forfeit: the sun has dried our carp pond to a muddy mess and tomorrow, if you fail, you'll have to stand in the centre and play 'Mummer's Boy'!"

I quietly groaned and shut my eyes. "Mummer's Boy' was an old village game: some unfortunate was made to stand in the middle of a mud pack on a three-legged stool whilst others flung clods of mud at him. The one who knocked him off three times was the winner. A stupid, cruel game. Henry would love it! My master stiffened and was about to protest but I tapped him on the knee. I also caught Wolsey's anxious gaze and winked quickly. He smiled back. Anne Boleyn, God bless her, lifted her head and — perhaps it was my fevered brain or the light wasn't so good — I am sure she blew me a kiss. Despite the cruelty she later inflicted on poor Queen Catherine, from that moment my heart was hers!

"Come on, Shallot!" the Hell-King roared. "Give us an answer!"

"Answer! Answer!" His cronies began to bang their cups on the tables chanting like naughty schoolboys.

"Quite easy," I replied, pushing back my chair and standing up. "It can be done in four crossings. First, the man takes the chicken to the other bank and returns to collect the grain. Secondly, the man takes the grain to the other bank and returns with the chicken. Thirdly, the man leaves the chicken and takes the fox to the other bank where he leaves the fox with the grain. Fourthly, the man then returns to collect the chicken. At no time," I concluded triumphantly, "is the fox left alone with the chicken or the chicken left alone with the grain."

My master clapped his hands. The rest, slightly befuddled, scratched their heads as they tried to work it out for themselves. Henry glared at me from under lowering brows.

"Correct, Roger," he purred. "So there will be no 'Mummer's Boy' for you. Let me show you your prize!"

He clicked his fingers at a servant who went to the far doors and flung them open. I heard a baying like the tolling of a bell, the sound of paws scraping the tiled floor, before the shaggiest, largest hunting dog I have ever clapped eyes on lurched into the room, two grooms hanging on to its leather leash for their very lives. The dog chased straight as an arrow to Henry, jumping at the table, knocking pots and dishes, trying to lick the fat bastard's face. Naturally, Henry loved the adulation and his mastery over the dog, popping pieces of meat into its mouth, even allowing it to drink from his water cup. The ladies screamed with delight as Henry scratched the dog's ears.

"Lovely boy!" he yelled. "Lovely boy, get down!"

Henry Norreys, emboldened by the dog's obvious affection, leaned across to give him a piece of meat. The change in that huge mastiff was chilling: ears back, lips curled over his huge teeth — I'd never seen Norreys move so swiftly in my life. Henry stroked the dog, smiling maliciously down at me.

"Your present, Roger!"

I just sat dumbstruck. The dog was massive: at least six to seven foot from the tip of his nose to the end of his tail. He stood four feet high, with a mangy grey coat, massive head and jaws like a huge pike. As the King spoke, the dog turned its head, tongue lolling, eyes gleaming as it glared at me. What could I do? To refuse a King's gift in public was lèse-majesté and, if I did, God knows what delights Henry would have ready for me?

"This is too much," my master whispered.

"Take him away!" Henry shouted. "Take Castor away to the chamber. Roger, make friends with my gift!"

I felt like running straight for the nearest jakes but I had deliberately not drunk too much. I remembered Cornelius's words and, whilst the King was engaged, I'd taken a piece of steak from the plate, opened my pouch and dusted it with some of the powder Cornelius had given me. It smelt sweet and cloying. I closed my eyes and prayed it wasn't poison. Wolsey was hiding the lower half of his face in his hands. Benjamin's fingers were not far from his dagger. Boleyn was no longer laughing. Even Norreys leaned over and murmured something in the King's ear. However, the King was obdurate: Castor the great mastiff was taken away and I had to follow.

The antechamber had two doors. As I went in they were closed and locked behind me. The grooms holding Castor glanced pityingly at me, released the leads and went out of the far door leaving me and the dog alone. The chamber was lit by sconce torches along all four walls: these cast the dog's huge shadow against the wall. Now, it is a universal belief of Shallot: I, who have been hunted by wolves, leopards and, on a number of occasions, flesh-eating rats, still believe that the most cruel animal on earth is of human kind. Moreover, I knew enough about dogs not to move quickly but tried to stare it out. The hound was a good-natured soul. It didn't bound towards me but squatted down on all fours, head up, tongue lolling, watching me intently. I crouched down as well, and took the piece of meat from my pouch. It was tender, easy to pull apart. Castor stood up. I stretched out my hand.

"Come on, lad," I murmured. "Don't eat old Shallot. Here's a nice piece of juicy meat."

The dog padded across. It stopped, sniffed at the meat, the saliva pouring like water from its huge jaws. The meat disappeared, another piece was given. Now, everyone likes a piece of steak, but Castor ate it as if his life depended on it. At last there was none left and he began to lick my hands. He growled at me. A growl that seemed to come from his very belly. I stood up and looked down at him.

"How dare you!" I declared, keeping my voice steady. "Sit!"

Well, down he went, whimpering ingratiatingly, eyes beseeching. I opened the pouch Cornelius had given me. I shook some powder on my fingers and allowed him to lick it.

"Good dog!"

I walked to the far end of the room. He made to follow.

"Sit down!" I shouted.

Down he went like a whore's knickers.

"Up!"

Castor came to attention, tail wagging, eyes intent on me.

"Here!" I snapped my fingers. I could see he was going to bound. "No, walk!"

I tell you, that dog was more intelligent than my chaplain and his parishioners multiplied by ten. He came across, licked the toe of my boot and lay down. I forgot about Henry and his sneering, snarling courtiers, I have had few friends and, in that darkened chamber, suddenly realised that I had another one for life.

Oh well, you should have seen it! I walked back into the royal banqueting chamber, Castor striding behind me. When I said 'down', he sat with me. When Henry called, Castor, God bless his heart, didn't bother even to look in his direction. The courtiers laughed and cheered. Silver purses were thrown. Even old Henry graciously conceded defeat: he hurled his drinking cup at me as a token of his pleasure, narrowly missing my head.

(Many years later, when Henry was syphilitic and I used to push him around the palaces in his wheelchair, he constantly asked me how I did it. Out of respect for Castor's memory, I never told the old rogue.)

The next morning Benjamin and I, with our new companion who insisted on sleeping in the same bed as myself, joined Cornelius in the gatehouse of Malevel Manor. I seized a moment when we were alone, to ask the Noctale what the powder had been and how he had known Henry would give me such a gift? Cornelius grinned: his teeth reminded me of Castor's, white and pointed.

"The riddle," he replied. "No riddle is beyond me, Master Shallot. As for the gift, Lord Egremont gave Henry two hounds. Your king said he only needed one but he intended to give the other to a good friend who least suspected it. When I heard about the riddle, I recalled the king's sniggers." He shrugged. "Castor loves aniseed powder. All dogs do. Give him that and he's yours for life."

"Does the King know?" I asked.

Cornelius shook his head. "The aniseed

powder is a sweet." Cornelius chucked me under the chin with his finger. "But Castor's also a good judge of character, Master Shallot. He apparently saw something in you that others do not."

I became embarrassed. Cornelius tapped me on the shoulder.

"Don't be shy, Master Shallot. I'm not praising you. It's just that I believe that all men are evil but some men less evil than others."

Later in the day, Egremont, Kempe and the rest of the Noctales swept into Malevel Manor. They were accompanied by two score archers from the Tower guarding a covered wagon in which the Orb lay sealed in its steel chest. For a while all was confusion as guards patrolled the grounds and carried out a thorough search of the manor from attic to cellar. Benjamin and I watched from the gatehouse and standing between us, staring out of the window, was Castor. When the grooms brought the royal hunting dogs who were to patrol the grounds at night, Castor threw his head back and barked in joyful anticipation. By now I was accustomed to the animal and the offer of two sweetmeats soon had him crouching on the floor gazing adoringly up at me. We watched as the chest was taken from the cart to the house. I

132

glimpsed Sir Hubert Berkeley amongst those who had come, as well as a young man and woman. I asked Cornelius who they were.

"Oswald and Imelda Petrel."

"Why are they here?"

"The guards have to eat. The Petrels will be allowed in every day at three o'clock to prepare an evening meal, and breakfast for the following morning, as well as to clean dishes in the kitchen. They are to be gone by six." He punched me playfully on the shoulder. "Don't worry, Shallot, Egremont has personally chosen them." He crouched down, patting Castor. "The Orb will be safe as long as your King practises no trickery."

"Not unless he has the power to make himself invisible!" Benjamin retorted. "How on earth, Master Cornelius, could anyone enter such a guarded manor, steal a precious relic and leave with impunity?"

"How indeed?" Cornelius murmured. "But I have seen your master's eyes. He wishes to be the Conqueror of France and, for that, he needs His Imperial Highness's help, but perhaps the return of the Orb is too high a price to pay!"

Two hours later we all met in the manor hall. Berkeley came over to greet me. He looked shamefaced and apologised that he had not known what had happened to me until it was too late. I reassured him and clasped his hand. Berkeley pointed to the steel casket on the table.

"I am glad that's finished, Roger. I am not sorry to see the back of it."

"Did you have any visitors?" I asked abruptly. "Footpads or bullyboys trying to break in?"

"No, no." Berkeley shook his head. "The casket was sealed the day after you were taken. Sir Thomas Kempe's men were seen in the alleyways and streets around. It was safe enough."

"Even from the King's trickery?" I whispered.

Berkeley, God bless him, blushed with embarrassment.

"Trust me, Roger," he whispered. "You would never believe the half of it . . . "

He walked away, called over by Egremont. I turned to the young man and woman I had glimpsed earlier in the day. A comely, married couple who owned a cookshop on the corner of Milkwell Street within chiming distance of St Giles'. Master Oswald was pleasant-faced, eager to please. He was totally over-awed by what was happening, so tongue-tied he could hardly speak. Imelda possessed the brains of the family: sharp-featured with a crisp, cool manner. She dismissed my flirtation with a mock-angry frown and explained how the Foreigner, her title for Egremont, had offered them five gold pieces to serve as cooks.

"How could I refuse?" she declared. "We will be able to extend our shop, even buy an adjoining cottage for an ale-house."

"Why did he choose you?" I asked.

"Why, Master Shallot, my pies are famous throughout London. I am a good cook. We sell to nobles, merchants and taverns. You must see for yourself."

I liked her bright, happy eyes. I was about to take her up on the offer when Egremont asked for the room to be cleared. I still remember the occasion: the Noctales, their cowls pulled over their heads; the rugged, weather-beaten archers, the best veterans in the King's troops with their long bows slung over their shoulders; young Master Oswald eager to please; Imelda smiling over her shoulder at me. They all went out of the chamber to wait in the gallery outside. Oh Lord, I close my eyes. As Macduff says: "I cannot but remember such things were, that were most precious to me." And what is more precious than a point in time when you see others full of life but, with hindsight, realise they were just sacrificial lambs and that bloody murder had already marked them out?

Ah well, they say the Orb of Charlemagne carried its own curse and I can well believe it. Kempe, Cornelius, one other Noctale, Berkeley, Benjamin and myself gathered around the table. Egremont broke the seals on the casket and swung back the lid. He opened the neck of the pouch, took out the Orb of Charlemagne and held it up for all to see.

"Behold!" he whispered. "The Imperial Orb! God's sign of empire: now restored to Charlemagne's rightful successor, His Most Imperial Highness Charles V, Holy Roman Emperor, King of Spain, God's Vice-Regent on earth!"

The Great Beast would have certainly quarrelled with that description but even I was overawed by the splendour and beauty of this famous relic. It was passed to Berkeley who studied it carefully.

"This is the Orb, is it not?" Egremont asked.

"It is," the goldsmith replied.

Egremont put it into the pouch and it was returned to the casket, which was again sealed.

"Right." Egremont faced us. "These are the arrangements. Eight of the Noctales under Jonathan — " Egremont pointed to the cadaverous-looking Noctale — "will stay and guard the Orb. They will be reinforced by six royal archers from the Tower. These men will not be allowed to leave this manor. At three o'clock every day the two cooks," Egremont's mouth curled contemptuously, "will be allowed in. They shall bring nothing in and take nothing out. The cooks will prepare food for the evening meal as well as breakfast for the following day. They must be gone by six." Egremont paused and stared around. "All windows will be shuttered. The front door will be locked from the outside. Cornelius will hold the keys. Once the cooks have left, the dogs will be released and the gatehouse closed. I understand the rest of the archers will camp outside the walls. Is that not right, Sir Thomas?"

Kempe nodded.

"At six in the morning and again at six in the evening Cornelius will light a lantern. Jonathan will reply." He paused. "Should the signal not be returned, Cornelius will immediately send for me. I and Sir Thomas will be staying at a local hostelry, The Golden Pyx." Egremont went across and placed his hand on Jonathan's shoulder. "I have every confidence in you, sir." He stared at him. "You are to carry out my orders precisely, do you understand? Even if a man falls ill, he must stay."

"How long will this last?" Kempe asked testily.

"I have told you, Sir Thomas, until the Imperial ship is ready." Egremont smiled sourly. "The ship will be accompanied by the English fleet, not to mention Imperial galleries. We do not want the French to interfere."

"When will that happen?"

"When I give the word in about five days. Now we should go."

Egremont and Kempe addressed the fifteen men left to guard the Orb, and then we left. It was the last time we saw any of them alive.

6

Cornelius, Benjamin, myself and, of course, darling Castor took up residence in the gatehouse. On the heath outside, the rest of the English archers set up their bothies and cooking-pots and, like soldiers anywhere, soon made themselves at home. They were all hardened veterans; constantly armed, they swept the roads keeping everyone away from Malevel. Egremont was a sly fox for, with Cornelius in the chamber above us, Benjamin and I found it very difficult to confer. Mind you, the German was a good companion. Despite his grim appearance, he had a fine singing voice and a very dry sense of humour. He was cultured and learned. On the evening Egremont left I found Cornelius in his chamber writing a letter. I asked if all was well.

"Oh yes," he replied. "I am writing to my daughter Louise. She's married to a merchant. In the spring I might be a grandfather." His face creased into a gentle smile.

You know the proverb: 'never judge a book by its cover'? This certainly applied

139

to Cornelius. He was a most dangerous adversary. I have met the kind before: he would question you gently and elicit more information than any torturer. He had a mocking look in his eyes. I knew that he knew that I knew that Henry planned some subtle trick. This made us all very knowledgeable but, as Benjamin and I wondered, God knows how we would achieve it.

We spent our first evening in the gatehouse whispering about this. Castor stood like a sentinel at the window, watching the royal mastiffs patrolling the grounds. He was an intelligent beast. He never howled but just growled softly in his throat as if he resented not being able to go down and play with them. Benjamin and I saw a window in the manor open and the lantern flickering. Up above we heard Cornelius's footsteps as he replied with the agreed signal.

"What on earth can we do?" Benjamin murmured. "The mastiffs would tear us to pieces if we tried to cross the grounds. No one can break in to the manor and, even if we did, how long would we survive?" He sighed. "Ergo, we cannot act until the Orb is moved. On this occasion, Roger, I think we are going to disappoint our royal master."

I sat on the edge of my bed and stared glumly at the wall. We had not seen Agrippa today but I had a feeling that he would soon arrive with dire warnings from the Great Beast.

"Even if we could get in," Benjamin continued, "we still don't have the replica."

"Oh, I am sure we soon will," I retorted.

I should have become a fortune-teller, a seer of things yet to come. The next morning, as Benjamin and I prepared to take Castor out on the heath, Kempe arrived. He was by himself and insisted on joining us. We walked out across the sun-dried grass, Kempe chattering about what was happening at court, discussing Skelton's latest satire against Wolsey. However, once we were in the woods and Castor was giving some poor rabbit a run for its life, Kempe led us deeper into the trees. There was an old stump, probably struck by lightning, around which bushes had grown. Kempe pushed his way through these. I glimpsed a hole in the hollowed trunk, into which Kempe put his hand and drew out a large leather bag. He undid the cord and gently shook the Orb of Charlemagne out. I tell you this, Berkeley was not only a brilliant goldsmith but the most skilled of counterfeiters. The Orb was an exact replica of the one I had seen at Malevel Manor. I weighed it carefully in my hands. It felt and looked the same.

"In a sense it's genuine," Kempe murmured. "Real gold." He pointed to the bands round the rim. "Precious stones. Only the most skilled craftsman could detect that it was made in London just a few weeks ago and is not a seven-hundred-year-old relic."

"And how in God's name," Benjamin asked, "are we to replace one with the other?"

Kempe shrugged. "The King has confidence in you and Master Shallot. It has to be done."

"Not now," I replied. "I don't want my leg chewed off or an arrow in my gullet."

"Do we know when the Orb will be moved?" Benjamin asked. "Or how?"

Kempe shook his head. Benjamin beat his gloves against his thigh.

"This is impossible."

Kempe pulled a face and put the Orb back in the bag.

"I have done my job, Master Daunbey. You must do yours. I will hold this till you are ready."

"Why not give the King the replica?" I scoffed. "Will he know the difference?"

Kempe smiled. "I wondered if you'd think of that, Shallot. Berkeley knows the difference and so do I. There's a secret to the genuine Orb." He brought his hand down on my shoulder. "But it's my little secret and you've had your orders."

We walked back to Malevel, Castor running ahead of us, ears flapping. Kempe collected his horse, hid the Orb in his saddlebag and rode back to The Golden Lion.

Benjamin and I returned to our constant watch. The days passed. The two cooks, Oswald and Imelda, always arrived on time and always left at six o'clock before the dogs were released. On the third occasion I waylaid them by the gate.

"How are things at the manor?" I asked.

"Very quiet," Oswald replied. "The place is beginning to smell a little, the jakes needs cleaning. The Noctales don't like the archers and the archers don't like the Noctales. They spend their time gambling, drinking and talking."

"And Jonathan their leader?"

"He seems nervous," Imelda replied. "Like a man walking on eggs; he never stays still."

"Is he worried?"

"Yes, I think he is. But less so than on the first day."

The following afternoon Oswald and Imelda left at six. As usual, Cornelius waited for the window to open and, when it did, made the signal back with his own lantern. We spent a desultory evening, my master lying on the bed staring up at the rafters. He had been quiet since his return from Venice. He was pining over the marvellous Miranda, though I also knew that he was deeply worried, not only about the present situation, but about the threats of the Poppletons. He had accepted my assurances that I was innocent of the Great Mouth's death yet he was worried about what would happen if, and when, we returned to Ipswich. I'll be honest: I drank too deeply. I fell asleep wondering how it would be to travel down the west coast of Africa. Nightmares plagued my mind. I envisaged a thousand fearful wrecks; fishes gnawing upon my bones; lying amongst dead mens' skulls or being cast up on some lonely shore waiting for the terrors to appear from the dark forest. I was woken roughly enough by Cornelius kicking at my bed. At first he was so excited he spoke in German but then he calmed down. It was the first time I had seen him look fearful.

"What's the matter?" Benjamin asked.

"It's well past dawn," Cornelius replied. "I have seen no signal from the manor!"

"Shouldn't we go up?" I asked.

"The dogs are still out. Egremont left strict instructions. If that light didn't appear, I was to send for him immediately. One of the archers is already galloping to his lodgings."

Castor, who had been taking up more of the bed than I, got up and walked towards the window: he stared, head rigid, towards the darkened manor house. I sensed a real nightmare was about to unfold. As if it sensed something was wrong, one of the guard dogs began to howl at the lightening sky and Castor joined in.

The bells of some distant church were ringing for morning Mass when Egremont and Kempe, the former accompanied by a large retinue of his personal retainers, galloped up to the gatehouse. The dogs had been put away. Cornelius had spent the time staring at the manor as if, through concentration alone, he could perceive what was amiss. We went up the path. Cornelius opened the door and we entered that hall of hellish murder. An archer lay just within the doorway; a broad pool of blood had gushed out from his slit throat and turned the floor slippery underneath. We went into the parlour where two more archers were sprawled. One had a crossbow bolt where his nose and mouth had been. Another, face down, also had his throat slashed from ear to ear. Cornelius rushed into the hall.

Egremont's followers thronged in after us. Lord Theodosius turned, ordering some of the men to go upstairs. Cornelius came rushing out of the hall, his face ashen.

"The coffer!" he shouted. "The clasp is broken off and the Orb is gone!"

"Impossible!" Egremont's face went slack.

Kempe glanced quickly at us but Benjamin shook his head.

Egremont clapped his hands.

"Everybody," he shouted, "into the hall! You and you." He pointed to some of his retainers. "Ride into the city! Tell the Cardinal that the Orb has gone. The ports should be watched, and guards placed on every city gate!"

For a while confusion reigned as Egremont despatched others on different tasks. We then went into the hall: the steel chest had its lid thrown back, Berkeley's intricate locks had simply been smashed and the lid prised loose. The Orb was gone. We made a thorough search of the house. On every gallery lay a corpse. Most had their throats cut or crossbow quarrels deep in their throats or chests. Jonathan, Cornelius's lieutenant, lay on his bed, eyes staring sightlessly up, his throat one great gaping wound, the blood drenching his jerkin and the sheets beneath.

Cornelius was beside himself. At Egremont's

orders, the front door of the manor was locked and more guards posted at the gatehouse. Kempe, as mystified as the rest, simply sat in the hall staring at the empty chest. He beckoned us across.

"No," Benjamin replied before Sir Thomas could even question us. "No, no, no. We saw nothing amiss."

The corpses were all collected and laid out in the parlour, a grisly line of fifteen cadavers. Each had died in the most horrible manner. The coffer was removed from the table, the hall cleared and guards posted outside. Egremont gathered myself, Cornelius, Benjamin and Kempe around the long trestle table. For a while he just sat, rocking himself to and fro.

"How?" he began in no more than a whisper. "How could this be done? Cornelius," he snapped. "There's no secret entrance or trap door?"

"None and, before you ask, Lord Theodosius, no shutters open or any sign of disturbance."

"Then how in God's name," Egremont replied, "did this happen? We have fifteen men here; six royal archers, nine of the most skilled Noctales. None of them would give up their lives easily."

"That's what I find strange," Benjamin

intervened. "Fifteen men were left on guard, yes?"

Kempe and Egremont nodded together.

"And there are fifteen corpses laid out in the parlour?"

"I counted them myself," Kempe replied.

"And no one was allowed in. Nor did we see anyone slip away."

"Anyone?" Egremont sneered. "For heaven's sake, Master Daunbey, it would take more than one man to kill fifteen veterans."

We all sat in silence, chilled by his words. Egremont was right. What force, what power, what skilled group of men could despatch fifteen veterans with such ease?

"I cannot imagine it," Benjamin spoke up, his eyes closed. "We have the manor guarded outside and in. Let us say an assassin strikes." He opened his eyes. "They might kill two or three but the alarm would be raised: all it would take is one man to cry for help. Some of them had their throats cut, which could happen in their sleep . . . but a crossbow bolt deep in the face? Loosed so close? They must have at least known what was happening?" He played with the ring on his finger. "And there's something else," he added. "Have you noticed there's no sign of any upset? No furniture in disarray? No marks on the walls? Not a shred of evidence that these fifteen men put up even token resistance."

He paused as the door was flung open. One of Kempe's men entered and whispered in Sir Thomas's ear.

"What is it?" Egremont snapped.

"We have checked the armaments," Sir Thomas replied. "The soldiers didn't even use their swords or daggers. The royal archers never put arrow to bow. No soldier used his weapons, with two exceptions." He glanced across the table at Cornelius. "Your Noctales each carried a long stabbing dirk, an arbalest and bolts. Yes?"

"Agreed."

"One crossbow was used and one dagger: the only weapons employed to kill fifteen men. But where did this assassin come from?"

"The cellar," Benjamin spoke up.

"I had it checked immediately," Egremont retorted. "Bare and empty as it was when we first arrived."

Kempe rubbed his face. "The King's rage can only be imagined!"

"It will be nothing," Cornelius declared sourly, "to that of His Imperial Highness!" He drummed his fingers on the table. "Fifteen men dead and the Orb gone. Well, Lord Theodosius, what do we do now?"

"Go back to London. I'll leave some of my retainers here." Egremont got to his feet. "Cornelius, I want this house searched again from top to bottom." He glanced at Kempe. "Sir Thomas, you'll accompany me? His Eminence the Cardinal and His Grace the King will demand witness to what I say."

"Wait a while." Cornelius walked to a side table and picked up a dish on which there were still crumbs. "We've forgotten two people; the cooks, Oswald and Imelda."

"Oh, that's ridiculous!" I declared. "You've seen them, two young people unarmed! How do you think they did it? Battered the garrison to death with a sausage?"

Cornelius sniffed. "Sir Thomas, my Lord of Egremont, I will send a despatch to the cookshop. Oswald and Imelda are to be brought here immediately."

Egremont looked as if he was going to object, surprised by the nature of Cornelius's request, but then he shrugged and, followed by Kempe, left the room.

The atmosphere of distrust he left only increased. Cornelius watched us narrow-eyed and, when we offered to search the house, he insisted on accompanying us. First we visited the cellar but we could find nothing amiss, and then we continued our search from room to room. Some of the beds showed that they

150

had been lain in: the sheets were soiled or crumpled. Yet it appeared as if the Angel of Death had swept through in a matter of seconds. In one chamber, dice and a cup lay on a table as if the game had suddenly ended. In another playing cards were spread out on the floor. In the kitchen two knives and a whetstone were placed on a stool as if their owner had been sharpening them when death struck. In exasperation we searched amongst the foodstuffs, sniffing at the bread, the dried bacon and fruit. Benjamin tasted from the wineskin. He picked up the cask of ale but it was empty. He placed it back on the floor and sat on it.

"How did this happen?" he asked, echoing Egremont's words.

Cornelius went and stood over him.

"Master Daunbey."

Benjamin looked up.

"Are you going to say that you were here to guard?" Cornelius asked. "Or will you not admit that you had secret instructions from your king to retrieve the Orb of Charlemagne?"

Benjamin stood up facing him squarely.

"Such words, Master Cornelius, might, in another place and at another time, lead to a duel."

"I shall remember that, Master Daunbey,

but my question still stands!"

I drew my own dagger. I went up and pricked the tip into the back of Cornelius's bulky neck.

"Ah, the ever-faithful dog!" Cornelius didn't even bother to turn.

"Stand back from my master!" I ordered. "Cornelius, you have your orders and so have we. You were in the gatehouse with us all the time. We never approached the manor. You, however, did. You let the cooks in and out. What else happened?"

Cornelius turned his head slightly, then he turned with breathtaking speed. One arm came shooting out, the edge of his hand caught me just beneath the chest and made me stagger back, the knife dropping from my hand. Then Cornelius, sword and dagger drawn, stood between me and Benjamin. The sound of the commotion brought others hurrying to the kitchen door. Cornelius was now balanced on the balls of his feet, the sword toward Benjamin, the dagger towards me. He was breathing in deeply through his nostrils, fighting hard to control the rage seething within him. Benjamin's hand was already on his sword. I was wondering whether to run or fight when I heard a commotion down the passageway. I turned and saw Castor in the doorway. No longer the friendly, bouncing dog, he crouched, head out, ears back, jaws half-open like some huge cat as he began to stalk across the floor towards Cornelius.

The Noctale moved his sword and dagger toward this new threat: he threw me a quick look and I knew I had a debt to pay.

"Castor!" I ordered.

The dog moved forward.

"Castor, sweetmeats. Stay!"

Castor's ears came up and he sat, almost smiling benevolently at Cornelius. I went up and stroked him. I took a sticky sweetmeat from my wallet. Castor took it, rolling it around in his mouth as happy as a child.

"Put up your sword and dagger!" Benjamin ordered. He waved at the people thronging in the kitchen doorway. "Go back to your duties. Anything you find, bring here!"

Castor fumed and growled, and within a twinkling the doorway was empty. Cornelius put his sword and dagger away and came forward, hands extended.

"I meant no offence, Shallot. Nor to you, Master Daunbey. However, if you are innocent of this crime then so am I." He pointed to the dog. "I wonder if he could help?"

After three more sweetmeats, Castor would have climbed to the moon if I had asked him.

Back round the house he went. He noticed nothing amiss in the upper chambers: only becoming excited when he found a scrap of food, a piece of chicken leg lying in the corner of a hearth.

After that it became a game: a search for food. We resumed to the lower gallery, but Castor refused to go into the parlour where the corpses were now stiffening under their bloody sheets. He crouched in the doorway and whined, looking beseechingly up at me. I stayed with him whilst Benjamin and Cornelius inspected the corpses. Now and again I glanced away as they pulled down sheets to display a bloody face, a chest smashed in by a crossbow bolt or a head lolling because of the deep gash in the neck.

Benjamin, however, scrutinised the corpses carefully, feeling the suppleness of their hands and legs, loosening belts, pulling up jerkins. At first, Cornelius was mystified until he realised what my master was looking for.

"They were all young men," he remarked.

"Yes, yes," Benjamin replied absent-mindedly. "The flesh is cold but the limbs still have a certain suppleness. What time did we enter this morning?"

"Somewhere between seven and eight o'clock," Cornelius replied.

"I think they were killed six or seven hours earlier," Benjamin said. "The blood has not yet thickened, the limbs haven't stiffened and there's no sign of poisoning." He pointed to the chest of one man. "Most potions leave some red or mulberry stain on the chest or stomach. There's none here."

They covered the corpses and we returned to the kitchen. Castor, smelling the food, immediately became excited. He went towards the cooking pot hanging over the hearth sniffing at it appreciatively. I dipped my finger in and tasted it.

One of Egremont's retainers came in to report that the cooks were at the gatehouse. We left the kitchen and passed the open door to the cellar. Castor immediately sprang down, like a ferret into a rabbit hole. We followed down the steps. The dog was waiting for us, legs apart, head up, eyes bright as if this was part of the game. Benjamin was intrigued by the dog's excitement. I gave Castor a sweetmeat and told him to go back up the steps which he did. The cellar had a plaster roof, brick walls on either side and an earth-beaten floor. The three of us began to examine and tap the brickwork. However, if we entertained any hopes of finding some secret passageway or door we were disappointed.

(It's different now, of course. Due to the persecution of the Catholic priests, every great house has caverns, trap doors and hiding-holes. I have at least three here. There should be four but I've forgotten where one of them was put! They were all built by that Jesuit lay brother, Nicholas Owen, a little man with a cheery face, God's own carpenter. Elizabeth's master spy caught him. Poor Nicholas went to the Tower; Topcliffe the executioner racked him so much his body had to be pinned together before they could take him away and hang him. He left a great legacy, did Owen, secret rooms and chambers up and down the kingdom. It will be hundreds of years before they are all discovered!)

Benjamin and Cornelius gave up in disgust.

"What made that dog so excited?" Benjamin asked.

I kicked at the floor. "Perhaps something here, master?"

Benjamin agreed. Servants were summoned and, armed with shovel and pick, hacked at the floor. Benjamin was very careful. He ordered another servant to bring down sacks and the earth was carefully placed in it.

"I've found something!" one of them cried.

Benjamin pushed him aside and, crouching

down, stared into the great, yawning hole. He leaned down and picked up a piece of yellowing fabric, covered in dirt and crumbling with age. He took the shovel from the groom and dug more carefully. We were forced back on to the steps as the cellar floor was turned into a gaping hole. Straining our necks we could see that Benjamin had unearthed a rolled-up piece of cloth.

At last it was all free. We carried it upstairs where Benjamin carefully unrolled it. In its prime, the cloth had been one of those thick tapestries that hung on a wall. Now it was faded, stained and contained its own grisly relic: a skeleton of a woman: the bones were brittle and grey strands of hair still clung to the gaping skull. One of the ribs was broken and the remnants of the dress around it were stained a dark maroon colour.

The servant swore and stepped away. Benjamin, however, laid the skeleton out carefully. One of the wrist bones snapped as he searched amongst the fabric and picked up a small locket inscribed with the letters 'I.M.'

"This has nothing to do with our search?" Cornelius asked.

Benjamin shook his head.

"What you are looking at, sir, are the

mortal remains of Isabella Malevel, once owner of this gloomy manor. Whoever broke into her house and plundered it, smashed one of her ribs, probably in an attempt to find out where she had hidden her wealth." Benjamin pointed to the dark stains on the rags. "They then cut her throat, wrapped her corpse in a tapestry and buried it in the cellar."

I kept staring at the locket. I had seen those same letters before — on a tapestry in Lord Charon's cavernous, underground chamber.

7

Benjamin ordered the remains to be taken into the parlour and laid with the rest of the corpses. Another courier was despatched to Westminster.

"I doubt if she had heirs or relatives," Benjamin declared. "So, what happens to the poor woman's remains is a matter for the King."

Accompanied by Cornelius we went to the gatehouse where Oswald and Imelda were waiting. The day was drawing on: halfway down the path, I stopped and looked back at Malevel with its shuttered windows and grim walls. A house of death! Was that the reason for the sense of evil? Did the old woman's ghost still walk there? Pleading, like Hamlet's father, for vengeance for a life snuffed out in such a cruel fashion? I had no doubt that Lord Charon and his coven had been responsible for the old woman's grisly murder: swarming in one night, like rats into a barn, plundering the house and torturing old Isabella to death. Afterwards, they must have wrapped her corpse in that cloth and buried it in the cellar, then swept the house clean, making it look as if everything and its owner had mysteriously disappeared. However, the important question was whether Lord Charon and his gang had stormed the front door or whether they had used some secret entrance and passageway as yet unfound?

"Roger?" Benjamin and Cornelius were looking at me strangely.

"I am sorry."

I joined them and went into the gatehouse. Oswald and Imelda were all a-tremble in the small guard room. They looked like ghosts sitting on a bench, clutching each other's hands; the archers had informed them about the grisly events that had occurred.

"We know nothing," Oswald declared, putting his arms round his wife's shoulders. "Sirs, we have been involved in no trickery."

Sometimes you can tell just from the first word: in my soul I knew Oswald was telling the truth. They were both innocents, caught up in this Byzantine game. A young man and his wife, eager to make their fortunes in the city, now cursed by their close acquaintance with the Great Ones of the land. Cornelius and Benjamin thought the same. We sat opposite them: Benjamin took Imelda's hand, assuring her of the Cardinal's protection.

"Just tell us what you know," he declared.

"What happened in those days?"

"We visited four times," Oswald replied. "We never noticed anything amiss."

"Tell us again," Benjamin declared.

"We always arrived just before three. Master Cornelius would take us up to the door and let us in. The manor was dark, it was not a pleasant place. The galleries and rooms were gloomy yet the soldiers were friendly enough, even the Noctales. Sometimes one or two would flirt with Imelda but they were no trouble."

"Did you go to any other part of the house?" Benjamin asked.

"Only once," Oswald replied. "Well, no, perhaps on two occasions, we used the latrines, a small closet down the gallery near the cellar."

"Most of the time," Imelda intervened, "we were in the kitchen. We would bake bread . . . "

"How many loaves?"

"Twenty-eight to thirty," she replied. "We took nothing with us. Lord Egremont insisted on that. The meats and other ingredients were already there."

"We baked and cooked," Oswald explained. "Cut up vegetables, cleaned the traunchers and platters: prepared oatmeal for breakfast the following morning and set the table for

161

the meal at nine o'clock."

"Were you always together?" I asked.

"I insisted on that," Cornelius retorted.

"And you never noticed anything amiss?" Benjamin asked.

"No, sir!" Oswald and Imelda shook their heads.

"How was Jonathan?" Cornelius asked.

"Silent, preoccupied. Rather nervous," Oswald replied. "I heard one of the guards say he would take a lot of food but never finish his meal."

"They were all nervous," Imelda offered.

"Nervous?" I asked.

"They didn't like the manor. They claimed it was haunted. One guard even said he heard sounds at night."

"Sounds?" Cornelius asked.

"I don't know what they meant," she replied. "But the old manor did creak. You should stay there yourself, sir. You'll find out."

"But there couldn't have been anyone hidden away?" Oswald added. "I noticed when the guards were walking up and down, the floorboards groaned, the stairs creaked. Master — " He glanced anxiously at Cornelius. "We have been told that they are all dead. One of the soldiers at the gate said their throats had been cut. It

162

would take a small army to do that." He laughed nervously. "Not a cook and his wife. Look — " He opened a small, leather bag he carried. "There are our draft bills: we have the finished accounts at home." He pushed the scraps into Benjamin's hand. "We were promised they would be paid."

"And they will be," Benjamin reassured him, getting to his feet.

He thanked the couple and they left. Cornelius stretched out his legs, folded his arms and leaned against the wall: with his heavy-lidded eyes half closed, he looked as if he were sleeping.

"What was Jonathan like?" Benjamin asked.

"A former officer in the Imperial Guard," Cornelius replied.

"And he would take orders from you?"

"No, from Lord Theodosius, as I am supposed to."

"Supposed to?" Benjamin asked.

"I'm different from the rest." Cornelius smiled wryly. "I am the Emperor's man in peace and war: his personal emissary. The rest are Egremont's men. Why do you ask?"

"There's no chance," I volunteered, grasping the drift of my master's questions, "that Egremont would give separate orders to Jonathan?"

"Why should he?" Cornelius retorted. "How could Jonathan be part of anything which led to his own death and those of his companions, not to mention the theft of the Orb. Whatever you are thinking, Master Benjamin, Lord Egremont has a great deal of explaining to do when he returns to the Imperial Court. No, no." Cornelius shook his head. "The real problem is how fifteen men, armed and dangerous, were all executed one after the other with no sign of resistance or any form of struggle. No one raised the alarm. No one saw anyone enter or leave." Cornelius got to his feet.

He walked to the window. Castor padded up and began to lick at his hand.

"This is a cursed place," Cornelius muttered, staring out at the manor. "I need to think, reflect." He opened his pouch and tossed two keys on a ring at Benjamin. "Malevel Manor is now yours."

"The Orb could still be there," Benjamin offered.

Cornelius shook his head. "I doubt it." He picked up his cloak. "I have to return to the city, to take counsel with Lord Theodosius. Will you see to the removal of the corpses?"

Benjamin agreed. Cornelius went back up to his chamber and, a few minutes later, we heard him leaving.

The next few hours were confusing. Benjamin ordered the soldiers into the manor. A cart had been hired and the corpses, including that of the old lady Isabella, were piled on, and hidden beneath a canvas sheet. Already the camp outside was beginning to break up, the soldiers going back to the Tower or Baynards Castle. By sunset all were gone: only Benjamin, myself and Castor remained. We closed the gates and, at Benjamin's insistence, locked ourselves in Malevel Manor. We were armed, and Castor was with us. Nevertheless, I'll never forget that night. Malevel in the daylight was grim enough but, when darkness fell and the wind drove against the shutters, I believe I walked with ghosts. The galleries and passageways were narrow and gloomy. The air became stale and every step we took made the floorboards creak. Both Benjamin and I were apprehensive, as if someone was watching us. Time and again, as we searched that house from cellar to garret, I would whirl round and look back down a shadow-filled gallery only to find there was nothing there. Even Castor lost his aggression. Now and again he would stop and whimper as if the animal could see things we did not. Nevertheless, Benjamin was thorough. We carried torches and searched every room, every fireplace. We found nothing! At last, long after midnight, we returned to the kitchen. We sat at the table, drinking some of the wine left, even cutting portions of the meat and bread but there was nothing amiss: no potion, no evidence that the garrison might have been poisoned.

Benjamin sat, chin in hand.

"Twenty-four hours ago," he began, "some time, about now, Roger, fifteen men were brutally murdered and the Orb stolen. But how?"

"This place is haunted," I replied. "A gateway for demons. You saw the old woman's skeleton."

"Ghosts may walk," Benjamin replied. "But they don't cut throats nor do they carry arbalests."

"They walk silently," I replied. "Master, how could an assassin even walk round this place without being noticed? Every step he took would make a noise."

Benjamin got up and walked to where the blackjacks had been cleaned and put on a table.

"One thing I did notice," he mused. "No food was left on the table. There were no dirty pots in the scullery."

"Which means?" I asked.

"Either they were killed before the evening

meal or long after. However, if they were killed after, the remains of their dirty traunchers and blackjacks would have been left out for the cooks to wash the following day."

"So they must have been killed before?"

"But that can't be," Benjamin replied. "The cooks told us they set the tables for the evening meal, yet we found no trace of that."

"Unless Jonathan ordered it to be cleared himself?" I declared. "I have another theory."

I explained about Lord Charon and my meeting with him: the initials 'I.M.' on the hangings in his chamber were identical to those on the locket buried with the remains of poor Lady Isabella. Benjamin, eyes closed, heard me out.

"It's possible." He opened his eyes. "It's possible that in his own devilish way, Lord Charon had a hand in this business." He tapped my hand. "You didn't tell me about your meeting in the sewers?"

"You never asked," I retorted. "And it's something I'd best soon forget."

Benjamin walked over towards where we had laid out our bedding for the night.

"Ah, that is not a matter for us, Roger, but for the authorities. The capture of Lord Charon will need troops." He took off his boots, lay down on the bedding and pulled a blanket up to his face. "A house of secrets," he murmured then fell asleep.

I sat for a while listening to the house creak. I grew agitated as I realised the Great Beast would soon make his anger felt. I went out into the passageway, took a torch from its sconce and stood at the entrance to the cellar. Castor, who had been asleep in the corner of the kitchen, roused himself and followed me out. He stood silently beside me as I stared into the darkness.

What had taken Castor down there in the first place? My master's questions about the setting out of the table and the cleaning of cups bothered me as well but I was too tired to think. I returned the torch, went back into the kitchen and lay down on the bedding with Castor sprawled beside me. I fell into an uneasy sleep thronged by nightmares, bloody-mouthed spectres in ghostly galleries and other terrors of the dark. (Oh, don't laugh at poor Shallot. I have seen ghosts! I have been at Hampton Court on the anniversary of Catherine Howard's arrest, and heard her scream as she did in life, as her ghost ran down to the royal chapel to beg the Great Beast's forgiveness for having slept with Thomas Culpepper. Once, following a wager with Master Walsingham, the Queen's master spy, I spent a night in the Bloody Tower. I was locked away in a cell — the result of some stupid remark or jest at court. I felt the ghosts throng around me: Thomas Cromwell, Henry's great minister who fell from power after taking lunch with the Duke of Norfolk. Or the poor Princes stifled in their beds. True, I never saw anything but, the next morning, when the captain of the guard came to open the cell and take me to the officers' quarters to break my fast, he stopped me on the stairs and said, "Sir Roger, you will have to pay your wager."

"Why?" I asked.

"Well, sir," the fellow replied. "You said you would be alone, but when I looked through the grille at midnight you were asleep in your bed . . ."

"Of course I was," I scoffed. "I was drunk."

"But there was someone with you."

My blood ran cold. "Who?" I asked.

"I don't know," the soldier replied. "Just a cowled and hooded figure sitting on a chair beside your bed staring down at you."

Oh yes, I believe in ghosts and that's the last night I ever slept in the Tower!)

The next morning the terrors of the living woke us: Doctor Agrippa, Kempe and Cornelius pounding on the door. I have never seen the Doctor so agitated. He brushed by me and swept into the kitchen: clutching his broad-brimmed hat, he looked like a country parson ready to pray, except for those eyes, which had turned pebble-black.

"The King wants your heads." He glared at Benjamin. "Either that or his Orb back."

"I didn't steal it!"

(Always the same old Shallot! Make sure you whine and protest your innocence!)

"He doesn't give a fig for that," Kempe intervened. He looked dreadful; unshaven, with black shadows under red-rimmed eyes. "His Grace," he continued, "held a banquet last night in Lord Egremont's honour. He drank deeply to restore his good humour but, beforehand, his rage can only be believed." Kempe pointed to his ear which was red and swollen. "He hit everyone he could!"

"And he'll not get my master's ships!" Egremont stood in the doorway. "No ships for the English king," he continued, walking into the kitchen. "No favours for you, Sir Thomas. Master Benjamin, being the Cardinal's nephew will not save you!"

"Our heads are our own!" Benjamin snapped back. "It won't be the first time the King has been displeased with us." He shrugged one shoulder. "At least for a while. Anyway, why are you here?"

Egremont sat himself down at the table. "To see if anything new has been discovered."

"Yes and no," my master replied.

He described our stay in the house the previous night, how every sound and footfall seemed to echo like a bell, and how difficult it would be for even the most soft-footed assassin to steal along the galleries.

"Naturally," Egremont scoffed. "That's why this house was chosen. It's lonely, off the beaten track and easily guarded, or so I thought. Is that all, Master Daunbey?"

"No, the discovery of Lady Isabella's remains yesterday has opened one interesting possibility. Isn't that so, Roger?"

I then described my meeting with Lord Charon and his ownership of one of the Malevel tapestries.

"It's possible," I concluded, "that Lord Charon heard, as he does everything in London, that the Orb had been moved here. He might well have organised the bloody onslaught to kill the guards and steal the relic."

"I have heard of Charon," Kempe intervened. "The sheriffs of London would dearly love to finger his collar and those of his coven."

"Is it possible to trace him?" Cornelius asked. "This wolfshead, this outlaw? And, if he has the Orb, what will he try and do with it?"

"Break it up," Kempe replied. "Sell the diamonds. Cut the Orb into gold pieces."

Egremont hit the table with his fist.

Sir Thomas continued, "Or he might try to find a buyer, either here or abroad."

The door opened and one of Kempe's men came in and thrust a small scroll into his hands. Sir Thomas unfolded and studied it.

"It's begun," he announced. "The news that the Orb has gone is already having effect. Sir Hubert Berkeley is missing from his shop. Apparently, he left last night and has not been seen since. Moreover, yesterday evening, a well-known seller of relics, Walter Henley, visited a chamber in the Rose and Crown tavern. He met a stranger, cowled and hooded. They went upstairs to the chamber, and the landlord took up a tray of food and drink. Henley was heard laughing. The stranger then left. They thought Henley was staying the night but a servant maid, going round to check the candles, noticed a pool of blood seeping out under the door. When the landlord opened it, Henley was found with his throat slit from ear to ear." He breathed in. "Since the Orb has disappeared, my men have had their eye on the likes of Henley."

Egremont got to his feet, indicating Cornelius to join him.

"These are matters for you," he declared. He put his bonnet on his head and looked even more like a falcon on its perch. "If the King of England cannot protect his treasures, and those of other princes, against outlaws and cutthroats, if he cannot rule his own city, let alone his kingdom, how, in heaven's name, can he take armies abroad?"

And, before any of us could reply, he and Cornelius swept out of the room. Benjamin immediately got to his feet, beckoning me to follow, and went out into the gallery.

"Master Cornelius, a word, if you please?"

The Noctale came back.

"You do want the return of the Orb?" Benjamin asked.

"Of course." Cornelius's eyes were as hard as flint.

"And you will agree that we have been as honest and as open with you as possible?"

Cornelius pulled a face. "So it would appear."

"But you, Master Cornelius, have not been so open with us!"

The Noctale's eyes widened.

"Every day," Benjamin continued, "you took the cooks into the manor and at six o'clock collected them again, locking and unlocking the front door, yes?"

Cornelius's face creased into a suspicion of a smile as if he knew what my master was going to ask.

"Now Jonathan would show the cooks into the house and out, yes? And, while you stood at the door, Master Cornelius, you must have asked for a report, if anything was wrong or amiss?"

Cornelius opened his mouth.

"Of course," Benjamin continued. "You might say that Jonathan had nothing to report, but that wouldn't be true, would it? Come with me!"

Benjamin took him down the passageway. Cornelius, ignoring Egremont's shouts, followed Benjamin and myself into the parlour where the corpses had lain. The weapons of the dead soldiers had been stacked against the wall. Most of them were gone but Benjamin opened a chest and took out a quiver and a long bow. "I noticed this," he said. "Count the arrows here. There are only six. However, in the other quivers, there were at least a baker's dozen. Now in the attack, only a dagger and arbalest were used, never a long bow."

"So?" Cornelius asked in mock innocence.

"The English archers were put here by Kempe," Benjamin replied. "Jonathan would

174

not have trusted them. He would have kept them under close watch. Now, the manor is well guarded from the front but, on both sides, it looks out beyond the walls to wild heathland."

Cornelius threw his head back and laughed.

"Master Daunbey, if you ever wish to leave England, you will find employment with my master, His Most August Imperial Highness. You are sharper than you look. I'll be honest with you. Jonathan was suspicious, particularly of Kempe's archers. He believed that one of these archers was communicating with Sir Thomas by sending messages wrapped round the end of one of his arrows. Your English archers and their long bows are famous. A master bowman could send an arrow out across the walls, aiming at a certain tree or other pre-arranged landmark."

"Why should Kempe want information?"

"I don't know," Cornelius replied. "But if Sir Thomas Kempe is going to watch us, I assure you, we will watch him."

And, patting Benjamin on the shoulder, Cornelius went out to where Lord Egremont waited.

"You never told me about that?" I said, pointing to the quiver.

Benjamin put it back in the chest.

"It's one of the first things I noticed. What intrigued me about all this, Roger, is that there was no sign of a struggle, so a half-empty quiver soon caught my attention."

"What is Kempe up to?" I asked.

"That," Benjamin replied, "like the rest of the mystery, remains to be seen."

"What are you whispering about?" Kempe stood in the doorway.

"About the subtleties of life," Benjamin replied enigmatically. "Sir Thomas, this relic-seller?"

"His corpse is still at the Rose and Crown," Kempe replied.

"We would like to see it."

"And see it you shall." Agrippa came out into the hallway, hat on his head, eyes twinkling.

I went and opened the door, to see that Egremont, Cornelius and their entourage were now sweeping through the gatehouse.

"What has happened to Lady Isabella's remains?" I asked.

"The Friar Minoresses at St Mary of Bethlehem have agreed to inter her remains," Kempe replied. "The archers and Noctales are to be buried in Charterhouse. The King has agreed to give grants to their relatives."

"And the Orb?" I asked. "The replica?"

"Safely stowed away," Kempe replied.

I stared at this most secret servant of the King's. Why should one of his archers send messages to him? Was he involved in this knavery? Was the Great Beast's rage genuine? But if Kempe had stolen the Orb, to whom would he sell it? Some merchant who would pay a fortune to have it hidden in his vaults? Or some foreign power? The French? Or even the Papacy?

"You mentioned Sir Hubert Berkeley?" Benjamin declared. "You said he was missing?"

"Left his home last night," Kempe replied. "Slipped out through an alleyway. He told no one where he was going or when he would be back. By dawn this morning his master journeyman, alarmed at his master's prolonged absence, sent word to the court."

"Could he be involved in this mischief?" I asked.

"God knows," Benjamin replied before Kempe could. "But, come, let's view the mortal remains of Walter Henley."

We gathered our horses. Benjamin himself locked up the manor and the gates. Kempe promised he would send some of the men to guard it as well as our few paltry possessions stowed away in the gatehouse. Castor also stayed, and I promised him that I would return with some sweetmeats. The dog just looked mournfully at me as I locked him in our room before going down to join the rest. Kempe informed us the Rose and Crown was just opposite the Priory of St Helen's, within sight of Cripplegate.

Benjamin, however, insisted on taking a detour and we stopped for a while at Master Oswald's cookshop. Benjamin threw the reins of his horse at me and went inside. It looked a cheerful, busy place, the ground floor of a three-storey house. The smells made my mouth water; I was tired of the dried meat and rather stale food at Malevel, so I went inside and bought a pie from a tray held by a boy. The crust was golden, carefully sculpted, and the meat was fresh and sweet. As I ate, a memory was jogged but I couldn't place it. I looked down towards the back of the shop, past the tables where customers sat on overturned barrels or hogsheads, to where Benjamin was busily talking to Oswald and Imelda. He was asking them questions, They replied quickly. After a while Benjamin shook their hands and came back to join me.

"Well, master?"

"One thing I have established, Roger. On the night all those men were killed, our good cooks roasted some meat and set the table. They are certain that Jonathan did not order the soldiers to clean up after the evening meal, which is strange, isn't it? Because, on the night they were all massacred, someone cleaned up that kitchen and removed all traces of the food and drink?"

"You mean the assassins?"

"Possibly." Benjamin grimaced. "But, there again, it may have been a mere coincidence. Imelda did say Jonathan was complaining about mice and the need to keep the kitchen clean."

"Then you have an answer," I replied.

"Of sorts," Benjamin declared. "But we'll see, we'll see."

We went out to join the other two. Kempe was waiting impatiently but Agrippa looked as if he was half asleep. When we had first arrived in the city, the market stalls were only just opening but now the crowds were milling about. I was glad to be out of Malevel Manor with its corpses, bloody mysteries and moonlit galleries. We had to dismount and walk our horses, and I fell behind watching a group of Lacrymosi. These belonged to a strange cult, men as well as women, who shaved the top part of their heads, painted their faces red and dressed from head to toe in brown serge cloth tied round the middle by a cord. They carried staves in one hand and Ave beads in the other: before Henry struck against Rome, they could often be seen in the great cities from Dover to Berwick. Their leader always bore a cross and they got their names because they were constantly crying — shrieking would be the more accurate description. They would throw their hands up in the air, mournfully exclaiming about their sins and those of others. This group of about sixteen helped the tears along by hitting each other with knotted ropes. An amusing set of noddle pates! Behind them a blind boy, his eyes covered in patches, beat on a drum whilst beside him two little girls, obviously the daughters of one of the Lacrymosi, held out begging bowls towards the crowds. I watched them pass. Benjamin called at me to keep up, and as I hurried to do so, I saw a shift in the crowd. Cerberus, Charon's dog-faced lieutenant, stood glaring at me. Apparently, Lord Charon had not forgotten me and, once again, I wondered if those deaths at Malevel Manor were his work.

At last we reached the Rose and Crown, a pleasant hostelry which stood fronting an alleyway. We left the horses with a groom and went inside. Mine host took one look at Sir Thomas's ermine-lined jerkin and came running up, his face bright at the prospect of profit.

"Some wine, my lords? A dish of meat,

your Excellencies?"

"Shut up!" Kempe retorted. "I want to see the corpse. You have not moved it, have you?"

The landlord's smile faded.

"It's on the upper gallery," the fellow whined. "A soldier still stands on guard."

He led us up the rickety staircase; halfway down the gallery, an archer lounged against the wall, chewing a piece of sausage. He clambered to his feet, licking his fingers as he recognised Sir Thomas. Mine host, taking a bunch of keys from his belt, unlocked the door. The room inside was no more than a garret, containing a trestle bed, a rather shaky lavarium with a cracked bowl and jug, a bench under the windows, a small table and two stools. The corpse lay just within the door, covered by a dirty blanket. Kempe pulled this back.

Henley had been no beauty in life. In death his fat face, with its popping eyes, half-open, slobbering lips and the angry red gash in his throat made him look grotesque. Agrippa, as if bored, went and sat on the bed, playing with a buckle on his belt. Kempe looked down at the corpse and turned away in disgust at the flies hovering over a pool of blood. I felt for the man's wallet but there was nothing there.

"I didn't take it," the landlord bleated from where he stood in the doorway.

Of course the thieving magpie had, but he wasn't going to admit it to us, was he?

"Tell us what happened?" Benjamin straightened up. He pulled the landlord inside the chamber by his jerkin.

The landlord wetted his lips, blinking as he considered whether to lie or not.

"Tell us the truth," Benjamin said, "and you can keep what you took from him. His coins, his rings: I also see the knife sheath on his belt is empty. You could hang for such thefts."

"He arrived here just after Vespers," the landlord replied in a rush. "He hired a chamber, a jug of wine and two cups. A short while later a stranger entered the room."

"What did he look like?"

"I am a busy man, not the parish constable," the landlord whined. "I saw a cowl and a hood: the lower half of his face was masked. His voice was gruff. He asked me where Henley was, and one of the scullions took him up. A short while later a message was sent down asking for a pure beeswax candle."

"Pure beeswax?" Benjamin asked.

"Yes."

"But they had a candle in here already." I pointed to the fat tallow sitting in its own grease in a small earthenware bowl.

"Look, I own a tavern. Some people like tallow candles. Others don't. I made a good profit from selling beeswax, so I sent it up. Afterwards, one of the maids," the fellow smirked, "was serving one of the customers in the adjoining chamber. Anyway, she heard Henley laugh, a deep-throated bellow as if his companion had told him an amusing story. A short while later the stranger left. We thought Henley was staying for the evening and that's all I know."

"Where's the beeswax candle now?" Benjamin asked.

The landlord sighed, hurried off and came back with it.

"Where did you find this?" Benjamin asked, taking the candle and scrutinising it carefully. "It's hardly been used."

"I know that," the landlord replied. "It was just left lying on the table and that," he added flatly, "is all I do know. I have a tavern to run." He gestured down. "What about the corpse?"

"Do you have a wheelbarrow?" Kempe asked.

"Yes."

"Pay the archer a penny," Kempe declared. "Some of the profits you stole from Henley's purse. Have the body taken to Greyfriars. The good brothers will bury his corpse in a pauper's grave."

8

We went downstairs into the street. Kempe muttered about continuing his searches for Hubert Berkeley, and Benjamin grasped him by the arm.

"Where did Henley live? You must know," he added, "if you were keeping a watch on his ilk?"

"Nearby." Kempe withdrew his arm. "That's right, in Old Jewry. Skinner's Lane, opposite the hospital of St Thomas of Acorn. Why?" Kempe's eyes slid to me. "Are you thinking of augmenting your relic collection? And what was all that business about the candle?"

Benjamin shook his head. "I was just intrigued."

"And so will the King be," Kempe added, hitching his fur robe round his shoulders.

His eyes strayed over my shoulder. I glanced round and saw two well-armed bullyboys standing in the mouth of the alleyway. Men like Kempe didn't go anywhere unless they were protected.

"I really must be going," he insisted. "It is important that we find Berkeley." He prodded me in the chest. "But meanwhile, what about this business of Lord Charon?"

"We also need to take counsel with His Eminence," Agrippa said, coming out of the tavern. He smiled apologetically and wiped his lips on the back of his glove. "They say a good ale is strong and clear. I, too, Master Daunbey, was thinking about candles. But, as Sir Thomas says, Berkeley has to be found and counsel has to be taken." He winked at both of us. "The court has moved to Sheen. I shall go there. Sir Thomas has Berkeley to find. Where were you when Charon," he added, turning to me, "first met you?"

"At the Flickering Lamp tavern," I replied.

"Go back there," Agrippa ordered. "Sir Thomas and I will meet you later on."

Agrippa collected his horse from the stable and nonchalantly rode off. Kempe followed a short while later.

"Why *were* you interested in the candle?" I asked, watching Kempe's bullyboys stride off.

"Collect our horses and I'll tell you."

Benjamin rode close beside me, as if he sensed we were being followed or watched.

"Describe the Orb to me. I know I have seen it but just describe it to me."

And so I did. Benjamin paused, absent-mindedly stroking his horse's muzzle, unaware

186

of the chaos and confusion he was causing in the narrow streets behind him.

"It's the amethyst," he declared.

"I beg your pardon, master?"

"Look around, Roger," he murmured, stooping to check his saddle as if there was something wrong. "Is that dog-faced man still following us?"

I glanced around but could see no sign of him.

"He'll be there," Benjamin declared, urging his horse on. "Anyway, Roger, I have a deep suspicion that the Orb taken from Malevel Manor was not the genuine one."

"But Egremont checked it!" I exclaimed. "And Kempe told us the real Orb contained a secret: surely Egremont would have known this."

"Roger," Benjamin laughed. "Gold and silver are easy to replicate and you can collect precious stones to match. However, I wager a jug of wine against a jug of wine that the amethyst on the top of the Orb is special: that's why Henley asked for a beeswax candle. The light from a tallow candle is not pure, the wick gives off a great deal of smoke and it splutters. The flame on a beeswax candle provides pure light. I suspect Henley was one of the few people who could recognise the true Orb of

Charlemagne. The person who stole it from Malevel Manor took it to Henley for our relic-seller to inspect. He did so, realised it was a forgery and burst out laughing."

"For which he promptly had his throat cut," I added.

"Oh yes, our assassin will be angry." Benjamin paused. "We really must check where Kempe, Egremont and Cornelius were yesterday evening."

"Not to forget Lord Charon?"

"Yes," Benjamin agreed. "Our assassin was not only angry, he had to keep Henley's mouth shut. The relic-seller was a fool. He was dead as soon as he entered that tavern garret."

"And you think something in Henley's house will reveal the secret?" I asked.

"Possibly," Benjamin replied.

We reached Old Jewry and made our way to the hospital of St Thomas Acorn. A beggar who sat squatting on the steps, scratching his sores, pointed across to a narrow, mean house wedged between two shops.

"That's where Henley lives," the fellow croaked. "We all know what he does. Often comes out to sell his trickery to pilgrims."

We left our horses in a nearby tavern, paid an ostler a coin, walked across and knocked at the door. It was locked but what are keys and bolts to a man like Shallot? I soon had the door open. Inside the house was dark, rather eerie, full of strange smells. The front parlour was all shuttered, cobwebs hung on the walls and dusty sheets covered the furniture. The kitchen and buttery were stale and ill washed. In a room at the back of the house we found Henley's workshop. Here the smell was so offensive we had to open the shutters. Benjamin looked at the pot suspended on an iron rod over the white ash in the hearth. He took his dagger out and fished amongst the contents. I gagged at the mess of cats' heads, birds and other small animals boiled in there. The stench was so bad I drew back and retched. Benjamin remained impervious and went around scrutinising the different items on tables and shelves.

"A cunning man," he breathed. "He could have taught you a trick or two, Roger. Relics are always bones, pieces of cloth, wood or leather." He picked up a small silver gilt case. "Henley must have made a prosperous living out of it. He'd take a bit of cat bone, boil it, clean it, place it in a silver-gilt case and there was part of the finger bone of St Amisias, or whoever you want."

My master must have caught the look in my eye.

"No, Roger, there'll be no more relics at our manor." He waved a finger at me. "Relics are forbidden."

He went across and looked at a shelf which contained some ledgers. He took them down and glanced through them: they were accounts, showing monies owing or salted away with the bankers.

"The King will be pleased," he murmured. "I am sure Agrippa will tell him about Henley's death and the Lords of the Treasury will soon have their fingers on all this."

A leather-bound folio was more interesting. It was an index drawn up by a Dutch scholar, published and printed in Bruges, which listed the principal relics of Western Christendom. Benjamin found the entry for the Orb of Charlemagne. There was a crude drawing above it which I recognised as the relic. The writing was more accurate: in the main it faithfully described the Orb; how it had been owned by the great Emperor and sent to Alfred of England and how the English kings had kept it in the most secret place. However, when it came to a detailed description of the amethyst the writer was silent. Instead Henley had scrawled in the margin: *'Per ig. Cruc. Ixthus vid'*.

"What is that?" I asked.

My master, who was skilled in secret ciphers, studied it.

"A mixture of Latin and Greek," he replied. "Ixthus is the Greek title for Jesus Our Saviour."

"And the rest?"

"Bearing in mind Henley's request for a candle, I'd say that *per ig* means *per ignem*, through fire. *Cruc* is Latin for cross: *vid* means *Videtur*, can be seen." Benjamin closed the book. "That's why Henley wanted the beeswax candle. Hold the Orb up, place the amethyst against a brilliant flame and, somehow or other, a cross can be seen in the centre of the stone."

"Can that be done?" I asked.

"Not artificially," Benjamin replied. "What I suspect is that, when the Orb was made for Charlemagne, this amethyst was particularly chosen because the goldsmith at the time thought it was of a sacred character. That amethyst," Benjamin continued, "is probably the only way of ensuring the Orb is genuine."

"But that's impossible, master. If Henley knew this, then surely the Emperor Charles V, not to mention his envoys Lord Egremont and Cornelius, would also have known?"

Benjamin sat down on a stool.

"When the Orb was placed in that sealed

casket in Berkeley's house," I insisted, "Egremont must have demanded that a light be held against the amethyst. He would then know that he was being tricked."

Benjamin rocked himself backwards and forwards, eyes closed.

"Did they know?" he asked.

"Oh come on, master. If a tawdry counterfeit-man like Henley knew, then surely Charles V's ambassadors would?"

"The only person who could answer that," Benjamin replied, "is Henley himself and he's now a member of the choir invisible. I suspect that Henley was not just a tawdry counterfeit man but an expert on relics. Somehow he found out the real secret and wrote it in the margin of this book." He sighed. "Yet, in the end, Henley didn't make the replica, Berkeley did. Is our goldsmith the villain of the piece?"

"No," I retorted. "Berkeley acted on the orders of the King." I paused. "And that's where the real mystery begins, doesn't it? If Berkeley put a replica in that chest, he must have done so on the orders of the King. If he did, why is Henry now raging? And I don't believe that he's playing one of his little games."

"It's possible," Benjamin replied slowly, "that Berkeley acted on his own: that he intended to dupe both Henry and Charles V. That the Orb is still hidden away in his shop or wherever Berkeley wanted to conceal it. Our goldsmith therefore might have fled, taking the Orb with him."

I recalled Berkeley's honest face. He would carry out the orders of his king in order to dupe a foreign envoy. But steal the Orb and flee?

"No, master," I voiced my doubts. "If Berkeley was ordered to make a replica, he would do so but I doubt he would steal the genuine article. However, that doesn't solve the real mystery. If the amethyst was special why didn't Egremont notice it was flawed?"

Benjamin opened the book and studied the inscription again.

"The cross of the Saviour can be seen," he read aloud. He placed the book back on the shelf. "Come on, Roger, I want to talk to someone."

We left Henley's house, collected our horses and walked through the crowds back to Cheapside. It was just after noon: the Angelus bell from St Mary Le Bow was tolling, calling the faithful to prayer. Most people ignored it, more intent on thronging the cookshops and taverns. Benjamin was growing enigmatic. He strode along the broad thoroughfare ignoring my questions.

"In a while, in a while, Roger," he murmured.

Near the Great Conduit, he gave a cry of exclamation and pointed to a goldsmith's sign.

"Pasteler!" he exclaimed. "John Pasteler!"

We walked across. Benjamin gave an urchin a penny to hold our horses. I followed him into the goldsmith's shop. Pasteler in many ways reminded me of Berkeley: an honest, well-to-do merchant busy amongst his apprentices and journeymen. The shelves and tables around the shop were littered with precious objects: cups, bracelets, brooches, ewers and bowls. Pasteler was surprised to see Benjamin but gave us a smile and a warm handshake.

"You have not come to buy, have you, Master Daunbey?" His smile faded. "I am sorry," he muttered. "I forgot, Johanna became ill."

This was a reference to Benjamin's betrothed who had lost her wits and been cloistered in a convent.

"The years hurry on," Benjamin replied. "No more wedding bands but, John, you have a collection of precious stones?"

"In my strongbox yes, rubies, emeralds . . ."

"Do you have any amethysts?"

Pasteler went away and came back with a

194

small metal-bound coffer fastened with three locks. He opened these carefully. I caught my breath: there must have been five or six amethysts lying on a satin cushion. Some of them were the size of small eggs, though none was as grand as the one I had seen on the so-called Orb of Charlemagne.

"I am not buying," Benjamin explained. "But, is it possible, Master Pasteler, to have an amethyst inside which, against a strong flame, a cross can be seen?"

"Of course." Pasteler picked up the largest amethyst. "Notice how they are cut, Benjamin: how many sides to this amethyst are there?"

"There must be at least seven or eight," Benjamin replied.

"Precisely," Pasteler declared. "This one is at least three hundred years old and has been cut in that way. Stay there!"

Pasteler went away. He brought back a small wax candle light. He struck a tinder, lit this and held the amethyst up against the flame. I peered over Benjamin's shoulder and caught my breath. The gem was many-sided, the lines crossed and within I could see a cross glowing. Benjamin studied it intently.

"And would this happen with any amethyst?"

"If it was pure and many-sided with lines

and sides crossing," the goldsmith replied, "yes, it's possible. It's a well-known trick in this type of stone."

Benjamin thanked him and we went and stood out in Cheapside.

"I think I have it, Roger," he declared. "The Orb of Charlemagne is surmounted by an amethyst. However, Henley's entry talks not only of a cross, as we've just seen, but the Cross of our Saviour. I suspect very few actually know what this cross is like. The amethyst on the Orb of Charlemagne may be unique: by some cut of the stone and trick of the light, one can not only see a cross but the figure of Christ nailed to it."

"And Henley would know that, but not the likes of Egremont?"

Benjamin grinned. "You know the world of relic selling: Henley, perhaps, stumbled on the secret and that is why he wrote the word, Saviour, in Greek. People like our Lord Theodosius would look for a cross, Henley would look for the figure of Christ." Benjamin sighed. "It must be the answer — that alone accounts for Henley's use of *Ixthus*."

"I agree," I replied. "So, when Egremont inspected the Orb at Berkeley's, he and anyone else would see the cross and think it was genuine. Henley knew otherwise. When he saw nothing but a simple cross in the amethyst shown to him, he knew it was false."

"I think so," Benjamin declared. "And he'd tell as much to whoever stole the Orb. Henley would then laugh at the way the thief had been duped. He had his throat cut for his pains, as well as to silence him for ever."

We went to a nearby tavern for something to eat and drink. We then collected our horses from the stables and rode slowly back to Malevel.

We expected to find it deserted but Kempe and his men were waiting: the soldiers lounged outside, Kempe sprawled in the keeper's small office.

"I tried to go up to your chambers," he explained, "but that bloody hound stopped me! You've got to come with me. We've found Berkeley."

"Where?" Benjamin asked.

"Amongst the ruins just north of the Tower. He's had his throat cut and he was tortured before he died."

Above us, Castor had obviously heard me and began to howl mournfully.

"How long has he been dead?" Benjamin asked.

"A few hours perhaps," Kempe replied.

Benjamin walked outside and stared at

Malevel Manor as if, through very thought, he could discern what had happened there. Kempe and I followed him out.

"We are to go now," Sir Thomas repeated. He glanced at me. "I suppose the bloody dog has to be fed?"

"Don't speak ill of your betters," I retorted.

Kempe just smirked.

"The King offered me two gold coins to find out how you placated the beast," he commented.

"Well, both you and he will have to wait, won't they?"

"Sir Thomas." Benjamin came back. "Sir Thomas," he repeated. "Before Roger and I go riding over the heathland to inspect some poor man's corpse, I have a question for you. You said that there was a way of knowing the Orb of Charlemagne was genuine?"

"That's correct."

"And the clue lies in the amethyst? If you hold it up against the flame you can see, inside the diamond, the faint outline of a cross and Our Saviour's body on it?"

"That's true," Kempe replied, his face full of surprise. "How did you find out?"

Benjamin just shrugged. "And you are sure," Benjamin persisted, "that the Orb which was given to Lord Egremont was the genuine one?" I saw a shift in Kempe's eyes, a slight flicker: his tongue came out to wet his upper lip, all the signs I've gathered over the years of a man about to lie.

"But that's ridiculous," he stammered. "Of course the Orb was genuine!"

"In which case," I spoke up, "you will not deny us the right to inspect the replica?"

"Of course, at an appropriate time and away from prying eyes."

"Good!" Benjamin declared. "And I have other requests, Sir Thomas." He pointed at the manor. "I want a guard left here." He tapped his pouch. "The windows are all shuttered and I hold the keys to the doors. No one is to go in there without my permission. Agreed?"

Kempe shouted an order at the captain of his guard telling him to leave four men.

"They can use the gatehouse," I declared. "My master and I, not to mention Castor, are moving to the Flickering Lamp."

"Do you have any other requests, Master Daunbey?" Kempe asked.

"Yes, I would like to know," Benjamin said, "why, when I inspected the quiver of one of your archers, Sir Thomas, some of the arrows were missing? Now in that silent massacre, no long bow was used. I just wondered, Sir Thomas, if one of the archers was sending messages?"

Kempe's face paled. He opened his mouth to reply but stamped his feet and looked up at the sky.

"We have to hurry," he declared. "I know nothing of what you say, Master Daunbey, but Berkeley's corpse is waiting. Lord Egremont and his creature Cornelius will be joining us."

Benjamin let the matter rest. I went up to our chamber where Castor threw himself on me, bouncing up and down, licking my face. I took him for a walk on the heathland and the mad beast ran around chasing crows and rooks and leaving any rabbit stupid enough to come out of its burrow in a state of mortal fear. At last, exhausted, he trotted back. We returned to the gatehouse where Benjamin had packed our saddlebags and, accompanied by a very sullen Kempe, we rode into the city to hire chambers at the Flickering Lamp.

We had no difficulty getting through the crowds. I tied a piece of rope round Castor's collar and everyone, including the beggars and counterfeit-men, gave us a wide berth. Boscombe seemed pleased to see me. He was in one of his strange moods and had changed his appearance, this time dressing in Lincoln green as if he was one of Robin Hood's men.

"It's good to see you again," he grinned. "I, too, have been away, business in the West Country. You still want your chamber and for your friend . . . ?"

Boscombe readily agreed to provide a further chamber. He also had the sense to offer Castor a piece of meat. The dog wolfed it down and immediately trotted after Boscombe to a make-shift kennel in a small plot behind the tavern stables. I left our saddlebags in my chamber, came down and pushed my way through the thronged taproom. Even as I did so I glimpsed Cerberus sitting in the corner watching me unblinkingly, his tankard half-raised to his lips.

We left by Cripplegate, galloping hard along the deserted path. It's a strange place north of the Tower. The soil is poor, its sprawling wild heathland is the haunt of footpads and outlaws. This bleak landscape is broken by thick copses of trees, small wood and the occasional dell where the land abruptly dips. A lonely, brooding place, the silence broken only by the sound of the crows which nested in the trees or the occasional howl of a dog from some lonely farm. At the top of a small hill, Kempe paused: behind us in the far distance I could make out the outlines of the Tower. We caught the salty taste of the river. Kempe pointed to a lonely copse further east, well away from the trackway which wound across the heathland.

"Amongst the trees," he explained, "there are ruins. Some people claim the Romans built an outstation there: others that it was a small castle built by William the Norman."

"It's a lonely place," I replied. "How was Berkeley's corpse discovered so quickly?"

"Two journeymen coming into the city," he replied, "stopped there last night. At first they didn't see anything wrong but, at dawn, they noticed the crows were massing on the walls at the far side of the ruin. They went over, and found Berkeley's body lying in a ditch. He was wearing a gilt bracelet with his name inscribed on it." Kempe cleared his throat and spat. "They brought this into the city and went straight to the Guildhall. I have a man there, a clerk, who brought the news to me."

I strained my eyes and caught a flash of colour amongst the trees.

"I think Lord Egremont is waiting for us."

Kempe put spurs to his horse and we galloped across the grass, not reining in until we entered the trees. We dismounted and followed Kempe into a large clearing where the ruins sprawled: crumbling walls and towers, covered in lichen and creeping ivy. Egremont and Cornelius were waiting for us inside: the Imperial envoy had his cowl pushed back, his long, dyed hair tumbling down on either side of his unshaven face.

"We've been waiting, Sir Thomas, at least a good half hour!" He looked sinister standing there, legs apart, sword and dagger in their sheaths. Beside him, Cornelius, hands pushed up the voluminous sleeves of his gown, looked even more threatening, the hilt of his dagger just peeping out from the edge of his cloak. Behind him was a silent half-circle of Noctales, an eerie sight with their shaven heads and monkish garb, yet all the more threatening as they were armed to the teeth. They stared at us without a flicker of friendship or camaraderie.

"They hold us responsible," I whispered to Benjamin. "You can see it in their eyes!"

"Where's Berkeley?" Kempe asked.

Cornelius snapped his fingers. Two of his men came forward, carrying a small stretcher, a piece of canvas between two poles. They pulled back the covering sheet. Lord have mercy! Berkeley was a good man, he deserved a better death. His boots and hose had been removed, his half-closed, blood-filled eyes gazed blankly up. His mouth was simply a gaping hole of blood and his throat had been slashed, drenching what had been a costly blue and gold jerkin.

"He was a good man, at least to me!"

I knelt down beside the corpse, closed my eyes and said a quick prayer. Benjamin on the other side was already examining the corpse.

"Look." He held up Berkeley's hand. "Someone has sliced off the top of each finger. The same with the left hand."

The soles of the poor man's feet were scorched, while long dagger furrows ran down either side of his bare legs.

"He was tortured," Cornelius exclaimed. "Tortured for a while. A small fire lit beneath his feet, the tips of his fingers removed. Now who would do that to Sir Hubert?"

"Anything else?" Benjamin asked. "How did he come here?"

"There are signs of horses," Cornelius replied, crouching beside us. "Whoever did this undoubtedly enjoys his work."

Benjamin got to his feet. "Sir Thomas, where were you last night?" he asked abruptly. "And you, my Lord Egremont?"

The Imperial envoy strode over, a riding crop in his hand. He laid this gently on Benjamin's cheek.

"Are you accusing me?"

I rose, hand on my dagger hilt. Egremont caught the movement and laughed deep in his throat.

"Tell him, Sir Thomas. Tell him where we both were last night."

"We were guests of His Grace the King and his Eminence Cardinal Wolsey. We were in the court from late afternoon. Master Daunbey, you know the King: we hunted, we feasted, we were entertained by one masque after another and the festivities went on until just before dawn. Master Berkeley here disappeared yesterday. He told his workers he was going out and that's the last we know of him."

"And where were you?" I asked Cornelius.

"We have lodgings in the old Temple buildings near Fleet Street," the Noctale replied.

"And?"

"Like you, Shallot, and you, Master Daunbey, I cannot guarantee where I was every single hour." He gestured at the corpse. "This is the work of a professional assassin. I believe he kidnapped Berkeley." He bent down and turned the corpse over. "Struck him on the back of the head and brought him here for questioning." He gazed slyly up at me. "But God knows why?" He pointed to the dagger marks on either side of the knee.

"These would be particularly painful; when a man tenses his legs and the muscles are tight beneath the knees such cuts would make him scream." He looked over his shoulder at Egremont and said something in German.

"What was that?" Benjamin asked, who knew a little of the tongue.

"We talked of the Schlachter, the Slaughterer. Years ago," Cornelius replied, "before I joined the Noctales and his Imperial Excellency was pleased to promote me in his favour, there was another Noctale, a master torturer, called the Schlachter. He served the Emperor Maximilian but — " Cornelius wiped his hands on his brown robes and stared up at the crows complaining raucously in the trees around the ruin. "This man became over-enthusiastic in his work. He made the mistake of torturing an innocent merchant and was dismissed by Emperor Charles. His name was Jakob." Cornelius narrowed his eyes. "That's right, Jakob von Archetel. He fled the empire and warrants were issued for his arrest. His apprehension was my first task." He smiled thinly. "At which I failed."

"Are you saying this could be the work of the Schlachter?" I asked.

"Possibly," Cornelius replied. "It bears all the hallmarks of his handiwork. The removal of the tips of fingers, the dagger wounds on the legs." His face became grave. "If Archetel is involved in this business, then it doesn't bode well. He would like to hurt the Emperor as well as line his own purse."

"And what about your outlaws?" Egremont intervened. "This Lord Charon you mentioned?"

"Ah yes." Kempe came forward, the bastard was smiling from ear to ear. "We discussed what you told us, Master Shallot, with His Grace the King. He wants Lord Charon trapped, arrested and interrogated." He tweaked my cheek. "And you, my dear Roger, are to be the bait."

9

We returned to the Flickering Lamp: it was late in the afternoon and I was torn between rage and fear.

"Always poor Shallot," I snarled as we sat in the taproom.

Boscombe came over: this time he was garbed as a friar, even his face was pulled in a sanctimonious expression and his little mockery did something to restore my good humour. Benjamin introduced himself fully, thanking Boscombe for his kindness to me during my recent troubles. The landlord simply pushed his hands up the sleeves of his gown, smiled beatifically, sketched a blessing in the air and walked away. Benjamin watched him go curiously.

"Master?" I asked.

Benjamin picked up his blackjack, tossing the remains of his chicken on the floor for Castor to eat.

"I am sure I have seen him before," Benjamin declared. He put his tankard down. "I am sure I have," he repeated.

"Perhaps when we came here first?" I retorted. (Oh yes, I regret I was so

208

dismissive.) "Maybe you glimpsed his face then? But, never mind him, what am I to do about Lord Charon?"

"Sir Thomas Kempe made it very clear," Benjamin replied. "Lord Charon may have had a hand in the business at Malevel Manor." He leaned across and gripped my wrist. "Roger, it's the only path we can follow: better that than being summoned to kneel before the King and listen to him rage or, even worse, have things thrown at us!" Benjamin glanced across the tavern to where Boscombe was standing beside the ale casks. "If we fail the King on this," he added, "it will no doubt mean spending months in the Tower, followed by some sea voyage down the coast of Africa."

He came over, sat beside me and leaned his back against the wall.

"Let's summarise, Roger, what we know. First," he said. "We have the Orb of Charlemagne. The King has really no intention of allowing that out of his realm. He therefore hires a royal goldsmith to fashion a replica. Secondly, this Orb contains a secret. If the amethyst on the top is held up against a flame, I believe the crucified Christ can be seen. This information is known to the King and to Sir Thomas Kempe. Now the relic-seller Henley also knew it but the thief did not. That is why Henley was killed and Berkeley was taken out on to that lonely heath, to be tortured and interrogated about the replica, before he was foully murdered."

"Thirdly," I added. "The replica that Berkeley fashioned apparently fooled both Lord Theodosius and Cornelius. Otherwise they would never have accepted it." I sipped at my ale. "This leads us to other interesting possibilities. Was the replica Kempe showed us the genuine article? Or did Berkeley make two?"

"And?" Benjamin asked.

"Where is the replica now?" I asked.

"I can't answer that," Benjamin replied. "However, Dearest Uncle told me that Henry has been negotiating with the Emperor for help against France for the last year. In that time Berkeley could have fashioned two or more replica Orbs." He sighed. "But we'll never know, will we? Well, Roger, what else have your sharp wits dug up?"

"Fourthly," I continued. "We know fifteen men were killed at Malevel Manor but how or by whom is a mystery. There's no evidence as to how the assassin was able to enter and massacre so many able men and then leave without disturbing a mouse. Fifthly, Sir Thomas Kempe is not above suspicion. We believe that at least one archer may have been sending him messages from Malevel Manor."

"But there again," Benjamin intervened, "we have no evidence that it was Kempe who was receiving such messages."

"Finally," I concluded. "Lord Charon may be involved in this wickedness. He was undoubtedly responsible for the murder of Lady Isabella Malevel and he may know some secret entrance into the manor."

"There is one other person," Benjamin added. "The man Cornelius referred to as the Schlachter, a former member of the Noctales who may be working for himself . . . "

"Or for Lord Charon?" I suggested.

I gazed round the taproom. The day was drawing on; traders, journeymen, porters, a few of the street trollops, two wandering musicians and a beggar with a fistful of pennies were now clamouring for wine and food, laughing loudly at Boscombe's imitation of a friar. One of the porters, a drunken oaf, caught my gaze and came lumbering across threateningly; Castor raised his head and growled and the fellow scuttled off like a beetle.

"I wonder if Cerberus, or another of Lord Charon's men, is here?"

Benjamin pulled a face.

"Boscombe!" I called. I held up my hand,

a silver piece between my fingers.

The taverner almost jumped across the room, knocking aside other customers.

"Master Roger?"

"If I wanted," I whispered, "to speak to Lord Charon, how would I do it?"

Boscombe took the silver piece and, before I could stop him, clapped his hands.

"Hear ye! Hear ye!" he bellowed, mimicking a town crier. "Know that Master Shallot, my guest and dearest friend, wishes to have words with the Lord Charon!" Boscombe put his hand on his chest and bowed. "Of course," he added, "at a time and place of Lord Charon's choosing."

The rest of the customers just gazed at him and a deathly silence held the taproom. Boscombe clapped his hands again and laughed.

"The scullions and tap boys will look after you: a free blackjack of ale." His eyes slid towards me. "On our good friend Master Shallot!"

He sat down on a stool.

"Was that really necessary?" I asked.

"It is the only way, my son," Boscombe replied unctuously. "Do it in any other manner and Lord Charon would become suspicious and you, my son, would be dead." He leaned across the table. "Why, Roger?"

he whispered. "Why Lord Charon? You were out at Malevel Manor, weren't you? There are terrible stories about a massacre taking place. Was Lord Charon . . . ?"

"They are all true," Benjamin retorted. "Will one of Lord Charon's men be here?"

"Oh, don't worry," Boscombe replied. "Within the hour he'll know all about it."

"Where do you come from?" Benjamin asked abruptly. "Your accent?"

"From the West Country," Boscombe replied cheerily, wiping his hands on his robe. "But there's not good custom along the south-western road, that's where my father had his tavern. Anyway, we sold up and moved into London, my wife and I. She's now lying in peace in St Botolph's churchyard." His smile widened. "And if she's at peace then so am I." He was about to push his stool back. "Ah, Master Roger, when Lord Charon took you and your belongings I found a bag under your bed." He got up, hurried away and then came back and thrust the bag at me.

I looked inside. Nothing much: the cup I had stolen from the Poppletons and a few of my makeshift relics. My smile of thanks faded as I realised that, when all this was over, I would have to go back to Ipswich and face their malice, King's pardon or not.

Such a thought would turn any man to drink and indeed I drank so deeply that I slept the night with Castor on the taproom floor. I spent the next day recovering, glad that Lord Charon did not strike immediately; my wits were so befuddled I would have been no use to anyone.

Now Sir Thomas Kempe had called me the bait so, naturally, I became anxious about what might happen if this self-styled lord of the underworld took me prisoner again. I pestered Benjamin but he was of very little help.

"Don't worry, don't worry," he replied absentmindedly. "Dearest Uncle will look after us."

I didn't believe him. However, on the morning of the second day as I sat in the tavern or walked the maze of alleyways around it, I became aware of men I had never seen before: traders and journeymen as well as beggars who looked as if they had eaten too well. Strangers called into the Flickering Lamp. Three or four self-styled merchants hired chambers in houses around whilst the old beldame who owned a tenement opposite the tavern, commented on how all her rooms, even the filthy cellar, had been hired.

Boscombe became suspicious and, after he served me breakfast, a succulent pie, gold and crusty, he decided to join me.

"What's the matter, Roger? I know your master is the Cardinal's nephew." His face became worried. "This invitation to Lord Charon: is it a trap?"

I glowered at him.

"I helped you once!"

"If it's a trap," I replied enigmatically, "stay well clear of it. If it's not, you have nothing to fear."

I looked down at the pie, so fresh and sweet, then at Castor who was looking at it longingly, tongue lolling, his great jaws drooling. I cut the pie in two. Castor growled with pleasure and Boscombe, seeing he was going to get nothing from me, shrugged and returned to his post by the ale casks.

Benjamin came in. He had been absent all night and I wondered if he had been across the city to see if the marvellous Miranda had returned. He was unshaven, out of sorts, his eyes red-rimmed. He ordered some food and sat down opposite me.

"The French have left," he snapped.

"I beg your pardon?"

"The French." Benjamin paused as Boscombe came over to serve us. "Don't you remember, Agrippa told us the French were in London? They, too, wanted the Orb of Charlemagne. The envoys had rented a large mansion in Westchepe. I went there yesterday afternoon." He shrugged. "To see if I could learn anything. Last night there appears to have been a banquet. Some form of celebration. Nobody we knew attended. Then, this morning, just before dawn, carts were drawn up outside the house, and the envoys' goods and baggage were piled high. I bribed one of the porters. He said the Messieurs were leaving, going down to their warship docked at East Watergate."

"Why the interest?" I asked.

"Who ever stole the Orb . . . " Benjamin replied. He put down a piece of the pie he was eating and stared at it.

"Master?" I asked.

"Nothing." He shook his head. "My memory was jogged but I am too confused to place it."

"You were talking about the thief and the Orb?"

"Ah yes. Who ever stole the Orb," Benjamin continued, "must have done it for personal gain. They would try to sell it . . . "

"To the French?" I asked.

"Well," Benjamin declared. "Let us say the thief did sell it to the French, is that why they celebrated and left London? They've got what they came for."

"Kempe should be able to help us there," I replied. "He'd keep the French under close scrutiny?"

"Sir Thomas has a great deal to answer but . . . "

"Master Daunbey! Master Shallot!"

We looked up at the travel-stained man who stood, hat in his hand, just inside the doorway. He came forward. Benjamin gave a cry of delight and rose to his feet, gesturing the man to a stool. I recognised Laxton, one of our manor officials: he looked after the horses and managed the stables.

"I rode through the night," Laxton explained, taking off his cloak and mopping at the dirt on his doublet. "Oh master, if you permit . . . ?" He began to ease his boots off. I helped him and he sighed with pleasure.

Benjamin ordered some food and meat. Boscombe, all curious, brought this across.

"How did you know we were here?" Benjamin asked.

Laxton pointed at me. "You wrote to Lucy. We found the letter on her." His face grew sad.

My heart skipped a beat.

"She's dead, isn't she?" I asked.

Laxton nodded. "I am sorry, master. She was found in a lane outside the village. She

217

had been attacked, beaten sorely about the head."

"What was she doing there?" I asked.

"We think she was going to the manor," Laxton replied. "She had a cloak and a pair of old battered boots on. She was carrying a small bag full of her possessions: some rosary beads, your letter and, I think, a lock of your hair."

Hot tears scalded my eyes.

"Who attacked her? Why?" I whispered. "Why Lucy? She was a merry soul."

"She wasn't dead when we found her," Laxton replied. "One of the grooms from the White Harte was going into the fields with his sweetheart, and heard her groaning. Lucy had tumbled into a ditch at the side of the road. They dragged her out. They thought she was dead but then she opened her eyes. She left a message for you." He closed his eyes. "Tell Roger," he repeated carefully. "Tell Roger the cup . . . " He opened his eyes. "She repeated that a number of times. The groom ran for help but, by the time we arrived, Lucy was dead." He paused. "What did she mean, master, about the cup?"

"'My cup is overflowing'." I brushed the tears from my eyes. "It's a quotation from the Bible. She always said that, when I was with her, her cup of happiness overflowed.

For some strange reason she thought this was funny."

"Does anyone know why she was attacked?" Benjamin intervened.

"No. Since Master Roger left she had been working at the White Harte. She made no enemies, though she steered well clear of the Poppletons. I know she had a disagreement with them over you and refused to work at their house. After she died, we had a parish meeting in the taproom," Laxton concluded. "It was decided that I should come and tell you. I reached the city just before dawn." He shook his head. "It's years since I've been to London. I'm glad I found you."

Benjamin, seeing I was upset, took Laxton away. For a while I just sat and cried. I then got up and walked out into the alleyway, knocking aside the costermongers and traders who thronged into the alleyway.

Now, you know old Shallot. I am not a man for prayer. I just like to sit and hope that God looks my way and, if he's in a good mood, smiles at me. I laugh and joke: it's the best way to hide the tears. However, Lucy was a soft young thing. She was a woman full of life with a keen sense of wit, lovable and kind. There wasn't a jot of malice in her beautiful body. She was born good and some bastard had killed her. I went down the narrow street and into the small church owned by the Crutched Friars, a little, dank place which suited my mood. I crouched on the floor before the statue of the Virgin Child and tried to pray for Lucy's soul. My usual prayer: 'This is Roger Shallot, sinner and stupid with it.' I was only halfway through when I heard the slither of footsteps. I was just thinking of fleeing when the club hit my head. I felt rough sacking and then it was down into the darkness. I woke up and, believe me, what a change! Not the Virgin and Child but Charon's ugly face peering at me. He didn't begin with some dramatic line like, "Welcome to my abode." He just kicked me in the groin and asked me what I was doing in church.

"I was praying," I moaned.

I stared around and, trust me, I began to gabble my prayers. I was back in the Lord Charon's abode, full of the opulent luxury which contrasted so strangely with the filthy surroundings and, in the background, I could hear the ominous slop of water. Shadows moved into the candlelight; Cerberus and all the other beauties of Lord Charon's household, twisted, leering faces, garbed in tawdry finery and armed to the teeth. I did what I always do in such circumstances: I knelt, clasped my hands and hoped my bowels would not betray me.

(Honestly, I can never stop trembling in such situations. Once, when the Great Beast had me sent to the execution block, the headsman told me to stay still.

"What do you expect me to do?" I screamed back. "Do a dance?"

And so I did a merry jig. I made the executioner chase me round the scaffold. God be thanked, Henry was playing one of his sick jokes and the courier bringing my pardon had taken a fall from his horse and been delayed!)

However, I did not jig that day. I just gazed beseechingly at Lord Charon.

"You wanted to see me?"

This king of villains, that mad, moustached, purple-hued, maltworm crouched down beside me.

"Well, ticklebrain?" He poked me in the shoulder. "You want to see the Lord Charon?"

"I know where those tapestries come from," I blurted out, pointing behind him. "Lady Malevel's house. You broke in, cleared out all her valuables, cut her throat and buried her in the cellar, didn't you?"

(You young men, take note, whenever you are captured by the enemy, none of this

221

stiff upper lip business. For goodness' sake, talk and talk fast. The longer you talk, the more hope there is and, where there's hope, there's life!)

"Now, here's a clever boy." Charon tapped me on the head.

"And you want to take it all back with you?"

"No! No!" I gabbled. "But the Orb of Charlemagne, the relic you stole . . . "

"Stole?"

And, throwing his head back, Charon laughed. The rest of his coven guffawed in ghastly chorus.

I stammered, thinking of the replica that Kempe still held, "I . . . I . . . I can get you the real Orb of Charlemagne."

Charon started to laugh again, until the tears rolled down his cheeks.

He waggled a finger at me. "We are not going to kill you just yet." He sighed. "Lord, I have never laughed so much since the Lady Isabella begged for her life." He glanced round at his lieutenants and edged a little closer. "Now, let me understand you, Shallot. On the one hand you think I stole the Orb, which I didn't. On the other — " One finger scratched at his blue, pockmarked face. "You say you can get it for me: that means you stole it! And you know what happens to thieves," he whispered. "They hang."

"No, no, you misunderstand me!"

"No, no, you misunderstand me!" The entire devilish crew chorused back.

Oh, pity me, I was in a nightmare: Charon's ugly, stained face; his cutthroat coven chanting my line like a chorus in one of Marlow's plays. And what about poor old Shallot? I just prayed that one of Kempe's men had seen me. Yet where was I? How would they rescue me? I started to cry. (Another of Shallot's rules; if you can't babble, blurt. Crying wastes time.) Charon dragged back my head.

"Didn't you ever think," he hissed, "that I knew about the Orb of Charlemagne? Do you really think I would have attacked a manor full of armed men? Do you really think I'm stupid enough not to realise how many strangers have appeared in the alleyways around that tavern? You are bait, aren't you, Shallot? A lure to catch old Charon? And that is very, very foolish of you!"

He was now talking like a schoolmaster confronting one of his dimmer scholars.

"I don't need the Orb of Charlemagne," he whispered. "I have taken it and I have sold it." He saw the surprise in my eyes. "And for you, Roger, I have a special gift.

Do you remember the rats?"

I moaned with fear.

After that Charon beat me around the head. The others joined in with kicks and blows before I was dragged out along the sewer side to another cavern, sealed by an iron grille. The small door was opened and I was thrown inside. I sat there wondering how in heaven's name I was to escape. I knelt and prayed. I vowed to become a monk but realised I was lying so I just crawled into a corner and listened to Charon and his henchmen carousing a few yards away. I didn't know whether it was night or day, but, a few hours later, they returned carrying torches. I was dragged out, back to Lord Charon's cave. The table was littered with food, goblets of wine, pieces of meat strewn on the floor. One of the villains had been killed in some drunken brawl, and now leaned against the table, his throat slashed from ear to ear. No, I don't lie! They just left him propped there, eyes popping, mouth gaping. I was laid out on the floor and ropes attached to my wrists and ankles. Charon, much the worse for drink, came and knelt beside me.

"You are going to die, Roger, in a way you can never imagine. Cerberus, show him our friend."

Dogface knelt on the other side. In his hand he held a cage. Inside was the longest and most ferocious-looking rat I have ever seen. This turd of iniquity was at least a yard long from the tip of his nose to the end of his tail; yellowing teeth jutted out, his belly sagged and his ribs showed through. He dashed himself against the cage and those eyes, pin-pricks of hell fire, glowered at me. I fainted.

I was roused by a bucket of filthy water. "Now, this is what's going to happen." Charon talked like some gentle priest. He pulled back my doublet and tapped my side. "We are going to attach a pipe here, the rat scuttles down and we light a small fire at the open end. The rat is hungry, ravenous. There is only one way out, dear Roger, and that's through you. Now, what do you think of that?"

I screamed and yelled, begging for mercy. I might as well have whistled across a graveyard. The pipe was attached, the rat went in. I could hear it rustling about, its sharp claws and teeth scrabbling against my clammy skin. I screamed, sobbing for mercy. The bastards were so drunk they could not light the fire at the other end. As they fumbled with the tinder, I heard a sound which, to my ears, was like an angel singing. A deep-throated bark. Castor had arrived! Confusion broke out, and there was a scramble for arms as Castor burst into the cavern like a hell hound. Intelligent beast, noble heart, Shallot's saviour! He took one look at Charon and lunged. The cavern became full of a confusion of figures. I heard the roar of an arquebus, the clash of steel. The pipe was kicked away from me, the rat fled. Benjamin, a bloody sword in his hands, crouched down and cut my bonds. I jumped to my feet. Archers, bullyboys, Kempe's men, as well as those of Egremont and the Noctales were now locked in a fierce life and death struggle with the outlaws. Charon was screaming, his body one bloody wound: he stabbed at Castor with a dagger but the hound refused to let go. I rushed towards them but stumbled over a corpse. I heard a splash and both the Lord of the Underworld and my noble hound disappeared beneath the surface of the sewer.

I ran to the edge but the current was strong. I could see no sign of either of them and I turned to defend myself as a villain, blood streaming from his mouth, lurched at me. Benjamin caught him midway with a cutting slash to the neck and the fellow fell, tumbling sideways into the water. Now, I have been in bloody struggles, I have watched the most horrible of battles. I have seen Mars in all its terrors, thankfully from some safe vantage point, yet that struggle in the sewers of London is one of the most memorable. A recurring nightmare. You see, Charon's men had no illusions. This was no honourable chivalrous fight where prisoners could be taken, ransoms obtained. These were bullyboys, the scum and the filth of the city who lived off the fat of the land with a deep-seated hatred for all authority. They asked for no quarter and none was given. I crouched in the shadows and watched. Benjamin moved effortlessly: a swordsman, he stood with his back to the wall and took on all comers. Cornelius moved beside him, a thin silent, deadly killer with his broad stabbing sword and thin Italian stiletto. A man born to kill. Lord Egremont and Kempe swirled by me. Kempe shouting orders, trying to stop the villains fleeing into the darkness whilst Egremont, and you can always tell from a man's face when he likes blood and dotes on killing, was in his element.

At last the fighting subsided. Most of Charon's men were dead but Cerberus and at least a score of others were alive or nearly so: their hands were bound, and soldiers and archers were pushing them away. Egremont, Cornelius, Benjamin and myself went into

227

Charon's cavern. Lord Egremont took the corpse from its seat at the table and, dragging it to the waterside, threw it in without a by your leave. He then cleared the table with his sword and sat down smiling, like a man who has done a good day's work.

"Your men are collecting the treasure?"

"We have clerks," Kempe replied, wiping the sweat from his face. "Everything will be collected and sealed."

Benjamin got up and, despite Kempe's protests, walked out. I followed. The caverns were now thronged with soldiers and clerks of the Exchequer. That's one thing about the English, they love good administration and Henry's Exchequer officials were the best there were. Years later I'd see them sweep into a monastery like Charterhouse or the great Abbey of Bury St Edmunds and, in a day, everything that could be moved was bagged, casked and sealed. They would scramble like ants round Lord Charon's treasure trove and sniff out gold like a mouse would cheese. Benjamin watched them, ignoring Kempe's protests to return. He then moved amongst them, asking if they had seen the Orb or any special relic? The clerks just shook their heads. I went and stood by the fast-running sewer, one of London's underground rivers, staring into the darkness.

I half expected to see that stupid dog with its great flapping ears and lolling tongue but he was gone.

Benjamin came up beside me and put a hand on my shoulder.

"He's dead, Roger. Charon struck him a number of blows."

"He was a good friend, master," I replied. This time my tears were genuine, silent, just running down my face. "He was a stupid dog. All fierce and loyal but with a heart as soft as honey."

Benjamin embraced me. "In which case, Roger, you had a lot in common." He stood away. "Castor saved you. When you failed to return to the tavern, I went out into the street. A beggar boy noticed you go into the church of the Crutched Friars but never come out. None of Kempe's men had seen anything untoward so I took Castor there. He immediately picked up your scent."

"But I was carried," I replied. I looked down at my boots, the tips were all scuffed.

"You were dragged but not far," Benjamin replied. "Castor was a hunting dog. In the cemetery behind the church, there's an entrance to the sewers beneath a grave stone. Kempe collected his men. Egremont and Cornelius were present when the messenger arrived and they insisted on coming too."

"You won't find the Orb down here," I replied, wiping my eyes. "Lord Charon, may God send him good judgement, said he had already sold it but, to whom, I don't know."

"You are sure of that?"

"As sure as I am of standing here."

"Someone like Charon," Benjamin mused, "would insist on being paid in gold or silver. Wait there, Roger."

He walked away, talking amongst the clerks opening casks and chests. I stood staring at the water, ignoring the chaos and confusion around me. Benjamin came back.

"The King is going to be a very contented man. Charon's treasure is a veritable hoard."

He linked his arm through mine and we walked further away from the clerks who were now dragging the casks and sacks out.

"We know the French envoys have left London," Benjamin continued. "If they bought the Orb they'd have paid in their own coin, Lord Charon would have insisted on it. However, apart from a few pieces, there's no sign of any French gold or silver. Nevertheless, one of the clerks told me that there's a casket full of gold, which looks new, as if Charon had just taken possession of it. It's not English, it's not French or German, but the best silver and gold from the mints of Italy."

My jaw sagged in surprise.

"Do you realise what you are saying, master?"

"Yes, yes, I do." Benjamin rubbed his face. "What I suspect happened is that Lord Charon took the Orb and sold it to the Papal Envoys. What I'd like to know is who sold the other replica to the French? And, the logical conclusion of that," he declared, looking over his shoulder, "is that since Kempe had the other replica, he must be the recipient of French gold."

10

While the clerks and soldiers removed the treasures to waiting carts, Egremont, Cornelius, Kempe, Benjamin and I gathered in Charon's cavern for a short meeting.

"There's no Orb," Egremont began. "No sign of it whatsoever. All we have done, Sir Thomas, Master Benjamin . . ."

The arrogant bastard barely deigned to notice me.

" . . . is help you arrest a coven of outlaws. There is no evidence that these villains were responsible for the stealing of the Orb, and yet . . . " He glanced sideways at Cornelius.

"What my Lord Theodosius is going to say," Cornelius's hooded eyes never left mine, "is that whilst Henry of England has come out of this well, we have not. Don't forget that we, too, can buy our spies in London: silver and gold need no tongue. We have heard rumours that the French, not to mention the Papal Envoys, are also looking for the Orb; that it is for sale and that the murders at Malevel are now well known to all those who are interested in the Orb."

"Soon," Egremont intervened, "we will have to leave. I have to go back to my master in Antwerp and tell him that the Orb is no longer his property or that of Henry of England. Naturally, I think it will be a miracle if any Imperial ships or galleys are seen in the Narrow Seas."

I just sat there with my head all in a whirl. Cornelius clearly suspected something was wrong. However, all I could grasp was that the Orb, which was a replica, had been stolen not by Lord Charon but by someone else. This mysterious thief had sold it to Charon and he, in turn, had sold it to the Papal Envoys.

★ ★ ★

"I need a bath." Lord Egremont spoke up, flicking dust from his sleeve. "Master Cornelius?"

Both men left the cavern. Kempe sat and waited for them to go, drumming his fingers on the table-top.

"They don't know the full truth, do they?" Benjamin spoke up. "Sir Thomas, you and I know that the Orb stolen from Malevel was only a replica. The thief took it to a relic-seller called Henley, who pronounced it a fake. Nevertheless, the thief, still determined on a profit, traded it to Lord Charon. I believe he sold it to the Papal Envoys in London."

Kempe lifted one shoulder elegantly. "You have proof for all this, Master Daunbey?"

"Yes, I have proof: when you go through Charon's treasures you will find freshly minted coins of Italy; a mixture of gold and silver, much used in Florence, Rome and Padua."

"Lord Charon acted quickly."

"Anyone would," Benjamin retorted. "Very few people could hold such monies: foreign envoys, however, are a different matter. Lord Charon would look for a speedy profit whilst the envoys could be out of the kingdom within the day, the Orb hidden in some diplomatic pouch."

"Are you saying," Kempe intervened, glancing towards the entrance, fearful of any eavesdropper, "that our King was prepared to dupe the Emperor?"

"I didn't say that," Benjamin replied quickly. "I am merely formulating a hypothesis which is based on considerable fact."

"But you have not finished, have you?" Kempe hissed back.

"No, I wish I had, Sir Thomas. It would be easier to say the Orb of Charlemagne has been stolen, that the Papal Envoys have it and that's the end of the matter. I have no real proof that the Orb was a forgery, just a suspicion. I might even travel back to Ipswich content that the English Crown, somewhere, still held the Imperial Orb. However, there are other, interesting developments."

"Such as?"

"Well — " Benjamin flicked away some crumbs from the tabletop. "The French, too, were in London. Doctor Agrippa informed us that they also wanted the Orb of Charlemagne and were prepared to pay dearly for it. According to what we have learnt, these French envoys have now left for Paris, highly pleased. I suspect they, too, think they have the Orb."

Kempe began to laugh though his eyes remained watchful.

"What are you saying, Master Daunbey? That there were two Orbs of Charlemagne? Both forgeries? That the one from Malevel Manor was sold by Charon to the Papal Envoys? Then who gave the French the other?"

"I don't know," Benjamin replied, "but I would like to see the replica you showed us in the woods near Malevel."

Sir Thomas rose to his feet in exasperation.

"Oh and I have another question," Benjamin added. "The archer in Malevel

Manor. He was sending messages to you, wasn't he, Sir Thomas?"

Kempe gave a dismissive motion with his hand and made to walk away.

"Either you tell me," Benjamin called out, "or I will demand an interview with Dearest Uncle!"

"Follow me," Kempe replied.

Sir Thomas walked out, shouting orders at his officials to ensure that everything was neatly tagged. He then led us down the sewer, the cold, fetid darkness broken only by the occasional soldier holding a blazing cresset torch. We must have walked half a mile before Sir Thomas reached some crumbling steps and led us up. We had to crawl out through a small hole at the top under a great slab of stone. The cold night air made me gasp and I exclaimed in surprise as I stared around. Night had fallen and the sky was bright with stars. In the light of flickering torches which had been fixed on wooden poles driven into the ground, I could see we were in a disused derelict cemetery and, some distance away, the dark mass of the church of the Crutched Friars. Usually derelict and empty, now the cemetery had been invaded by soldiers and clerks. Carts waited to take away the treasure, horses chomped at the long grass. Men-at-arms and archers were driving away the curious sight-seekers. Sir Thomas led us across, through the corpse door and into the church. He closed the door, struck a tinder and lit a candle in the Lady Chapel. I did likewise. I had not yet finished my prayers, so rudely interrupted by Lord Charon's henchmen. I lit two candles: one for Lucy, the other for Castor. I then joined Sir Thomas and Benjamin where they sat on a bench against the rood screen.

"There's no one here," Sir Thomas began. "Churches are the best place to plot."

"It was you, wasn't it?" Benjamin asked. "You were the one the archer was sending the messages to?"

"Yes, yes, it was." Kempe eased his legs. "I feel tired," he declared leaning back against the rood screen. "But it was a good night's work, Master Daunbey."

I was sitting on Benjamin's right, and I looked across. In the dim candlelight, I was sure the devious bastard was laughing at us.

"Why?" I asked. "Sir Thomas, I am cold. I am hungry. I've been manhandled by Charon's ruffians. I would love a hot meal, two cups of claret and a soft bed."

"There's no great mystery," Kempe replied. "Lord Egremont and his creature Cornelius had the upper hand at Malevel. However, the King was determined to know that all went well so I chose an archer called Yeovil. Whenever possible, he was to send me a message fired from a window at the side of the house. A master bowman, Yeovil chose his target well, an ash tree just beyond the walls. It was simple enough for any skilled archer."

"And what did Yeovil report?" Benjamin asked.

"Nothing." Kempe got to his feet: tucking his thumbs in his war-belt, he stared down at Benjamin. "Oh, he said the leader of the Noctales, Jonathan, was nervous and that the men were bored. But the casket was still sealed, the Orb was safe and all was well."

"Can I read these messages?" Benjamin asked.

Kempe shook his head. "They have been destroyed."

"And the replica Orb?" Benjamin asked.

Kempe tapped his foot against the paving stone: he stared up through the rood screen at the tabernacle on the high altar.

"The brothers," he remarked quietly, "will protest at us destroying their churchyard."

"Sir Thomas!" Benjamin snapped. "The replica Orb?"

"Tomorrow at first light," Kempe replied,

leaning down, "you will come to the Tower. What remains of Charon's gang will be summarily tried, found guilty, tortured and, by this time tomorrow, will be hanging on a gallows in Tower Green. They are going to be questioned closely about the Orb of Charlemagne."

"The replica?" Benjamin insisted.

"Oh, you can see that as well," Kempe replied. "It's still safe and sound in a Tower storeroom. You really shouldn't worry about that. You see, Master Daunbey, you have it all wrong. The real Orb of Charlemagne was kept at Malevel Manor. It was stolen and now the King wants it back — which is your task." He jabbed a finger in Benjamin's face. "Whatever you think, the real Orb was stolen." He shrugged. "I admit the King had Berkeley fashion replicas: one to keep, the other — " He smirked. "Perhaps to make a profit at some future time. So, good night, sirs." And, spinning on his heel, Kempe walked out of the church.

Benjamin sighed and got to his feet.

"Did you believe that, master?" I asked.

"I don't know," he replied. "Roger, I don't know any more. Perhaps we do have it all wrong. Perhaps the thief did sell the real Orb to Lord Charon and he, in turn, sold it to the Papal Envoys. Perhaps Henley was only killed so as to keep his mouth shut. But, who the thief was and how he did it remains a mystery." He sighed. "Oh, a cup of wine! And, talking of cups, Roger, I have something to show you."

We left the church and walked back through the alleyways to the Flickering Lamp. Boscombe was waiting, all attentive. He played the part of the inquisitive taverner and we were faced with a volley of questions. Believe me, that man was a better actor than Shakespeare's Burbage!

"And where's your dog?" he cried. "Where's poor Castor?"

"He's dead, God rest him!" I snapped. "And, if you don't bring us food and wine, Boscombe, you'll join him!" A good response, I hate hypocrisy — except in myself.

The taverner grinned and hurried away. I noticed with some amusement that this time he was no longer dressed in the garb of a friar, but that of a scrivener, a long grey robe with an ink pot and quill fastened on his belt. Benjamin had gone up to our chamber: when he returned, he was carrying the cup I had stolen from the Poppleton house. He ignored my questions.

"Let's eat and drink," he declared and asked Boscombe for some water and salt.

I was busy finishing my meal but, when I drained my wine cup and was about to ask for more, Benjamin held out the Poppleton cup.

"Drink, Roger!"

I took it and sniffed. "Water?"

"From the rain butt. Drink it!"

I sipped from it and handed it back. Benjamin cradled it in his hands whilst I shouted for more claret.

"Now drink again, Roger."

I grabbed it from him, slurped from it and then gagged.

"Master, it's got salt in it!" I grasped his wine bowl and sipped from it. "Some sort of trick, master?"

"No." Benjamin threw the water on to the rushes. "Look, Roger, look into the cup!"

"Nothing remarkable," I declared.

"Do you see anything?"

"Nothing but brass," I replied.

"No, at the bottom."

I poked my finger in. At the base of the cup was a circular piece of brass.

"Nothing but this," I retorted. "It's where the stem and cup meet."

"Watch again." Benjamin now held the cup. He did something with the stem and the innocuous clasp at the bottom moved slightly to the side revealing a small hole.

"How did you do that?" I exclaimed.

Benjamin held the cup up, pointing to a small imitation jewel in the middle of the stem.

"You just press that very firmly and the clasp opens. Whilst you were eating I put some salt in the hole. I cleaned the cup then poured in some water. On the first occasion you drank water. I pressed the clasp, swirled the water about and you tasted salt."

"That's how they did it!" I exclaimed, half rising to my feet. "That's how those two bastards killed their mother! They must have suspected how I first cured Lucy. They knew I used a potion so they brought that cup up; but first they put poison in the hole at the base."

Benjamin pushed me back into my seat.

"I listened very carefully to what you told me," he replied, "and I realised the Poppletons had tricked you." His face became grim. (It was one of those few occasions in my life when I realised Benjamin was not just the dreamy scholar: there was a darkness in him. He had not forgotten how, earlier in the year, the Poppletons had spread scandal that he had only opened his school because he liked little boys. Oh yes, the darkness in him could be murderous, but that was for the future.) On that night Benjamin smiled bleakly into the cup. "When Laxton came and told us about Lucy's death," he continued, "how her last words were, 'Tell Roger the cup,' I sensed something was wrong."

"Of course," I replied. "Otherwise she would have said, 'My cup is overflowing'!"

"What I think happened," Benjamin continued, "is that, somehow or other, Lucy herself discovered the Poppletons had tricked you. Perhaps she overheard a conversation on how keen the Poppletons were to have that cup back. Poor girl! She might have found it hard to keep it secret and . . . "

"So the Poppletons killed her?" I said.

"Oh yes. It has all their hallmarks: attacking a poor girl in a country lane and beating the very life out of her."

"We should go back," I replied. "Let's take horse and ride to Ipswich."

"That poses difficulties," Benjamin replied. "We have no real proof. No, the Poppletons would claim it was not their cup and there's very little evidence for their involvement in Lucy's murder. Moreover, Dearest Uncle and the King want us here." He picked up his wine bowl. "Let the evil ones fester for a while, Roger. Tonight, let's drink, celebrate your escape and toast the memories of Lucy and Castor!"

Drink we did and heard the chimes at

midnight from the nearby church. Nevertheless, we were up early the next morning,
long before the sun peeped its head above St
Paul's Cathedral. However, when we arrived
at the Tower, we found Justice was an even
earlier riser. A royal commission had been
set up on the green before the great Norman
keep and already the executions were taking
place. A long pole had been slung on two
uprights which had been driven deep into the
ground. From this six of Lord Charon's men
were already dangling, whilst others were
being tried in front of three Justices brought
up especially from Westminster. I tell you
this, in Henry's time, justice was short and
brutal. "Give him a fair trial and hang
him!" was one of the old bastard's favourite
aphorisms and he wasn't joking. There were
no hand-wringing pleas for mercy. Henry was
as swift and as merciless as a hawk swooping
for the kill. On this occasion the process was
no different: the trial consisted of little more
than a barrage of questions to which the
felons, all bloody-mouthed and black-eyed,
mumbled some response. The Chief Justice
then passed judgement, a black silk cap was
placed on his head and the felons despatched
to the gallows. The poor unfortunates were
made to stand on a table whilst nooses were
put round their necks, and then the table was

kicked away and they were left to dangle.

On one side of the Justices, Lord Egremont, in a throne chair, watched with interest. Behind him stood the cowled and hooded Noctales. Egremont seemed to be enjoying himself but I glimpsed the distaste on Cornelius's face. Kempe was busy: he was the chief prosecution witness. He simply described the attack on Lord Charon's stronghold, the treasures they had found and, above all, 'the abduction of the King's most loyal servant Roger Shallot'. Can you believe that? Men being hanged because of old Roger!

"In the Empire," Egremont spoke up, "they'd be boiled like chickens in a cauldron or burnt at the stake." He looked over his shoulder at Cornelius. "But it's good to see a felon dance on air, is it not?"

The Noctale crossed himself and glanced away.

Do you know, my heart warmed to that hard-faced, enigmatic man. In a way he reminded me of Cecil and others I had worked with: ruthless but not bloodthirsty men. If someone had to die then let it be done quickly. No relish, no licking of the lips!

"There are some missing?" Benjamin replied.

"Yes, there are," Kempe replied. He came across whilst the Justices waited for more of Charon's gang to be dragged out before them. "The King is insisting that these all be dead by dusk. Some have been tortured. They know nothing about the Orb but they have admitted that Lord Charon's lieutenant is William Doddshall."

"Doddshall?" I queried.

"More commonly known as Cerberus," Kempe explained. He went to stand behind the Justices. "Oh," he called over his shoulder, "Cerberus is on the rack." He pointed across to the dungeon at the base of the Norman keep. "He said he'll talk to no one but you, Shallot. You'd best see what the bastard wants before he dies."

"And we have a meeting with you, Sir Thomas," Benjamin called out.

Kempe glanced quickly at Egremont and then nodded.

Benjamin and I left the execution ground and walked over to the Keep. I would like to say it was pleasant to be back in the Tower but I've always hated the place. Benjamin and I had been there only a few months previously, seeking out the mysterious assassin who had created such bloody havoc amongst the Guild of Hangmen.

I wanted to flee. Nevertheless, I was

intrigued that Cerberus wished to talk to me. We went down the steps and into a maze of corridors. A sentry took us into the torture room.

Now this was a strange place, or at least it was when I visited. It looked more like a hospital with its white-washed walls. The floor was clean and swept and flowers, arranged in baskets, stood on small shelves beneath the open windows. A child's toy hung on a string from a hook on the wall. The chief interrogator was a kindly, soft-spoken man with watery eyes and slack lips. He came and shook our hands, waved us in, pointing across to a table where there was wine and sweetmeats. Perhaps it was all the more dreadful because of that. Nevertheless, nothing could detract from the terror of Exeter's Daughter: a huge rack in the centre of the room like a large four-poster bed with rollers at the top and bottom. (It was called Exeter's Daughter because a Duke of Exeter had introduced the rack into England in the fifteenth century. Oh, for you students of History, the English were racking and renting long before then, but this rack was regarded as a work of art. It pulled your arms and legs out slowly. It gave the torturers a chance to relax, take some refreshment before turning the wheels again.

247

I'm not being brutish. You read my journals yet to come. I've been on that bloody rack! My arms became half an inch longer than they should be, before that bastard, John Dudley Duke of Northumberland, changed his mind and had me pardoned.)

On that particular morning poor old Cerberus was Exeter's guest. He was stripped naked except for a loin cloth, his hands and feet lashed to the rollers, the poor man's body pulled as tight as a bishop's garter. He was unconscious when we came in, his ugly, ruddy face slack. The torturer tossed a bucket of water over him and held a piece of burnt cork beneath his nose. Cerberus began to shake and moan.

"No, no," the master torturer whispered. "Master Doddshall, you have a visitor; the man you asked to see, Roger Shallot."

Cerberus turned his eyes. He tried to speak but his tongue was too large.

"For pity's sake," I ordered. "Slacken his legs and arms."

"Anything to oblige," the master torturer squeaked.

"And a cup of wine?" I asked.

The wheel was pulled back. Cerberus relaxed. I went up and forced the wine between his lips.

"You wanted to speak to me?" I asked.

"Damn you, Shallot!" he whispered, the blood bubbling on his lips.

"If you've brought me here to curse," I replied. "I won't stay long."

"No, no," Cerberus shook his head. "But I'll speak alone."

"I don't want to leave," the master torturer spoke up. "This is my chamber and my responsibility."

"Leave!" Benjamin ordered.

"But . . . ?" the fellow stuttered.

"On the Lord Cardinal's orders!" Benjamin insisted.

"Oh well, if you put it like that," the fellow replied. "I am only too pleased."

Everyone, the watching soldiers, the torturer's apprentices scrambled out of the room, and Benjamin followed, closing the door behind him.

I stood over Cerberus. "We are alone."

"I want to ask you a favour."

I stared back, surprised. "A favour, a boon?" I exclaimed. "You cheeky bastard! It's not so long ago you were trying to have a rat nest in my stomach!"

"It's all the luck of the dice," Cerberus replied. "But, for what it's worth, Shallot, Charon did like you. He wouldn't have allowed the rat to dig deep, just a bite or two."

"When you get to Hell," I said, "thank him for me."

"I don't want to hang," Cerberus replied.

"Neither do I but there's nothing I can do for you."

"I have a horror of hanging," Cerberus insisted. "Do this favour for me. Please!"

"And in return?"

"I'll tell you what I know. Oh, one thing more, Master Shallot, send my parents a letter."

I just stared in disbelief.

"Please!" Cerberus insisted, "To John and Christina Doddshall of the Silver Wyvern on the High Pavement in Nottingham. They think I am a clerk with a good benefice in a nobleman's household. Tell them I died of the plague or the sweating sickness, that I was honoured and loved. Oh, and one thing more."

I closed my eyes.

"Before I die, I want a priest to shrive me. Promise me that!"

What could I do? The poor bastard was going to die and, but for the love of God and the favour of my master Benjamin, I could have well ended up as a member of a gang like Charon's. I gave him my word.

"Now," I began. "The Orb of Charlemagne?"

"Lord Charon, may he rot in hell,"

Cerberus replied, "bought the Orb from the Schlachter."

"I have heard of that name before. Who is he?"

"No one knows," Cerberus replied. "He is one of London's most skilful assassins. If he accepts a task, he always carries it out himself: poison, the garrotte, the dagger, the sword."

"Was he responsible for the deaths at Malevel?"

Cerberus closed his eyes. I gently pushed up his head and forced more of the coarse wine into his mouth. Cerberus blew on his lips, coughing as the wine stung his throat.

"I heard what you said," he gasped. "It's possible but, how he could do it by himself is a mystery."

"How did the Schlachter tell Charon he had the Orb?"

"He sent us a message," Cerberus replied. "Told us to meet him in a copse to the north of the hospital of St Mary of Bethlehem. Only Charon and myself were to go. He named his price: two thousand pounds in gold. Charon and I were to come just after dark as the hospital bell rang for Compline. There was to be no trickery or he'd take our lives as well as the money." Cerberus closed his eyes.

I thought he had lost consciousness but then he stirred and looked up at me.

"This was about two or three nights ago. Charon was curious about the deaths at Malevel. After all, that was our handiwork, the murder of the old lady, the stripping of the manor. Anyway, he brought the gold in barrels on a sumpter pony. We stood at the edge of the copse and, when the Compline bell sounded we entered the trees. On a log lying in the centre of the clearing was a small wine tun. We went across and took the lid off: the Orb was inside. We took it, left the gold and rode back into London."

"And you never saw the Schlachter?"

Cerberus gasped and shook his head.

"No one ever does. Lord Charon had hired him before." He grinned. "Certain rivals who had to disappear when Charon could prove he was elsewhere."

"How would you hire him?" I asked. "There must be a way?"

"Isn't it strange?" Cerberus gasped. "Very few people claim to know the Schlachter yet it's remarkable how many people use his services. If you want to hire an assassin in London," he continued, "you make it known in ale-houses or amongst the market sellers in St Paul's churchyard. However, for the Schlachter, go to Scribes' Corner, a small alcove just within the door of St Paul's. Seek out a clerk called Richard Notley. He's a lean-faced knave. Tell him you wish to hire a slaughterer and say where you reside. The Schlachter will make himself known."

"And the Orb?" I asked.

"Lord Charon sold it to the Papal Envoys. It was over and done with in a matter of hours. Charon thought it was most amusing."

"Did he know it was a replica?" I asked.

"Neither he nor I gave a pig's turd!" Cerberus scoffed. "The Italians paid good silver and gold. Charon was content." He licked his chapped lips. "That's all I know, Shallot," he gasped. "As God is my witness. Now, be a gentle boy, pour the rest of that wine between my lips and, if you don't keep your word, damn you to hell!"

I fed him the wine and left. I took Benjamin aside and briefly described what Cerberus had told me. Benjamin immediately ordered a friar to be sent for and told the torturers to desist from any further questioning.

We went out and sat on a bench at the top of the steps whilst, across the green, the remaining members of Charon's gang were summarily despatched. A ghoulsome sight: four gallows, their long poles forming a square. I saw what Henry's troops did when they crushed the Northern rebellion under Robert Aske. There were corpses hanging on every gibbet and on every tree along the Great North Road. But, on Tower Green, with the sun growing strong and birds whirling against the blue sky, it was macabre to see this square of hanged men. Most hung silent, only a few still twitched and jerked in their death throes. At last Cerberus was dragged out: he was carried across on a door and laid before the judges. They asked him how he was to plead. He told them to go to Hell so they sentenced him to hang but Benjamin intervened.

"Master Cerberus," he began. "Master Cerberus was most cooperative in telling us about these outlaws' depredations. He is not to hang. His head is to be severed from his body."

Isn't life strange? Cerberus cackled with laughter when he heard this and began to bless my name as if I had given him a king's pardon. Kempe and the judges objected but Benjamin was obdurate.

"He is not to hang!"

A squabble would have broken out but Egremont got to his feet, clapping his gloved hands. He said something to one of his retainers. The man ran across and brought back a small log from a pile heaped at the far end of the green.

"If he is not to hang," Egremont declared, "justice will still be done."

He rapped out another order. Two of his liveried servants rolled Cerberus off the door and positioned him so his neck lay against the log. Egremont took off his cloak, drew his sword and positioned himself carefully. He brought the sword up and, in one clean sweep, took Cerberus's head sheer off at the neck.

Of course, I had walked away, hand to my mouth. I don't like the sight of blood, even if it's not my own. By the time I returned, archers from the garrison had placed Cerberus's body and severed head on the door and were taking them away to be buried in a lime pit in a desolate part of the Tower.

Egremont looked like a man who has done a good day's work. He accepted Kempe's offer of refreshment but first walked round the scaffold, carefully inspecting the corpses as if he was suspicious that one of them might still be alive. Eventually he conferred with Kempe, then Benjamin, Cornelius and myself followed them across the green and up into the great hall.

"A satisfactory morning's work," Kempe

announced as he sat at the top of the great table waving us to the benches on either side. "But the last man," he continued, "the one who didn't want to hang: what did he have to say to you? What did he confess?"

My master's boot tapped my leg.

"Nothing much," I replied.

"Come, come." Egremont beat his wine cup against the table.

"Did he mention the Orb?" Cornelius snapped.

"He said that the outlaws and wolfsheads had heard about the theft but nothing else."

Cornelius's eyes slid away. He knew that I was lying.

"Surely," my master intervened. "Surely, Lord Egremont, you, too, have made careful searches?"

"Oh yes, we have." Lord Egremont took his gloves off and played with the small, leather tassel on one of them. "Rumours spring as thick as weeds." His voice took on a harsh tone.

"Such as?" I asked.

Egremont didn't even look at me.

"Rumours that the Orb is in the hands of the French or the Papal Envoys. His Imperial Highness Charles V will not be pleased."

"My Lord Theodosius, your command of

the English tongue is admirable," Benjamin commented.

"I studied in the Halls of Cambridge," Egremont replied. "The quadrivium, the trivium, logic and metaphysics."

"And you, Master Cornelius?" I asked.

"For a while I lived in England," Cornelius retorted. "Many years ago I was apprenticed to a cloth merchant, a Hanse at the Steelyard."

"What has this got to do with the Orb of Charlemagne?" Egremont snapped.

"Nothing," Benjamin murmured.

"In which case — " Egremont got up and, smacking his gloves against his thigh, he bowed to Sir Thomas and Benjamin and strode from the room.

Cornelius followed as silently as a shadow. Kempe watched them go.

"Are you skilled in tongues?" Benjamin asked him.

Sir Thomas narrowed his eyes. "In French, Italian," he replied.

"And German?" Benjamin asked.

"Yes."

"And you have worked in the Empire?"

Sir Thomas became uneasy. He opened his mouth to reply and looked longingly at the door, as if he wished to be gone.

"These matters are not your business," he

snapped. "But to answer you bluntly, yes, I have been a royal envoy to Lubeck and yes, Master Daunbey, before you ask, I have met Lord Egremont and Cornelius on a number of occasions. However, I believe I have got something to show you." And Kempe strode from the hall.

"Why these questions?" I asked.

"What," Benjamin whispered, "if this is all one plot, Roger? An alliance between Egremont and Kempe, with Cornelius party to it, to steal from both the Emperor and our King and so become rich on the profits?"

11

We sat and murmured about the possibilities. What proof did we have that this mysterious assassin, the Schlachter existed? Or, even if we did, that he was involved in the theft of the Orb? Our discussion was cut short by a soldier who came in and shouted that Sir Thomas was ready for us. He led us out of the hall and across to Wakefield Tower. Kempe was waiting for us in a chamber on the second storey. He locked the door behind us, opened a chest and, taking out the Orb, held it up. Benjamin almost snatched it from his hands. He ordered me to light a candle and then held the amethyst against the flame. I crouched down and peered as the jewels became brighter. I saw the cross but no figure of the Saviour hanging on it.

"It is a replica?" Benjamin asked.

"Oh yes," Kempe replied.

Benjamin weighed it in his hands.

"And fashioned by poor Berkeley?"

"Of course."

Benjamin handed it back. The chest was closed. We were about to leave when we heard hurried footsteps and a pounding on the door. Doctor Agrippa swept into the room. He took off his broad-brimmed hat and gave a mocking bow.

"I come direct from the court. What news?"

"You've seen for yourself," Kempe retorted. "The wolfsheads are hanged but the Orb of Charlemagne is still missing."

Agrippa shrugged. He pulled two small warrants out of his jerkin and handed them to Benjamin and myself. My letter was quite simple: it bore the King's personal signature and seal and informed me that the royal ship *Peppercorn* was due to leave the Thames in ten days time. It was sailing to explore and navigate the waters down the West Coast of Africa: both Benjamin and myself were appointed as officers. Oh, I could have wept! I could have sat upon the ground and howled. I hate water. I don't like the sea and I certainly didn't like the prospect of going on a sea voyage and never returning. Benjamin read his, folded it neatly and slipped it into his wallet.

"The King is angry?" he asked.

"It would be best," Agrippa replied, "if you do not show your faces at the court. Egremont is going to leave soon and, if he doesn't have the Orb, the King's wrath will fall on you."

With that warning ringing in our ears, Benjamin and I left the Tower and returned to the Flickering Lamp. I was all nervous and agitated, jumping like a grasshopper but Benjamin remained stony-faced. He took me into the taproom and sat me down. He ordered some victuals from Boscombe and began to list the possibilities.

"Look at me, Roger," he declared. "I do not want to go on my travels either."

"It's vindictive of the King," I retorted. "The bastard . . . !"

Benjamin brought his finger to his lips. "Hush now, that's the way of the world, Roger. The King has lost his treasure. Whatever subtle schemes he has been plotting, he has also been publicly humiliated. Someone will have to pay for that and what better victims than the Cardinal's beloved nephew and his rapscallion of a servant? Henry will no doubt plead that it's not his fault: he must show the Emperor that someone has been punished. Moreover, my uncle is no longer as high in the King's favour as he once was. By exiling us from England, Henry gently raps Dear Uncle's knuckles." He took a deep breath. "So, we can sit around and moan, or fathom this mystery and discover a satisfactory answer. Now, let's concentrate on what we know." He leaned closer over the table so no one could hear us. "First, Henry has the Orb of Charlemagne: the Emperor wants it. Secondly, the King orders Berkeley to make at least one replica."

"At least?" I queried.

"Oh yes. We were shown one this morning. We know another was in that chest at Malevel." Benjamin sighed. "And, unless we have it wrong, the French have a third."

"Is that possible?" I asked.

"So it would seem."

"But why?" I asked.

"If we knew that," Benjamin retorted, "we could solve this. However, let's continue. Thirdly, the Orb was taken to Malevel, where there are no secret passageways or entrances. No one entered or left that house except those two cooks. Yet we know that every man jack of the garrison was brutally slaughtered without the alarm being raised. Fourthly, we know an archer was communicating with Sir Thomas Kempe. We have to accept Kempe's word that nothing untoward was reported. What else?"

"Fifthly," I added, "we know Cornelius had the keys to the house, to let the cooks in and out. Perhaps he was engaged in some subtle stratagem but, there again, why should Cornelius, the most faithful Imperial servant, turn traitor?"

"Sixthly," Benjamin intervened, "we know that, if this Schlachter exists, he certainly sold the Orb stolen from Malevel to the Papal Envoys. Now that poses even more interesting questions. Who sold the Orb to the French? And where is the real Orb?"

Benjamin paused as Boscombe came back and pushed two bowls of meat on to the table.

"Somehow, master," I took out my horn spoon, "the solution lies at Malevel Manor. I have been wondering what led poor Castor to that cellar? It wasn't the remains of some poor, old woman. What did Castor smell? What was so attractive?"

Benjamin pointed at his dish of meat. "Food. Let us say," he continued, "the killers sheltered there. How did they escape unnoticed? Were they there with someone's permission?"

He sat for a while eating, lost in his own thoughts.

"We always come back to food," he remarked. "Why had the table been cleared away, the kitchen and the blackjacks washed? Food!" he repeated. "Perhaps it's time we visited those cooks: perhaps they did see something? Tomorrow at first light we'll go there. In the meantime, search out this scrivener at St Paul's. Give him your full name, tell him we're staying at the Flickering Lamp, and say you want to hire the services of a slaughterer."

Of course I protested but Benjamin was insistent. So, after a quiet sleep on my bed, I braved the afternoon crowds and made my way up into St Paul's Cathedral. It brought back memories of being hired by Sir Hubert Berkeley. I lit a taper in his memory. As I did so, a serving wench caught my eye: her black curly hair framed the sweetest, prettiest face. She reminded me of Lucy and so I fell to talking. Well, you know how it goes, one things leads to another. We shared a loving cup in a nearby tavern, followed by a most energetic two hours on the bed in a small chamber above.

It was dusk before I returned to the Cathedral but the scriveners' corner was still busy. I espied Master Richard Notley, a cadaver-faced, wispy-haired man. He sat, legs crossed under the table, lips pursed, pen ready to dictate any messages. I remembered my promise to Cerberus so I sat down and dictated a letter to his parents in Nottingham. Notley acted the professional scribe. He faithfully wrote down my farrago of lies, about how young William had lived, then died, in something akin to the odour of sanctity. Now and again Notley's pen faltered and I wondered if he knew the truth. When he had finished I signed it, paid him a fee, plus an extra coin so that a reputable carrier would take it to Nottingham.

"Is there anything else, sir?" His close-set eyes studied me curiously.

"My name is Roger Shallot," I replied. "I can be found at the Flickering Lamp tavern."

"Yes," he interrupted quickly. "I know where it is."

"I am a farmer," I continued. "I am looking for a slaughterer: certain beasts have to be killed before Michaelmas. I want someone skilled, not a butcher's lad."

"That will be one silver piece, sir, just for my searches."

I paid the coin over.

"And when will I meet him?" I asked.

"Oh, don't worry, sir. You will be informed as soon as possible. Now — " He pushed back the table and pointed to the hour candle burning in its small glass holder. "My day's work is done."

I thanked him and left. Once outside the cathedral, I remembered poor Berkeley so I went along the lanes and alleyways to his house. His steward let me in. The man's face was tear-streaked, the household still in mourning. All the walls were covered in mourning cloths and the rooms were shuttered; it was no longer the convivial, merry household I had joined.

"You see, Master Shallot, Sir Hubert had no heirs," the steward explained. "His Will has still to go through Chancery. All work has stopped."

I expressed my condolences and accepted his offer of white wine and some marzipan wafers.

"It's about his work I've come. Are Sir Hubert's accounts here?"

"Oh no, sir. Sir Thomas Kempe came and took them all away."

"What was Sir Hubert working on?" I asked. "I mean, what different artefacts?"

"None of us know," the fellow replied. "For the last year Sir Hubert was hired by the court. He worked by himself without any of his apprentices. God knows what he was doing!"

"Did Sir Thomas Kempe come here often?"

"Yes, he did, sometimes carrying clinking saddlebags. We suspected they contained gold to be melted down. Only once," the steward continued, "did I catch a glimpse of Sir Hubert at work. I was in a chamber upstairs. I looked down into the garden, and saw that Sir Hubert had taken a lantern out: he was holding something precious up against the light. I caught a glint . . . " he faltered.

"A jewel?" I asked.

"Yes, probably a jewel, some precious stone."

I finished my wine, once again expressed my condolences and left.

Darkness had fallen. A watchman stumped along the lane.

"Nine o'clock! he bawled. "And the night is fine! Pray to God for grace divine!"

The villains who stood in the doorways of the inns and taverns slunk away at his approach, though these did not bother me. Old Shallot can easily act the ruffler, cloak thrown back, sword and dagger hanging from my belt, chest out like a cock of the walk. Thank God we cannot judge a book by its cover. I was strutting along, thinking about what I had learnt, when two shadows came out of an alleyway, cloaked and hooded. My hand was seized before I could grab my dagger and I was dragged into the doorway of a tumbled-down house. I was getting ready to plead for mercy, to offer my assailants anything I carried, when one of the figures pulled back his hood. Cornelius's heavy-lidded eyes studied me.

"Going for an evening stroll, Master Shallot?"

"Yes, yes," I snarled. "Taking the night air."

"A busy, busy man," Cornelius retorted. "Writing letters for poor old William Doddshall; asking for a slaughterer to kill some beast; then down to the late lamented Sir Hubert Berkeley's house. To find out what?"

Oh, I could have kicked myself. However, you must remember those were my green days. I had not yet learnt to crawl about the streets and so give the slip to any pursuer. Cornelius, his companion standing behind me, grasped my jerkin and pulled me closer.

"Every step you take, Master Shallot, I am there. When you meet the Slaughterer, you will thank God. In Germany we have a proverb: 'He who plans to sell the bearskin, even before he goes hunting, often ends up as the bear's dinner'."

"And we have a proverb in England," I retorted. "'A stitch in time saves nine.'"

He looked at me curiously. "And what does that mean?"

To be quite honest I didn't know either,

but it sounded clever! I pulled myself away and strolled off down the alleyway. (Always remember that: if you are ever in doubt, say something enigmatic and walk away. People will think you are wise and cunning. It's a device used by the playwrights. I have never understood certain lines in Marlowe's *Edward II*. I was going to invite him to supper to ask him what they meant but then poor Kit was killed in a lodging house on the Isle of Dogs, stabbed in the eye by that bastard Poley!)

I reached the Flickering Lamp and found Benjamin in his chamber, lying on his bed looking up at the ceiling. I told him all I had done, including my visit to Berkeley.

"Why did you come here in the first place?" he asked abruptly. "I mean, to the Flickering Lamp?"

I told him about the relic-seller I had met whilst he was on his travels in Italy. Benjamin just nodded.

"Why?" I asked.

"And Boscombe gave you licence to sell relics?"

"Yes," I replied. "But the Lord Charon had other ideas. I was too successful."

We heard laughter from the taproom below so we went down for our supper: lamb cutlets in rosemary sauce, followed by quince tarts. It was a merry evening: Boscombe was dressed up as a bawdy man and he had brought others in for some entertainment. These were the most fantastical-looking creatures: men and women who were known as 'Bawdy Folk'. They were dressed in the skins of animals, mostly otter and fox, whilst some of them wore masks of bears and wolves on their heads. They didn't wear hose but instead had leather aprons across the groin. The men were otherwise naked, crotch to neck. The women had soft woollen bands to cover their generous breasts. They all wore bangles on their ankles and wrists. Large earrings hung from their ear lobes whilst they had painted their faces grotesque colours.

They began with a shuffling dance and followed this with acrobatics, somersaults, and an act of swallowing knives and spoons. They then performed a most scurrilous play about a vicar, a bishop, an inn-keeper and two whores. I will not offend your susceptibilities. It was absolutely disgusting but very, very funny. Boscombe joined in, ever the actor, and the jokes and jests became sharper and more pointed. Benjamin murmured that he had seen enough and went off to bed. I, however, joined in with glee, drinking and dancing until I lost all memory of what followed. I woke up in an outhouse dressed in a bearskin with one of the bawdy women lying by my side. I went out and washed, pouring buckets of water from the small well in the courtyard. I dried myself off, collected my belongings and went upstairs for a few hours' proper sleep: it was good preparation for a day of horrors and bloody murder.

It started well enough. Benjamin kicked me awake. We broke our fast and then made our way along Cripplegate to Oswald's and Imelda's cookshop. It was a bright, clear autumn morning as we passed the traders and merchants preparing for a day's haggling. When we reached the cookshop I rapped on the door but there was no answer.

"Strange," Benjamin murmured. "They should be up, baking fresh pies."

We went down the narrow runnel which ran alongside the house, through a small wicket gate into a narrow garden. The door to the scullery was open and we went in. The first corpse was lying there. In life she had been an old, plump, cherry-faced woman. In death, ashen-checked, she lay face down in the pool of blood that had gushed from her slashed neck. In the kitchen a young apprentice lay, flung like a rag doll in the corner, the wound to his neck looking like a gaping mouth. Oswald was in the shop, lying slumped in a chair; his wife was in her chamber on the second floor. Both had been killed silently, quickly, with a jagged cut running from ear to ear. A ghastly sight! Nothing else had been disturbed. The sweet smell of baking mixed with that of blood and gore.

Benjamin felt the ovens.

"They were killed either very late last night or early this morning," he declared. "No baking has been done for the day and their cadavers are cold." He chewed the corner of his lip. "As at Malevel, there is no sign of any resistance or disturbance. It's as if they knew their killer; who waited until they were separated and then struck."

Benjamin walked across and looked down at the tray of pies which had been left unsold from the previous day. He picked one up and looked at it curiously.

"Murder again eh, Master Daunbey?"

Benjamin dropped the pie. I spun round. Cornelius and two of the Noctales stood in the doorway.

"Don't you ever sleep?" I snarled.

"No one sleeps, Master Shallot," Cornelius crouched down and studied the apprentice's face, "when a mad wolf is on the prowl!"

"Why are you here?" I asked.

"I told you last night: we follow you. I have answered your question." He got to his feet, wiping his hands on his robe. "Why are you here?"

"Because nobody went into Malevel Manor except these cooks," Benjamin replied. "They must have seen something."

"Master Daunbey, I don't treat you as a fool," Cornelius sneered. "I'd be grateful if you would return the compliment." Cornelius walked over and sat in a small rocking chair near the hearth, pushing himself gently backwards and forwards. "We noticed," he continued, "the arrows missing from the quiver. Jonathan told me about that. But I can see nothing wrong in Sir Thomas Kempe being informed on what was happening in the manor." He smiled bleakly. "After all, Jonathan did the same for me."

"Did he?" Benjamin asked.

Cornelius narrowed his eyes.

"Did he?" Benjamin persisted. "You take orders from the Lord Egremont; did Jonathan do so too?"

Cornelius just waved his hand. "True, true. However, we also noticed, Master Daunbey, how clean the kitchen and scullery were. Now I don't know about English archers, but it certainly made me wonder why a group of soldiers would spend their evening cleaning the table and washing the blackjacks. Why not just pile them in a heap for someone else to wash? After all, that is why those two cooks were hired. So, I ask you again, why are you here?"

He turned and said something in German to his companions, who left.

"What are you looking for?" Benjamin asked. "I understood something of what you said."

"The same as you, my dear Benjamin: Master Oswald's finished accounts." He waved a hand. "Not the scrap of paper he gave you but the finished bill that might contain some interesting information."

"Such as what?" Benjamin asked.

Cornelius wagged a finger at him. "I don't know and neither do you, yet there may be something, evidence you might not recognise until you see it." He sighed and let his hand drop. "Oh, perhaps you're right, the cooks did notice something untoward? Something which they later remembered." He breathed out noisily. "Though God knows what?"

One of the Noctales came in and whispered into his master's ear.

"Now, isn't that strange?" Cornelius looked up. "There are no accounts and the strong box containing all these poor people's savings has been broken into and rifled. So, it will be dismissed as the work of some housebreaker. One of your London nightbirds who came in quietly through the scullery, slashed their throats and then stole both the money and the accounts." Cornelius got to his feet. "However, we know differently, don't we? Our assassin worked quickly and expertly. Whoever he was, he was known and respected by these people. They allowed him into their house. Mistress Imelda went to her chamber, perhaps to change her working clothes or put paint on her face."

"Yes, it must have been something like that," Benjamin replied.

"Then the assassin struck, starting with the old woman in the scullery, then the apprentice boy. It would have been quick. A hand over their mouths, a quick slash to their throats. Oswald and Imelda came next. My question is, who did it and why?"

Cornelius slipped his hands up the sleeves of his gown. He reminded me of some monk at his prayers. His brain must have been teeming. He knew we were lying and holding back information on what had happened at Malevel. He tapped his foot against the paved kitchen floor.

"Who has the authority," he said, "to walk into a house like this?" He glanced sideways at me. "You were friendly with Imelda and Oswald."

"I am Roger's friend," Benjamin replied,

"but that doesn't mean that I would want to cut his throat."

"True," Cornelius replied. "But there are others such as Doctor Agrippa or even Sir Thomas Kempe . . . ."

"That's true," I intervened. "And there's also Master Cornelius and Lord Egremont. After all, these poor cooks were hired by you to undertake this lucrative work: you would have been even more welcome here."

"I know," Cornelius snapped, "where Lord Egremont was last night." He rubbed his face, stared at me then snapped his fingers and, the Noctales following, left the house as quietly as he had arrived.

My master and I went out into the street and along an alleyway to a small open space like a village green: there was a duck pond in the centre with battered wooden benches around it. We sat on one of these and watched children play on a hobby horse and chase an inflated pig's bladder.

"I think we'd best go back to Malevel," Benjamin said.

"You have a theory, master?"

He scratched the tip of his nose. "The beginnings of one, Roger, but they're still shadows in my mind."

"And the murders in the cookshop?" I asked.

"I don't know. True, there could be something of interest in the accounts but don't forget, Roger, we have a rough copy of these. Perhaps those cooks knew something else and had to be silenced before they remembered it and began to talk."

"The work of the Slaughterer?" I asked.

"Possibly, but how could even a professional assassin enter a house with four people in it and slay them all without meeting any resistance?" He got to his feet, fingers drumming the hilt of his sword.

"You are apprehensive, master?"

"No, Roger, I am frightened. If we leave on that ship, then it's the end for both of us. I don't think we're intended to come back. In ancient Israel the Jews used a scapegoat, an animal they burdened with their sins, to cast out into the desert to die. We are the King's scapegoats: that sea voyage will be our death."

"This theory of yours?" I asked.

"It's based on the King," Benjamin replied. "I know your true opinion of him, Roger, and I agree with it. Henry of England would never give anything away. Oh, Henry wanted Imperial ships but he also wanted to make a fool of Europe's princes and collect as much silver and gold as he could. Such a ploy would please Henry: he could retreat into his private chamber with Norreys and the others to laugh and sneer until his sides were fit to burst. But come on, Roger, let's return. I am sure the Slaughterer will soon make his presence felt."

"Do you think he will, master?"

"Oh yes. But not to help us. I believe we are about to enter the lion's den."

"And Master Cornelius?" I asked.

"Oh, one of his men is watching us from a corner of a nearby alleyway." Benjamin slipped his dagger in and out of the sheath. "I do wonder about him," he murmured. "Could he be the Slaughterer, the assassin? All he has to do is wait until his master gets bored and returns to the Imperial court."

"Aye," I added, "and leave us poor bastards to the mercy of our King!"

12

We returned to the Flickering Lamp not in the best of humours. Benjamin sent a constable to the Guildhall about the murders at the cookshop. He then became lost in his own thoughts, sitting at the table in his chamber talking to himself, writing out comments in that strange cipher he always used. I hung around the taproom looking for any villainy which might emerge. Yet, I'll be honest, I began to wonder if it was time Benjamin and I bolted like rabbits for France or Spain, well clear of Henry's wrath. I drank and ate a little too much. I became mournful about Castor and Lucy and decided to write a poem about both of them. Boscombe tried to rally my spirits, recalling my escapades the previous evening with the Bawdy folk. But I wasn't in the mood. Doctor Agrippa visited us. He was closeted with Benjamin and then left as mysteriously as he had arrived. Towards dusk I decided to take the air. I was in the alleyway outside the tavern when a beggar boy caught my finger. He was a thin-faced little waif, with eyes almost as large as his face under greasy, spiked hair.

"Come, come . . . " the poor, little bugger stuttered. "The man is waiting for . . . " He closed his eyes. "I have forgotten," he moaned, "the rest of the message . . . "

"Message?" I asked.

"Yes," he replied. "But come . . . "

Like the fool I was, I followed him up the street. The little boy led me through a side door of the Church of the Crutched Friars. It was deserted, and the sound of my boots rang hollow through the nave. Someone had lit candles before the statue of the Virgin. I remembered Lord Charon and my spine began to tingle so I stopped the boy and crouched down.

"Who sent you?" I asked.

"Come," the child repeated. "Your friend is waiting."

He led me across, out through the corpse door at the other side of the church and into the overgrown cemetery towards the charnel house. This was the Ossuary or, if you aren't too well educated, the Bone House. When the graveyard becomes too full, bodies are dug up and the bones simply slung into this long, open shed. The boy took me to a gravestone near the Ossuary and told me to sit down. I did so and drew my dagger, which I gripped beneath my cloak. When I looked round, the boy had gone. Now there's something about old Shallot: on the one hand I am the most cowardly of cowards but, on the other, I hate to show it. I didn't want to go running back to the tavern with my knees knocking so instead I sat and quivered like a jelly. My imagination was stirred by the shrieks of some bloody owl until my nerve broke. I turned and screamed into the darkness for the bird to piss off. Only then did I see it. Across the graveyard was a huge plinth, some tomb built by a London merchant who wanted to be remembered but who was probably forgotten before his corpse grew cold in his grave. The huge, rectangular stone slab was covered in moss and lichen. Now, candles arranged along it glowed eerily through the darkness.

"Who's there?" I called. I stood up and walked slowly across. "Who's there?" I repeated.

I drew closer. I stopped and blinked, believing my mind or eyes were playing tricks on me. In the candlelight a face, framed by long, straggly hair, peered at me, two hands on either side of the tomb, as if someone was hiding behind it and peering above it. I realised what I was looking at. Someone had severed the head of the scrivener I had met in St Paul's Cathedral. Both the head and hands of Richard Notley had been cut from his body and placed on the tomb, garishly illuminated by the lighted candles like some macabre child's game on Samain Eve. Oh horrors! Oh bloody murder! For a while I stood rooted to the spot. I could do nothing but stare at that ghastly head, the half-open eyes and blood-encrusted lips, with the hands on either side. I gave a scream which must have frightened even that bloody owl before I fled like a greyhound across the graveyard. I tripped on a grave and fell flat on my face. I got up. For a while I was lost. I screamed for the boy or to find the door to the church. In the darkness around me, someone gave a low and chilling laugh. I turned round, screaming abuse as I walked backwards. My elbow caught something. I darted around and, with a sob of satisfaction, threw myself into the church, slamming the door behind me. I ran towards the other side door but then the candles in front of the Lady statue were abruptly extinguished. I reached the door; it was locked, the bolts pushed fast across.

Oh Lord, then the whistling began. A most chilling though mundane sound, like a labourer going about his work: a man immersed in his task and happy to do it. The whistling drew nearer. Sobbing and crying, I fled back through the darkness towards the corpse door. A crossbow quarrel zipped by my head, smacking into the wall of the church. I stumbled over a bench, bruising my shins and legs. The whistling began again. I heard another click and a crossbow quarrel cut the air above me.

Imagine poor Shallot! Weep for old Roger! For his legs shaking like leaves in a storm; for his belly rolling like a drum; for the tears which scalded his eyes; for the sheer, bone-wrenching terror which sent me crashing around that church like a pea in a barrel. And, all the time, came that dreadful whistling. I flitted around in the dark like a bat, the assassin following me. Oh, that's what I hate about killers — although, at the same time, it has been my salvation on many occasion — assassins enjoy their work. They like to see their victims suffer and recognise their power, accept they are going to die. It's true, isn't it? Those murders that take place in a family, the product of strong drink or hot blood, are quick and sudden like a brawl in a tavern over a dice or a wench. However, the born killer, the man who lives on human blood, wants his victim to know that death is about to stretch out its cold, hard hand! All I can say is, thank God! For, if they play such a game, it at least gives you a chance for the good Lord or his Holy Father, or some angel of light to intervene. On that night they did. As I hid behind the high altar there was sudden pounding on the corpse door. Angry voices were raised. I crouched, promising the good Lord everything he wanted: a life of fasting, of chastity, of bread and water. I heard the bolts of the side door being drawn. The assassin, fearful of being trapped himself, slipped out into the night. I ran across to the corpse door and drew back the bolts: outside, holding a sconce torch, were two venerable, but very aggrieved, friars.

"What's going on here?" one of them shouted. "This is a house of God, not some tavern! Why are the doors locked? Compline bell hasn't sounded!"

"I was trapped," I replied.

"Trapped? Who trapped you?"

I was too terrified to explain. I emptied the contents of my purse into their hands, stumbled back through the church, out into the lane and back up to the Flickering Lamp. I ignored Boscombe's curious gaze but pounded on my master's door. He threw it open and I almost collapsed into his arms. After two cups of claret and a meat pie, I felt better and told my master what had happened. He was too kind to upbraid me for my foolishness in going alone but listened very carefully.

"The Slaughterer has struck." He pulled the shutters across the window and drew the bar down. "The Slaughterer is sending us a message."

"But why kill Notley?"

"Oh, the scrivener was punished. People like ourselves, Roger, should know nothing about the Slaughterer or how to hire him. He obviously suspected that we might return with some soldiers, and that Master Notley might have been asked to visit the Tower and forced to confess all he did now about this terrible assassin. So Notley had to die and the Slaughterer used his corpse to send us a grisly message. Now, Roger — " Benjamin pulled his stool closer. "I have been studying everything that has happened since my arrival in London. You have told me a little about your own adventures. However, this time I want you to go back to the beginning. Tell me everything with whatever detail you can recall. Take your time."

I lay back on the bed and told my master all I could remember from the moment he left our manor to his fortuitous arrival at Newgate prison. Now and again Benjamin would stop and question me about some point and then I'd continue. Sometimes he'd ask me to stop whilst he wrote something down on a piece of parchment. I must have spoken for at least an hour.

"Why is all this so important?" I concluded.

"Pies," Benjamin enigmatically replied. "It's all about pies." He wouldn't say any more. I became cross but Benjamin had already returned to his papers, muttering under his breath. Now, full of wine and safe from the terrors, I drifted into sleep and spent the next day in bed, grieving over Lucy and wondering what revenge I could inflict on the Poppletons. Now and again my little brain (Excuse me a while — I see my chaplain sniggering. A sharp rap across his knuckles brings him back into order so I can return to the turmoil of my youth) would come up with some brilliant scheme of vengeance, before returning to our present troubles.

Now, the more I thought of Malevel the more convinced I became that, if Castor could have talked, we would have now known why the cellar was so important. Benjamin kept well away from me all day, being more busy in the taproom. Late that evening he shook me awake from my slumbers.

"Get up, Roger! Up now! Arm yourself!"

His face was grim. I noticed he had his leather wrist guards on and his war-belt strapped around his waist, sword and dagger hung in the Italian style. He had his guarded look, the same expression that had threatened violent retribution if I approached the marvellous Miranda.

"Where are we going?" I asked, pulling my boots on.

"We are going for supper," Benjamin replied.

I glanced at the hour candle burning in its glass on a shelf.

"Boscombe will not be pleased. The ovens will be out . . . "

"I don't give a fig what Boscombe thinks!" Benjamin retorted. "It will happen on the turn of a card." He smiled wryly. "Or, in this case, a knock on the door."

We went down to the taproom. Boscombe grumbled but brought across two tankards of ale and a platter of cold meat, onions and apples neatly sliced. The pot boys and scullions had long left. The taproom was empty. Boscombe busied himself about, humming under his breath. A watchman stopped in the lane outside.

"It's eleven o'clock and all is well! Pray for your souls that they stay out of Hell!"

Benjamin stopped, a piece of food halfway to his mouth.

There was a loud rapping on the door.

"Answer that, Shallot," Boscombe called.

"Master Boscombe, we are eating," Benjamin replied.

Cursing and muttering under his breath, the taverner went to the door and pulled it open. I heard someone say something and Boscombe's exclamation.

"What? Impossible! I . . . !" His voice took on a nervous stammer. "I don't know what you're talking about!"

I pricked up my ears because I am sure I caught mention of the names Berkeley and Notley. The change in Benjamin was startling. He stood up and drew his sword. I watched, open-mouthed, as Boscombe closed the door: drawing the bolts across, he turned slowly. He saw my master's drawn sword and smiled.

"Oh, Master Benjamin, what's the matter?"

"You know full well," my master replied. "The constable just knocked on the door and told you a strange story: how he met two men outside the church of Crutched Friars who gave their names as Berkeley and Notley, and said they had an appointment with you to discuss certain matters."

Boscombe took a step forward, his genial smile faded, his eyes watchful. I noticed he was standing differently now, on the balls of his feet, like a man ready to run or leap.

"And I heard your reply," my master said

softly. "You used the word 'impossible'. You were caught on the hop, were you not, Master Boscombe? Why is it impossible to meet two men who, in theory, you shouldn't know at all? Both men are dead. Notley's corpse hasn't even been discovered. Roger knows because he has seen his severed head. You know because you killed him. You are Jakob von Archetel, nicknamed the Schlachter."

Boscombe drew a bit closer.

"Earlier this evening," my master continued, "I took the constable into my confidence. I asked him to deliver that message tonight, just after the watchman had proclaimed the eleventh hour."

"My name is Andrew Boscombe," the taverner replied. "I hail from the West Country."

"The real Andrew Boscombe probably did," Benjamin replied. "But you are no more English than poor old Castor. I've listened to your tongue quite carefully. Now and again I can catch the rolling 'R', the guttural 'G'. You are a Hainaulter — probably from around the town of Dordrecht. Once you were not only a subject of the Emperor Charles V but a high-ranking official, engaged in his secret business as a Noctale. About fifteen years ago you fled to England. You

289

are a consummate actor, a born mimic. You probably did live in the West country for a while but, later, used your wealth to travel to London and buy this tavern. To all intents and purposes, Andrew Boscombe, the honest, jovial taverner, the man who loves a jest, play-acting and mummery. But, when the candles are extinguished, when the darkness comes, you are the Slaughterer, London's most skilful and subtle assassin. You are responsible for the deaths of many: Notley, Berkeley, those two poor cooks Oswald and Imelda. Above all, sir, you are responsible for those deaths at Malevel though how you did it and who you worked with is still a mystery."

Boscombe moved to a stool.

"Master Daunbey, you have me wrong. This is preposterous. I am what I claim to be. A taverner, your servant's close friend. Tell him, Roger."

I stared at him narrow-eyed. Benjamin's allegations seemed fantastic yet I recalled my master's close interrogation of what had happened since I had arrived in London: Boscombe's initial refusal to lodge me and then his abrupt change of mind. The way Lord Charon had seized and interrogated me. Boscombe's ability to disguise himself and then . . .

(Ah, excuse me, my little clerk is murmuring about coincidences. So what? Ask yourself, is anything in life planned? It may have started with coincidence, oh yes, but once I was in Boscombe's power, he had worked to keep me there.)

My suspicions deepened as I remembered how Boscombe had claimed to have made a trip to the West Country whilst we had been at Malevel. My change of mood must have been obvious.

Boscombe's lips curled. "We have all night," he said soothingly, "to discuss these matters!"

Benjamin, his sword in hand, stepped back and sat down on the stool. "I could have had you arrested," he replied. "Taken to the Tower for interrogation. However, men like you don't break, do they, Boscombe? Something untoward would happen: you might even escape, and there again, my evidence is not as strong as I would like."

Boscombe pulled the stool closer, his eyes sliding to his warbelt hanging on a hook in the wall. I drew my own poignard.

"Let's hear your story." Boscombe waggled a finger. "And, if it's good, I'll put my hands behind my back and you can cart me off to Newgate."

"You are an assassin," Benjamin declared.

"A Hainaulter. My servant, Roger, came here to sell relics. Now, not all of life is planned and plotted; sometimes Fickle Fortune spins her wheel and kingdoms are won and lost on a single blow. If Prince Arthur hadn't caught a cold in the marshes of Wales, he would now be king and Henry would simply be a royal prince . . . "

"Or who would think," Boscombe sneered, "that a butcher's son would become Cardinal and First Minister of the Realm?"

"Ah, you catch my drift," Benjamin replied, ignoring the taunt at Dearest Uncle. "At first you saw Roger as a trickster, but when you discovered that Shallot worked for me and I for the Cardinal you gave him a comfortable berth here. You were intrigued. You couldn't accept he was working by himself, and thought there was some secret, subtle trickery. Nevertheless, he was dangerous to have about. You had ties with the Lord Charon, not close, but a sharing of information, so when you were laying your plans to seize the Orb, you asked Lord Charon a favour. Roger was seized, frightened and beaten and this provided you with a golden opportunity. You knew Sir Hubert Berkeley was involved in arranging for the Orb of Charlemagne to be handed over to the Imperial envoys. Accordingly,

Roger, down on his luck, was provided with new clothes and sent along to St Paul's; at the same time you let it be known to Sir Hubert that my manservant was looking for employment in London. Berkeley was working on a secret assignment for the King, and was persuaded Roger would be the best person to offer him protection. How did you arrange it, Boscombe? Send Berkeley a message, saying it came from me?" Benjamin glanced at me. "Remember, Roger, Berkeley seemed to know you'd be in St Paul's."

I nodded, my eyes never leaving Boscombe. The taverner just stared at Benjamin. Never once did he look at me: his cold, calculating gaze was for Benjamin and Benjamin alone. The hair on the nape of my neck curled, this man was intent on our murder. I could only sit and blink as I recalled Berkeley's words on hiring me. I also realised how Lord Charon had found me so quickly.

"Roger's imprisonment was an unforeseen occurrence," Benjamin continued. "However, he was released from Newgate and came back here. How could you leave such a tender friend in his adversity? You offered us both chambers, even taking in poor Castor; anything to keep us under close scrutiny." Benjamin paused, tapping the tip of his sword on the paving stones. "And then we come to the business at Malevel! God knows how it was done. Boscombe the taverner supposedly left for the West Country; but in reality you adopted your secret profession: the Schlachter, the Slaughterer! Somehow or other — " Benjamin jabbed a finger at him " — you were responsible for the deaths of those men. You stole the Orb and left."

"Oh come, Master Benjamin," Boscombe scoffed. "And how did I do that? Just walk up to the manor, knock on the front door and fifteen burly men offered their throats to be cut?"

"Who told you there were fifteen?" Benjamin asked.

Boscombe's sneer faded.

"As for how you did it . . . Well, Master Boscombe, when I came here two things struck me as odd. First, here's a taverner who is also a master of disguise. You revel in it. Secondly, I had seen you before: something about your features struck a chord in my memory. On the day that the massacre was discovered, when Kempe and others were milling about Malevel Manor, I am sure I glimpsed your face. To be sure, it was hidden by some disguise, but there was something familiar."

"Mistaken identity!" Boscombe sneered.

"Perhaps," Benjamin replied. "However,

we now come to another matter: Berkeley's murder. You lured the goldsmith out into that lonely copse north of the Tower. The Orb you had stolen from Malevel was a forgery: Henley the professional relic-seller had told you so when he met you in that tavern. He must have been surprised to see the Orb of Charlemagne given to him for scrutiny but his surprise turned to laughter when he realised it was a fake."

"Henley?" Boscombe retorted. "I don't know any Henley!"

"Oh, you not only knew him but killed him," Benjamin retorted. "And then, full of fury, you and your accomplice — and you do have an accomplice, don't you? — lured the hapless goldsmith to that lonely glade where you tortured him. Asking the same question, time and time again: where was the real Orb?"

"Very interesting." Boscombe got up and moved towards the wine vats. "Thirsty work, Master Daunbey, do you wish some wine? My good friend, Roger?"

We both refused. Benjamin now stood up, his sword out, but Boscombe coolly filled his goblet and returned to his stool. I noticed he moved it a few inches nearer the wall. He toasted us both silently but there was something in his eyes that convinced me my master was right. Boscombe was the Slaughterer and he was only biding his time.

"You eavesdropped," Benjamin continued, "on our conversations. When Roger expressed a desire to meet the Lord Charon you happily obliged. Now, the Lord of London's underworld should have been pleased that Roger was ready to offer him the Orb of Charlemagne but he wasn't. Why? Because he already had it. Roger was, therefore, an unnecessary nuisance and had to be despatched. He would have been, if it hadn't been for that dog. The rest you know: except that Cerberus, Charon's lieutenant, on the brink of death, gave Roger information on how to contact the Slaughterer." Benjamin paused, watching Boscombe sip his drink. "Only then did you become afraid. Perhaps the net was closing in? Notley was stupid, a possible threat, so you killed him and used his corpse to frighten Roger before you attacked him in the Church of the Crutched Friars. However, being disturbed, you fled and, once out into the darkened lane, became again Boscombe the genial taverner, the purveyor of wine and pies."

"The pies!" I exclaimed. "Of course, master, the pies!" I half rose from my stool. "You bought pies from Imelda and

Oswald — I have eaten them here myself — that's how you could get into their shop so easily."

"I noticed the same," Benjamin declared. "And after Oswald and Imelda were killed, I realised someone had entered their house who knew them well. Friendly, genial Boscombe coming round to place another order. However, once you were in the house you became the Slaughterer: a dagger thrust here and another there, and an entire family was wiped out. Then you stole their accounts. Why, Boscombe? Was there something which had to be left hidden? Or, in their conversation with you, had they let drop that they'd seen something wrong at Malevel Manor? I don't know how you killed those soldiers but, for some reason, you spent a great deal of time cleaning that kitchen, scrubbing down the traunchers, washing out the blackjacks. Why, Boscombe?" Benjamin advanced towards him. "More importantly, who did you work for? Who hired you? How did you get in and out of Malevel so easily?"

Boscombe shook his head and stared into his wine cup.

"Master Daunbey, this is a merry tale for a dark evening. Yet, it's nothing more than old wives muttering round the fire and gossiping.

Go through this tavern, search my private chamber, you'll find nothing untoward."

"Oh, I agree." Benjamin declared. "Much suspected, nothing proved. Indeed, it all rests on coincidence: if Roger had not met the relic-seller and then come here; if we had not hired chambers at the Flickering Lamp after our return from Malevel." He smiled thinly. "But God is good. Perhaps he grew tired of your bloody-handed ways and Roger is his vengeance."

"I'll say nothing!" Boscombe yelled.

"You could be taken to the Tower," I retorted. "Spread out on the rack like Cerberus was whilst royal messengers are sent to the West Country, to discover all they can about Andrew Boscombe."

The taverner stared at me round-eyed. "Is that so, Roger? Now tell me, what do you think I'll do? Saunter into the barge, sit in the Tower and tell all to Fat Henry's questioners? Oh yes." He clapped his hands together. "Have mercy on me for I am a traitor and an assassin. I stole the Orb of Charlemagne. I sold it to the Lord Charon." He paused and grinned. "I shouldn't have said that, should I? I'm not supposed to know that, dearie, dearie me!"

One second Boscombe was shaking his head, the next the wine cup went flying at

Benjamin's head. Boscombe sprang across the room, snatching his sword and dagger from his war-belt. He came back, moving sideways like a dancer.

"I'm not going to the Tower!" he hissed. "And you are never leaving this tavern! Both of you will die and I've got all night to dispose of your corpses."

He came skipping forward, sword and dagger whirling. My master, skilled at fencing, blocked his blows. Boscombe stood back. Again they closed. It was obvious that Boscombe was no taverner: the way he moved, slightly sideways trying to draw out my master's sword and expose his body for a killing thrust of the dagger, showed him to be a professional, a skilled swordsman. The deadly dance continued; the slap of boots against the stone floor; the screeching clash of steel; and the grunts and groans of both combatants. My master was at a disadvantage, he did not know the room like Boscombe did. Twice he nearly slipped. Each time Boscombe closed for the kill. I tried to intervene but Benjamin waved me away. Boscombe stood back grinning, chest heaving.

"Oh, you fops!" he breathed. "Ever the gentleman."

His sword and dagger went down as he

studied my master. Now Benjamin may have been a fop, a gentleman, but old Roger was not. As Boscombe shuffled forward, I did what I was good at. I threw my dagger with all my force and caught him low in the neck, the point rupturing soft flesh and nerve. The blood spouted out like wine from a broached cask. Boscombe dropped his sword, hands clawing at the hilt of my dagger, his face contorted in pain. He stepped back, turning as if he wished to flee to the door. He collapsed, his life blood pouring out through nose and mouth as well as the jagged wound in his throat. I went to turn him over but Benjamin grasped me.

"Let him die!"

For what seemed an age Boscombe's body jerked and moved on the floor. He tried to turn over, move sideways before his body gave a final shudder. Benjamin kicked at his boots.

"It's a pity, as a prisoner he might have talked."

"Aye," I replied. "And as an assassin he might have killed you."

I turned him over. Boscombe's eyes stared sightlessly up into mine.

"This was no time for the rules of the duel," I exclaimed, pulling my dagger out and wiping it on Boscombe's jerkin. "If he had killed you, what chance would I have had?" I stood up, resheathing my dagger. "I'm glad the bastard's dead!"

Benjamin grasped my shoulder and turned me round.

"I would like to protest, Roger," he declared. "I would like to say it was swordsman against swordsman but I'm glad for what you did: I thank you for that."

Benjamin dropped his own sword and dagger on a table. He then went round the tavern securing the windows and doors.

"Intriguing," he remarked. "Did you notice, Roger? In all the taverns I know, either here or on the Scottish march, the scullions, maids and tapsters sleep on the kitchen floor. Boscombe, however, lived alone and, since we arrived here, no other customers have hired a chamber. The tavern was a mere front," he continued. "A fitting disguise for a man who earned his gold by cutting throats. So now, let's see what proof we can find."

We scoured that tavern from the garret to the cellar but Boscombe was like all the professional killers I have met. A very tidy man, neat and precise. Not a stick was out of place, nothing seemed untoward. At last we broke into his own chamber but, there again there seemed to be nothing

301

remarkable — a sword, a dagger, tavern accounts, some silver and gold in a small chest — until we searched the large aumbry or cupboard which stood beside the bed. It contained more clothes than a simple taverner should have owned. Robes, cloaks, broad-brimmed hats, satin breeches, jerkins of different textures and colours, boots and shoes, wigs and hair-pieces. On the floor at the back was a small chest full of face paints, the sort mummers and players use to daub their faces when making a presentation.

"His disguises," Benjamin remarked. "But what else?"

On a shelf was a sheaf of documents, all associated with the tavern, though we did find bills bearing the marks of Oswald and Imelda for pies and other pastries sold to the Flickering Lamp. We then searched the bed and at last Benjamin's suspicions were proved correct. Behind the chest, at the foot of the small fourposter, was a secret cupboard, noticeable only to someone making a thorough search. Inside were a few personal items: a letter in French, the ink faded; a lock of hair, neatly waxed to the bottom.

"Some lady love," Benjamin remarked.

He pulled out the rest: a receipt from a goldsmith in Nottingham; a gilt-edged dagger and a small box containing about four or five phials. Benjamin sniffed at these and pulled a face.

"Poisons!" he declared.

Finally he pulled out a large flask with a stopper on. Benjamin undid this. He told me to bring a cup from the bedside table and poured a little in. For a while he sniffed at it, then laughed softly.

"What is it?" I asked.

"Valerian," he replied.

"He had trouble sleeping!" I exclaimed.

"I don't think so," Benjamin replied, putting the stopper back in. "Men like Boscombe have no conscience. They sleep like a babe, as did those poor soldiers at Malevel Manor."

13

Benjamin refused to say any more, becoming more concerned about Boscombe's corpse.

"It's important," my master insisted, "that no one at court learns that he has been killed."

We went back to the taproom, took the cadaver and put it in a cellar behind some vats. After that we packed our belongings and collected our horses from the nearby stable.

"Where to, master?" I asked. "Eltham? Westminster?"

"No," Benjamin replied. "Malevel. We need to be there."

We rode through the night. Benjamin showed the guards at the city gates his special pass and we were allowed through. The first streaks of dawn were lighting the sky as we approached Malevel Manor: in the half-light, its shadowy shape reminded me of some animal crouched, ready to spring. Kempe's men were still on guard at the gatehouse. Benjamin told them to stay at their posts and look after our horses whilst we were at the manor. We opened the front door and went in. An eerie place, black as Hell!

The air was stale, yet something else filled my senses. A reek of evil, of wickedness. I wondered if the ghosts of Lady Isabella and the fifteen soldiers slaughtered there watched and waited for justice to be done. Dirt from the cellar still lay heaped on the gallery floor. Dust covered the tables and chairs in the kitchen. For a while Benjamin wandered around: up and down stairs, along galleries. I could hear him as he went, floorboards creaking, the house groaning as if it resented our presence. I sat in the kitchen trying to control my own fears and reflecting on my master's confrontation with Boscombe. Everything had now started to fit into place yet it still didn't explain the mystery surrounding the Orb, or how the dreadful murders at Malevel had been carried out.

Benjamin came back.

"What now, master?" I asked. "And why didn't you tell me about Boscombe?" I challenged.

"Roger, Roger." Benjamin patted me reassuringly on the shoulder. "I didn't really know myself. Only after the attack on you in the church did my suspicions harden into certainty. You see, whilst you were gone, I grew concerned. I went looking for Boscombe, only to find that he himself was nowhere in the tavern."

"But he must have been working with someone else?"

"Yes, yes, he was . . ."

(Well, Benjamin actually did voice his suspicions and now my secretary, that little marmoset, that ticklebrain of a quillpusher, that smelly pudding-bag, is jumping up and down. "Tell me! Tell me!" he cries. I rap him across the knuckles with my new ash cane. A gentle tap to remind him of his duties. I can't tell him now! The Queen would object: she wants my memoirs to be written as events unfolded. I mean, here is my little puddlebrain of a chaplain; who runs to London to watch Coriolanus and Faust: he'd certainly object if someone came on the stage at the beginning of Act Three and said, "Well, that's it! The play has ended, this is what happened!" Ah, the little pudding-bag nods wisely. I have his attention again.)

Benjamin became busy. I just sat rather surprised by what he had told me. However, once my master was immersed in a task, he was deaf to any questioning. Letters were written to Sir Thomas Kempe, Doctor Agrippa, Lord Theodosius and Master Cornelius. Kempe's ruffians at the gatehouse were given a penny each and despatched to deliver them. I went to a small ale-house nearby and bought some provisions: when I returned, Benjamin had cleaned the kitchen, wiping away the dust from the table and chairs.

Kempe was the first to swagger in, accompanied by Agrippa and his lovely bullyboys. The sun had risen and it was good to have the sound of voices shattering the eerie silence of Malevel. Kempe swaggered into the kitchen.

"Well, Daunbey?" He tossed his hat on the table and took a chair at the far end. "You have a solution to this mystery?"

"Of a sorts, Sir Thomas. But, first, Doctor Agrippa."

The warlock looked up expectantly. He sat on the stool to Kempe's right, his face wreathed in a smile like some benevolent parson greeting one of his parishioners.

"Benjamin," he declared, his eyes now blue, dancing with merriment. "I can sense the end of a hunt! So you'll not be sailing on the *Peppercorn*?"

"Perhaps not," I snapped. I glanced at Sir Thomas. "But others might."

"Now, now!" Agrippa stretched out one black-gloved hand, admiring the ring on one of his fingers.

(A little affectation. Agrippa sometimes pushed a blood-red ruby ring over one of his gloved fingers. One of his henchmen once told me that it was a magical ring that housed a demon. I think that was a lie. Agrippa may have had his strange ways but he was as fallible as the rest of us.)

"I have a favour to ask you," Benjamin declared. "Your lovely lads outside . . . ?"

"Ah yes, my little boys."

Agrippa said it in such a way that I wondered about the true relationship between him and some of the rather girlish-looking young men who made up his retinue.

(Oh, don't get me wrong, appearances can be deceptive: as Will put it in the 'Merchant of Venice': 'The world is still deceived with ornament'. Agrippa's men were killers, one and all, professional assassins.)

"I would like to borrow them," Benjamin said.

"To do what?"

"A little game. A military exercise."

Agrippa agreed and called his henchmen into the hall.

"Which of you?" Benjamin asked, studying their grinning faces. "Can move as silently as a shadow? Stick a dagger into a man's back without him even hearing you come?"

A young man, his hair falling in lovelocks down to his shoulders, minced forward looking rather bashful. He had a thin face, clean-shaven, with bright red lips but his eyes were dead.

"I have been known to do that," he offered. He grinned over his shoulder at his comrades.

"Then all of you," Benjamin declared, "apart from this young man, scatter throughout the house. Take a seat in each room. And you? Your name?"

"Robert," 'Lovelocks' replied.

"Ah yes, Robert. Once this is done, see how near you can get to each of your comrades without being discovered."

"And don't steal anything!" I shouted. "I know you lot. A cozening gang, light-fingered . . . !"

"As if we would!" they all chorused back.

"Do as Shallot says!" Agrippa snapped. "No, no, Sir Thomas." Agrippa pressed Kempe back in his chair. "Now is not the time to protest. Let us see what happens?"

The game began. Agrippa's men dispersed. Benjamin told Robert to count to one hundred but the fellow could only go to twenty before he became confused so I had to count for him and then he went hunting. Now 'Lovelocks' could move like a cat but the game soon ended. A shout from a chamber further down the gallery showed he had been apprehended. Benjamin called him and the rest back into the kitchen.

"It's impossible," 'Lovelocks' declared. "The floor is uneven. No footpad, not even a fellow with cloths around his boots, could move round this manor without being detected."

Agrippa thanked and dismissed them.

"Why all these games? This deception?" Kempe snapped.

Benjamin closed the doors. He went and sat at the far end of the table, with myself on his right.

"Deception, Sir Thomas?" he asked. "Deception? How dare you sit there and talk about deception! Where is the Orb of Charlemagne?"

Sir Thomas made to rise.

"Oh, sit down and don't look so aggrieved," Benjamin mocked. "You know full well what I'm talking about, Sir Thomas. The Orb of Charlemagne, the great relic?"

"Are you witless?" Kempe retorted, sliding back in his chair. "It was stolen! Stolen from here. You were given the task of recovering it!"

"Oh, don't be ridiculous!" Benjamin snapped. "How can I recover something that has not been stolen? You have the Orb of Charlemagne." He pointed down the table. "You, Sir Thomas. You've known where it is all the time, whilst we have been chasing moonbeams."

Sir Thomas made to rise again.

"No, you can't leave." Agrippa took off his hat, running his fingers through his raven-black hair. "You will stay, Sir Thomas. Your henchmen may be outside but so are mine."

"You don't know, do you?" Benjamin asked Agrippa. "Not even you, sir, know the truth of this. I am glad because that means Dearest Uncle is also innocent of any deception. Now, Sir Thomas, I shall tell you a story."

Kempe sulked in his chair.

"It won't take long," Benjamin said. "Our noble king was the proud owner of the Orb of Charlemagne. This precious relic had been in the hands of English kings since the time of Alfred. Now, although I love the King dearly, I recognise his anxiety: fourteen years on the throne and he has not produced a living male heir. He would not let so powerful a relic as the Orb be given away so lightly: it would not only be a betrayal of those ancestors who wore the crown of St Edward but also a source of power which the King needs in his daily prayers, that his wife Catherine of Aragon conceive and bear a son."

"Be careful what you say, Daunbey," Kempe warned.

"Oh, I'll be very careful," Benjamin replied. "I am not criticising the King but rather those who give him advice and counsel. For His Grace not only wants an heir, he also wants to humiliate the power of France. Emperor Charles V, nephew of our Queen Catherine of Aragon, has the fleets and armies to do this, and Henry asked for his support. In return instead of an alliance cemented by a marriage or division of the spoils, Charles made one demand, and one demand only: the return of the Orb of Charlemagne which, the Emperor believes, is rightfully his. Is that not true, Doctor?"

Agrippa nodded. "Agreed, agreed!"

"What could Henry do?" Benjamin continued. "If he refused, he wouldn't get the ships and troops and would have made a powerful enemy. Of course, the Emperor's demand was made public, and throughout Christendom interest was reawakened in the Orb. France laid its claim, and so did the Papacy. Both these parties sent envoys to England to counter Imperial pressure on our noble King."

"What has this to do with the theft of the Orb?" Kempe snapped.

"Everything," Benjamin replied. "Henry

312

was now in a quandary. He sought advice. One of his councillors offered a subtle plot. A stratagem which would not only allow Henry to keep the Orb but also mock his enemies abroad and so enrich the Exchequer that England might not need foreign armies and ships."

"Are you talking about me?" Kempe asked sardonically.

"If the cap fits!" I taunted. "Wear it!"

"The plan laid before the King," Benjamin declared, "required precious metals and the work of a master goldsmith. Sir Hubert Berkeley was chosen and sworn to silence. The Orb was taken down to his shops where he was to make a replica. But, once Berkeley had finished one, how many more was he ordered to make? Eh, Sir Thomas? Two, three, four or five? After all, it would cost the King little: golden cups and precious ornaments litter the palaces but not hard cash. Golden artefacts were collected and melted down. The King's jewel house was raided for amethysts and precious stones. And so the replicas were ready. I am speaking the truth, am I not?"

"Finish your tale," Kempe snarled.

"Oh, I'll finish it, Sir Thomas. But, in the end, you must tell the truth. Your plan was as follows. A replica Orb would be handed over to the Lord Egremont made out of genuine gold with precious stones. The work of a cunning goldsmith, it might have been years, if ever, before the Emperor realised he had been fooled. And if he did realise?" Benjamin shrugged. "The English crown would protest its innocence, point out that the genuine Orb had left England and that what had happened to it after that was not their concern."

"And the other replicas?" Agrippa asked.

"Ah well," Benjamin smiled. "Like a trader in a market, Henry had raised interest in the Orb, so why not satisfy it? However, the Imperial envoys had to be satisfied first: a replica Orb was moved here. One of your archers kept you informed and you rejoiced: the replica Orb had been accepted and was closely guarded. The Emperor Charles would be satisfied and the King would get his troops and Imperial gold. Nevertheless, the French were still in London and then matters took a comical turn. You, Sir Thomas, sold another replica to the French. Heaven knows what story you peddled?" Benjamin smoothed the top of the table with his fingers. "Do you know, sir, I suspect the King does not really intend to go to war at all? He'll take Charon's gold and the vast profits he has made in selling these relics to replenish his coffers."

"This is nonsense!" Kempe scoffed.

"No, it isn't," Agrippa intervened. "Our King has a subtle mind. He hates the Emperor Charles. His resentment of the Spanish alliance is only surpassed by his deep contempt for the King of France." Agrippa spread his black gloved hands. "What I say is not treason but the truth."

"The King would love it," I intervened. "He has made fools of his fellow monarchs and a vast profit to boot."

"Of course things went wrong," Benjamin continued. "When the Orb was stolen from Malevel, Henry was furious. Matters might become even more tangled if the Emperor learned that an Orb was now held by the French. The Emperor might even accuse Henry of stealing it himself in order that the French should have it."

"Wouldn't that happen anyway?" Kempe retorted. "If both countries claimed to possess the Orb?"

"Oh no," Benjamin retorted. "If the Emperor had the Orb and the French claimed they had one as well, the King would play both sides off against each other. He would tell the Emperor that the French were only acting as a dog in the manger and, in time, whisper the same response to the French. I am also certain another Orb would have been sold to the Papal Envoys."

"Preposterous!" Kempe sneered.

Thoroughly enjoying myself, I rapped the table with my knuckles.

"Is it, Sir Thomas?" I asked. "Is it really preposterous? What do you know about relics?" I ticked the points off on my fingers. "There are enough pieces of the true cross to build a navy. At least five cities in Spain claim to possess the right arm of St James. The veil that Veronica is supposed to have used to wipe the face of Christ can be venerated in cities from Warsaw to Cadiz. Who would object if there were three Orbs of Charlemagne, with each owner claiming he had the original one?"

"Roger speaks the truth," Agrippa declared. "Very few people have seen the true Orb of Charlemagne. It was stored in a coffer in a secret chamber in the Tower."

"The thefts," Benjamin declared. "Let us return to the thefts. We were ordered to steal the Orb from here. Of course that was nonsense, a mere diversion intended to make the Imperial envoys believe the Orb must be genuine — and Cornelius for one fell into the trap — for otherwise why would Henry send two agents with secret orders to steal it back? However — " Benjamin smiled thinly. "When it was indeed stolen Henry was furious because his plans had been upset. He would have to get the stolen Orb back but how could he do that? If the Imperial envoys had stolen it themselves, and he just gave them a replica, then he'd turn himself into a public mockery. Indeed — " Benjamin leaned back in his chair and stared up at the ceiling, " — Henry might even have suspected that the Orb had been stolen so that the Imperial envoys could establish the truth."

"And if it had been stolen by others?" Agrippa asked.

"The thieves might try to sell it to the French," Benjamin replied. "That's why you, Sir Thomas, moved quickly, ensuring the King made some profit from his trickery. What we have established," Benjamin continued, "is that those who did steal the Orb from Malevel did so to line their pockets. They traded it to Lord Charon who, in turn, sold it to the Papal Envoys. Now that would have infuriated our King: an expected source of profit had been abruptly cut off."

"So?" Agrippa scraped back his chair. He stood up and stretched. "In the end the French have an Orb, the Papal Envoys have an Orb but the one the King is supposed to have given Charles V is missing. Very clever," he commented. "Very subtle."

"And who," Kempe asked, "was responsible?"

"Oh, we'll come to that by and by. But, Sir Thomas, am I speaking the truth?"

"A farrago of lies and tittle-tattle, based on conjecture. All this mummery!" Kempe waved his hands. "Sending Agrippa's men round the house . . . "

"That wasn't mummery," Benjamin intervened. "I have just established proof, at least in my own mind, of how the massacre here took place. Now, Sir Thomas, either you tell me the truth and I'll prove who stole the Orb, or I'll take the swiftest horse and ride direct to my Dearest Uncle." Benjamin leaned on the table, narrowing his eyes. "He doesn't know anything about this, does he? He'll reproach the King for not taking him into his confidence. I will have to tell His Grace what a marvellous opportunity was missed, all frustrated by Sir Thomas Kempe. Who knows, Sir Thomas," Benjamin added. "Could you prove to the King that you acted wisely in these matters? Suspicion might fall on you. You know I am speaking the truth. You have Sir Hubert Berkeley's accounts, which show how long Sir Hubert was working on this matter. At court there are many suspicious minds, and the

King himself, in certain moods, will suspect anyone. He might ask how many orbs were really made, and whether Sir Thomas Kempe was engaged in a little private profit?"

"How dare you?" Kempe sprang to his feet.

"Oh, quite easily, and sit down!" Benjamin snapped. "I'm not accusing you but others might."

Kempe was no fool. He would have liked to have swept out of the room. However, such dramatic gestures might look fitting in certain circumstances but Benjamin's words must have chilled his sly heart. The Great Beast trusted no one and, once suspicion was sown in his wicked brain, it always came to full flower! Kempe sat down and breathed in deeply.

"What I tell you," he began, "is the King's own secret. Henry does not want Imperial ships. Oh, he'll take the gold but you won't see English troops in France." He licked his lips. "Henry is more concerned that he has no heir. The Queen, how can I put it, is past child-bearing. There is only the Princess Mary."

(So, in that dusty, shabby room at Malevel I heard the first rumble of the storm that was about to break. And what a storm! Slowly, surely, Henry was about to take those steps which would deluge the kingdom in blood; send men like More and Fisher to the block; tear England from the Church of Rome; cause the north to rise in bloody revolt; and queens to be accused of treason and barbarously hacked to death. Merlin's prophecy was about to be fulfilled.)

Kempe appeared to be lost in his own thoughts, perhaps even he was fearful.

"Continue," Agrippa said quietly.

"Henry cannot understand why God has not given him a male heir," Kempe continued in a rush. "He has studied the Bible. He believes his marriage is cursed because Catherine was once married to his elder brother Arthur."

"But the marriage was never consummated," Benjamin declared. "Arthur was a mere stripling. A weak, sickly child."

"Who told you that?" Kempe retorted. "Has Dearest Uncle confided in you?" Kempe pointed a finger. "Master Daunbey, you should be very careful. The King believes otherwise. He believes the marriage was consummated: accordingly, he should never have married Catherine of Aragon and that's why his marriage has been cursed and is without a male heir."

So, there it was. Henry had tired of Catherine. He had consulted with God and realised that he should not have married her in the first place. Now Henry's brain was a box of teeming worms. He often found it very difficult to draw a distinction between his will and that of God. Once he had got it into his fat head that God was displeased with him, or that God wanted him to do something, then nothing on earth would stop it, as thousands found to their cost.

"Is that why His Excellency the Cardinal has not been informed of these matters?" Agrippa asked.

"Yes, yes it is," Kempe retorted. "The King — " He paused. "His Grace believes he should marry again."

"And who's the lucky girl?" I quipped before I could stop myself.

"Haven't you learned your lesson, Shallot? Are you so clod-witted? Don't you remember the banquet where the King gave you a present, a German hunting dog that was supposed to rip your balls off? It wasn't because you won a riddle — the King caught you making eyes at his beloved!"

I recalled Anne Boleyn. Kempe was right. Henry was jealous and I had paid the price for my little flirtation.

"Boleyn?" Benjamin exclaimed.

"Anne Boleyn. The King is smitten with her," Kempe replied. "You know some of the game, Master Daunbey, but not all of it. Of course, the King would like to make a profit. Of course, he will take gold from the Empire, from the Papacy, from the French. Aye, even from the Devil himself! But it's not money the King is really after — or even to take his armies to France. He wants a divorce. Charles V is Catherine's nephew. He'll have to be persuaded to support the King."

"And, of course, the same is true of the Holy Father in Rome?" Benjamin asked.

"Precisely. Not to mention the French. The University of Paris, and the French cardinals will be asked for an opinion and the King wants them to agree with him. Now," Kempe continued, "about fifteen months ago, I hatched a scheme whereby the King could win Imperial favour, not to mention gold, and at the same time woo the French and the Papacy as well as make them pay. Henry was delighted. He laughed till the tears rolled down his cheeks. He said he would relish till his dying day how we had fooled them all in one fell swoop."

"As well as win a new wife to boot," I interjected.

"Of course," Kempe smiled. "And it really didn't take much. Henry raided his treasury and cups, plate and dishes were melted down. The royal jewel house was rifled, and appropriate amethysts given to Berkeley, who was sworn to silence. He was given a glimpse of the real Orb, provided with precise drawings by me and set to work on the King's secret assignment. I then let it be known in the Empire, in France and in Rome that the Orb of Charlemagne was for sale. They all rose like fish to the bait. The King, of course, had chosen to do business with Emperor Charles. Lord Theodosius of Egremont arrived in England. I thought there would be no difficulty." He paused at the sound of horses outside.

"That will be Lord Egremont," Benjamin declared. "Agrippa, can you keep him busy?"

The good doctor agreed and left.

"Naturally, the theft upset the King," Kempe continued. "Not to mention myself. Can't you see, it's the one thing we hadn't planned on? No one was to steal that Orb: the King's merriment soon turned to anger."

"And you know nothing else?" Benjamin asked.

"All I know, you now know," Kempe concluded. "Naturally, the King has been mollified by the treasure found in Lord Charon's stronghold. To a certain extent the King received his profits from the Papacy with interest and, of course, the French, having paid a small fortune, also believe they have the true Orb."

"Very well." Benjamin got up and unhitched his cloak from the back of the chair. "Sir Thomas, I am going to unmask the assassin. To do that, I need your co-operation. Whatever I say, you will agree to. Understood?"

Kempe swallowed his pride and nodded. Benjamin went to the door and opened it. Lord Egremont, followed by Master Cornelius, almost knocked him aside as he swept into the room.

"What is it?" he snapped, glaring at me as if he'd like to take my head.

Kempe vacated his chair. Egremont took it, throwing his cloak and hat at Agrippa. The good doctor picked them up and tossed them unceremoniously on to a bench.

"Sit down, my lord." Benjamin returned to his own chair. "Sir Thomas, too, and Master Cornelius, by my side."

"You've found the Orb?" Egremont asked.

"No, I am afraid I haven't," Benjamin replied. "Boscombe has that."

"Who?"

"Boscombe, the tavern-keeper at the Flickering Lamp."

"What has that knave got to do with it?"

"That knave," Benjamin repeated. "That

knave, my lord? Do you know him?"

Egremont shifted in the chair.

"You should," Benjamin continued. "His real name is Jakob von Archetel, a former member of the Noctales." Benjamin turned to Cornelius. "I believe he fled the Empire. What was he nicknamed, the Slaughterer? He's responsible for the murders here at Malevel."

Oh, to see the confusion break out! To watch virtue outraged! Oh, the huffing and the puffing! Agrippa sat like an imp come to judgement. Egremont made to leave but the good doctor shook his head.

"Stay, sir! Stay or you'll be arrested! My men are outside."

I glanced at Cornelius and he threw me a look. Isn't it strange how in a few seconds you can learn something? I did then, in that one glance! Firstly, Cornelius was innocent of any crime. Secondly, and rather surprisingly, he hated Egremont. Cornelius got up, took out his sword and laid it on the table with its point towards Egremont. He shouted something in German. Egremont replied, his face now suffused with rage yet he was fearful. This shouting match went on for a few minutes until Cornelius dipped inside his cloak and brought out a small, purple wax seal. He held this up and jabbed a finger at Egremont who sullenly sat down. He knew he was trapped but, even at that moment, did not realise what great danger he was in.

"Master Daunbey," Cornelius declared. "I have told my Lord of Egremont that he is to stay. Unbeknown to him I carry the Emperor's personal seal."

"Why?" Agrippa asked. "I thought Egremont headed this embassy to the English court?"

Cornelius sat down. "Oh, he is here for the Orb of Charlemagne but I am the Emperor's personal emissary to his beloved aunt, Catherine of Aragon." He grinned openly at Kempe. "I bring her the Emperor's most tender regards. Indeed, the Emperor has deigned to choose me, his most humble of servants, to have secret talks with his beloved aunt."

"About what?" Kempe shouted, then his hand went to his lips as if regretting what he had said.

"Oh come, come, Sir Thomas," Cornelius jibed. "Your king has his secrets and so has the Emperor. Master Daunbey, would you please continue?"

Benjamin waved round the kitchen. "Malevel is a lonely, deserted manor house. When the Orb was brought here, I wondered why it had been decided to keep it under strict security in such a place?"

"It was well protected and guarded!" Egremont shouted.

"You could have asked the King to keep it under guard until you sailed."

"Impossible!" Egremont retorted. "The Orb was the Emperor's. It was in my care. It was my duty to decide how best it be guarded until the Imperial ships arrived in the Thames."

"Good." Benjamin smiled thinly. "I am glad you have conceded that Malevel Manor was your choice. The guards placed there were at your behest. The leader of the Noctales, Jonathan, answered directly to you."

Egremont just stared back.

"Now, this is what happened," Benjamin continued. "You are not a German, my Lord Egremont, you are from Hainault. You have studied in England. Years ago Von Archetel fled to England. If the Imperial records are searched I am sure it will be found that some link between you and this Von Archetel exists. During your stay in England you and he, now calling himself Boscombe, communicated. You probably have no love for the Empire or its Emperor and being sent here to collect the Orb was a temptation you could not resist. You wanted it for yourself. You and your accomplice would steal it, sell it and make a small fortune whilst the English Crown and its servants would be held responsible."

"You have proof of this?" Cornelius asked.

"Oh, yes, we have proof, haven't we, Sir Thomas?"

Kempe nodded.

"Let's go back to when the Orb was moved here," Benjamin continued. "Do you remember? People milling about, then the doors of the manor were secured. What we didn't know was that you, my Lord of Egremont, had brought in your own special assassin, the taverner we know as Boscombe. God knows how he was dressed — in the garb of a Noctale or probably as one of your retinue. It wouldn't have been hard as Boscombe is a master of disguises. Anyway, he hid in the cellar."

Egremont sneered but the shift of his eyes showed his surprise.

"Now, of course, Boscombe didn't stay there all the time. He had to eat and drink. So he made contact with Jonathan, who would accept him."

"I don't think so," Cornelius intervened.

"No, listen," Benjamin continued. "Boscombe, by birth and upbringing, was a

Hainaulter. He is fluent in the tongue so he could dismiss very quickly any suspicions that he was an English spy. I suspect as well that he carried a letter from my Lord of Egremont." Benjamin waved his hand. "Saying that he was on a secret assignment to help the Noctales, so his presence must not be revealed to anyone."

"Yes . . ." Cornelius said. "If this man Boscombe spoke fluent Hainault and carried a letter from my Lord of Egremont which hinted at possible treachery on the part of the English . . . Yes, Jonathan would have accepted such an order."

"After that it would be easy," Benjamin continued. "Of course, Jonathan would also have received secret instructions to tell no one outside the manor house, including you, Master Cornelius. Nevertheless, he had been alerted to the possibility of treachery, and was both nervous and withdrawn as a result." Benjamin coughed to clear his throat. "Once Jonathan accepted that letter, everything fell into place."

"And if Jonathan hadn't accepted it?" Agrippa interrupted. "If he protested, made Boscombe's presence known?"

"Then Egremont could have explained it away," Benjamin replied. "However, Boscombe was safe in the cellar. Jonathan would have supplied him with food. On the second day, according to the notes listing the quantity of cooking ingredients used, Imelda and Oswald began to make slightly more of everything. I suspect this was at Jonathan's orders because he had another mouth to feed. Now the days passed, any reservations Jonathan had would be allayed, and then Boscombe struck. One evening, before the small garrison gathered for their supper at nine, he went into the kitchen and poured valerian into the ale cask." Benjamin shrugged. "Dressed in the gown and cowl of a Noctale, he would not alert suspicion and he was only there for a short while. He lifted the cork from the bung-hole and poured the potion in. Remember, Boscombe is a taverner, an assassin and a master of disguise: he'd have chosen his moment carefully. Now, valerian is a powerful sleeping drug; within an hour the entire garrison was fast asleep. Drugged so deeply that Boscombe could move round the manor at will. And if someone, perhaps, didn't drink, Boscombe a professional assassin, with surprise on his side could soon take care of them."

"But we found corpses all over the manor," Kempe declared.

"Of course we did," Benjamin replied. "That's because Boscombe had all night to arrange matters. He dragged the bodies from the kitchen, placed them in different locations and then he killed them: this one with a dagger, another with an arbalest. Those poor soldiers were so drugged they would never even know they were dying: that's why we found no sign of any struggle, not even token resistance. Boscombe still had to be careful, any crash, any cry might have alerted the dogs outside. He also retrieved Egremont's letter from Jonathan's body and tidied up the kitchen. He took especial care with the blackjacks to remove any stains or odour of the valerian. He poured the rest of the ale down the privy, washed out the keg and returned to the kitchen."

Egremont sat at the far end of the table looking down at his fingers, playing with his rings, moving them to catch the poor light.

"The Orb was taken out of its casket," Benjamin continued. "Boscombe had cleaned any traces of his presence from the cellar and he hid there until the alarm was raised. We broke into the house, Lord Egremont with us." He pointed down the table. "You, my Lord, had left strict instructions, that if the alarm was raised, the doors to Malevel were not to be opened without you being present. When we entered the manor, confusion reigned with servants and retainers milling about. Boscombe, now clothed in his disguise as Egremont's retainer, joined them. Don't you remember Egremont sending people hither and thither? Boscombe just walked out of the house, took a horse and rode back into the city. We, of course, were confronted with the mystery of how fifteen soldiers could be brutally slain and the Orb stolen, without us finding any trace of how the killers had carried out their gruesome task."

"Except for old Castor?" I intervened.

"Yes, on reflection, the dog had more sense than us: he smelt the food Boscombe must have taken down into the cellar. In such a confined, closed space the dog could still detect the odour. In the end we discovered something else which distracted us; in digging out that corpse, we also destroyed any traces of Boscombe's stay in the cellar.

"It's true, isn't it?" Kempe taunted Egremont. "It's true what Daunbey says? When we arrived here, both before and after the murders, your retainers were swarming about, no one would stop any of them."

"When I met Boscombe at the Flickering Lamp," Benjamin declared. "There was something about his face, his walk . . . I was sure I had seen him before. Now I know that I caught a glimpse of him when we entered Malevel after the alarm was raised."

He sighed. "But that is in hindsight. At the time, no one would have suspected his presence, all he had to do in the confusion was walk out of the door and take horse."

"Why was the goldsmith tortured and killed?" Cornelius asked abruptly.

"Ah!" Benjamin glanced quickly at me.

"I think," I intervened smoothly, "that Egremont and Boscombe were intent on ensuring the Orb was the genuine relic, which is why they also murdered Henley the relic-seller. Once he had validated the Orb, he had to be silenced. Berkeley was next: they had to be sure their relic was genuine before they approached a prospective buyer."

Lord be thanked that Cornelius did not realise how many replicas there were, or the real truth behind Henley's death!

"It is obvious," I continued, "that a leading goldsmith like Sir Hubert Berkeley would never go out and meet someone like Boscombe. Sir Thomas didn't send him the invitation, and neither did my master. However, Berkeley would accept an invitation from Lord Egremont. The goldsmith, still observing his vow of secrecy, went along but, instead of meeting Lord Egremont or Master Cornelius, Boscombe the Schlachter was waiting. Berkeley was pinioned, taken to that lonely place and brutally questioned. Lord Egremont, of course, was elsewhere, well seen by all, whilst his accomplice was busy torturing and interrogating Berkeley to find the truth."

"They snuffed out Berkeley's life," Benjamin declared, "and then they sold the Orb to the outlaw leader, Lord Charon. Do you remember Lord Egremont involving himself in that fight in the sewers? He wanted to make sure that the Orb had gone. Of course it had, sold to the Papal Envoys."

"So the Orb is in Rome or shortly will be?" Cornelius asked testily.

"No," my master smiled. "By a very clever subterfuge, Sir Thomas's agents at Dover replaced the genuine Orb with a replica. Isn't that right, Sir Thomas?"

Kempe, all smug and righteous, nodded solemnly.

"The Orb has been brought back to London," he declared sonorously. "But, Master Daunbey told me to keep it a secret."

"Lord Egremont, you are a traitor and an assassin," Benjamin said, getting to his feet. "You are responsible for the deaths of six English archers and nine of your own countrymen. Men with families, lovers, wives and children. You and Boscombe killed, and killed mercilessly, for the sake of filthy gain."

"You have no proof," Egremont shouted back, half rising. "Not one shred of evidence."

"Oh, but we have," Benjamin replied. "Boscombe is in the Tower suing for a royal pardon. He has told us everything, including details of his former life. He even told us where we can find the valerian he used, in a secret compartment in his chamber. He blames you, holds you responsible . . . " Benjamin looked at Kempe. "Your men hold him closely, don't they?"

"He's in Byward Tower," Kempe retorted. "And has been since late last night."

"He holds you responsible, Lord Theodosius," Benjamin taunted. "He even claims you forced him to do it."

"He's a villain and a liar!" Egremont shouted back. "It was his idea from the start!" He stood up and breathed in deeply. "I am not a subject of your king," he declared.

"So what will you do, my lord?" Kempe taunted. "Ride down to the Thames and take ship to France?"

"I'll deny everything."

"Theodosius, Lord of Egremont." Cornelius got to his feet, holding out the purple seal.

"In my eyes you are guilty of high treason. My men will arrest you and take you back to the Emperor, where you and your family will suffer for your crimes. However, if you confess now . . . "

Egremont rose and turned his back to us, staring at the wall as if he did not want us to see the expression on his face.

"I confess." He did not turn round. "I confess, Master Cornelius, to save my family in the Empire. I do not want them to suffer for what I have done." He turned and came back to sit in his chair. "I was born in Hainault," he began defiantly, "and have always found it difficult to acknowledge the authority of the Hapsburgs, and being despatched here and there as the Emperor's lackey. Many years ago, Master Cornelius, before you joined the Noctales, I met Jakob von Archetel, a clever, subtle clerk. He stole a relic and murdered its owner. He was tried, found guilty, sentenced to death and was imprisoned in the dungeons of a small castle outside Dordrecht overlooking the sea. I helped him to escape. When I came to England, Von Archetel and I met again. I sometimes used him to collect information about the English court. Boscombe, as he now called himself, was deeply interested in relics. Time and again he'd talk of the Orb of Charlemagne." He paused as if choosing his words.

I recalled Agrippa's warning that interest in that famous relic was rife amongst London's underworld. I now knew the reason.

"I couldn't believe my luck," Egremont continued, "when the Emperor chose me to go to England to receive the Orb from your king. I wrote to Von Archetel, who suggested Malevel as an appropriate setting for our scheme."

"Thank you," Benjamin spoke up. "I always wondered, as I put the pieces of the puzzle together, how a lord from Hainault would know so much about this manor."

"We were going to steal the Orb and sell it," Egremont continued. "We would divide the profits: Boscombe wanted to move on, and I decided to use the gold we earned to leave the Imperial service."

"Did you know Lord Charon?" Benjamin asked.

"No, but Boscombe did. He said the outlaws would pay a good price. When we attacked Charon in his cavern I had to make sure he was dead." He smiled grimly. "But your dog took care of that. And you, Master Daunbey and Shallot, who must be the luckiest man alive, took care of the rest. Ah well!" He shrugged. "*Sic transit gloria mundi*. Boscombe was as guilty as I — the bastard should die!"

"Theodosius, Lord of Egremont." Master Cornelius walked towards him. "You are an envoy of his most Imperial Highness. Sir Thomas, is it not true that this manor was given into our care?"

"Yes, yes, it was," Kempe replied.

"So, in theory, we are within the Imperial jurisdiction?"

"According to all diplomatic protocols," Kempe replied, his eyes watchful as he sensed what was coming next. "Yes, this is Imperial territory."

"In which case," Cornelius pointed to Egremont. "you, Lord Theodosius, have been accused, have confessed and been found guilty of treason and heinous murder. You are sentenced to death. I, by carrying this seal, have the Imperial authority to see it done!" Cornelius drew himself up. "Sentence is to be carried out immediately!"

Egremont's face went white. He clutched the back of his chair.

"You have no authority," he gasped.

"I have every authority, sir."

Benjamin went to stop him but Cornelius knocked his hand away.

"The law is on my side." He turned and shouted an order.

The Noctales who had accompanied him crowded into the room. He spoke to them in German, showing them the seal. The Noctales seized Egremont, plucking off his chain of office and taking off his war-belt. Egremont shouted something in German. Cornelius paused and nodded, then Egremont was thrust out of the room. Kempe made to protest but Cornelius ignored him.

"One of my men is a priest," he declared, "so he will be shriven and then he will die."

He swept out of the room, and Kempe followed, with Agrippa trailing behind. Benjamin and I just sat and listened. We heard the sound of footsteps going out through the front door, and Cornelius shouting for a log to be brought from the store behind the manor. There was chattering, the murmur of voices, and then Cornelius shouted in German. This was followed by silence, cut short by the sound of a loud thump. A little later Cornelius came back into the hall. In one hand he held his bloody sword, in the other, Lord Egremont's cloak which he was using to wipe the weapon. He re-sheathed his sword and stared at us.

"Imperial justice has been done. Egremont's remains will be sent to St Mary of Bethlehem, north of the Tower. If his family want his body returned, they will have to pay for it." He pulled the cowl over his head, pushing his arms up the voluminous sleeves of his gown. He walked towards us. "Master Daunbey, I thank you. The Emperor will make his pleasure known."

"You are a hard man, Master Cornelius," Benjamin replied.

"I am his Imperial Highness's most humble servant."

Cornelius's words were tinged with humour. "Egremont was not a traitor," he continued. "He was just a thief. If I have understood Sir Thomas correctly, King Henry would have blamed both of you for what happened and I and the Noctales would have returned to Germany in disgrace." Cornelius took his hands out of his sleeves. "Egremont deserved to die, yet his was a more merciful death than that of poor Berkeley." He smiled and, leaning over, brushed some dust from my shoulders. "Sir Thomas seems a little confused." He grinned. "Boscombe isn't really in the Tower, is he?"

"No," Benjamin replied. "He's dead. I killed him last night and hid his corpse in the cellar of the Flickering Lamp."

"I'll go there," Cornelius replied. "I want to make sure the Slaughterer is really dead."

"And then?" I asked.

Cornelius struggled to keep his face straight.

"Tonight I shall take the Imperial Orb from Sir Thomas and, tomorrow, I shall leave on the first available ship — no more of this nonsense. The Emperor will be pleased to see his great relic."

"Are you sure it will be the genuine one?" (Old Shallot couldn't resist the taunt.)

Cornelius bowed his head, his shoulders shaking with laughter.

"Come, Roger! Master Daunbey, please excuse us."

Cornelius took me by the shoulder and led me through the hall and out into the courtyard. The Noctales were bustling about; Egremont's retainers already had the bloody corpse wrapped in a roll of blankets. One groom was taking away the log whilst another was bringing buckets of water to wash away the pool of blood congealing there. Kempe, Agrippa and others of their party had now gathered under the gateway.

"You wished to have words with me, Master Cornelius?"

The Noctale led me along the side of the house.

"You remind me of my brother, Roger." He stopped and faced me squarely. "Though you have more than his luck. You and your

341

master unmasked a traitor. The Emperor will be well pleased." He poked me playfully in the chest. "You will always be welcome in the Empire." His face grew serious. "I will also give you a warning. Your king is planning to divorce Catherine of Aragon, my master's aunt. Whatever Henry tries to bribe him with, the Emperor will not agree to this. Imperial troops will soon be in Rome: the Pope will not grant that divorce. Cardinal Thomas Wolsey will bear the brunt of your king's fury and, when that happens, remember the German proverb, 'If lightning strikes, don't shelter under the tallest tree'." He clasped my hand. "And as for relics," he whispered, "Roger, who really gives a fig?" The Noctale grinned. "I know there's a great deal about this Orb which you, Master Benjamin and Sir Thomas have not told us. Why was Henley really killed, and Sir Hubert? What is the real secret of the Orb?" He shrugged. "But, in the end, what does it really matter? True religion is a matter of the heart, not the pocket." And then that strange man walked away, shouting for his retainers.

Oh, I have met the Noctales since but that's another story. Suffice to say they discovered Boscombe's corpse and, within the day, it was gibbeted at Tyburn for

342

all to see. A short while later the Imperial envoys left the English court. Benjamin and I took lodgings in a different tavern until the Great Beast summoned us to call on him. Oh, he was in his most generous of moods! It was 'dearest Benjamin' and 'most beloved Roger'. He pawed and he kissed me. I could understand why: in his eyes, everything had gone according to plan and Henry was now a richer man: all Berkeley's goods and wealth came to him for the man had been a bachelor; Lord Charon's treasure was now in the Exchequer and, of course, the Flickering Lamp tavern, another source of wealth, also fell forfeit to the Crown. The Great Bastard loved treason: it meant forfeiture of all the traitor's goods and made him richer. Benjamin and I were given purses of gold and assurances of friendship.

"And don't worry, Roger," the King shouted down to us at a banquet. "There'll be no sea voyages for you on the *Peppercorn*. Go back, my faithful dogs!" he intoned dramatically. "Go back and enjoy your well-earned rest!"

Beside him Tom Wolsey was not so happy. Oh, he forced a smile but I could see he was worried and I recalled Cornelius's warning.

Just before we left London, Wolsey called me to his private chamber. This was not so proud Tom, the great Cardinal: his purple robes were doffed and he sat in black hose and open-neck shirt, fanning himself on a window seat. He looked like some prosperous merchant rather than a Prince of the Church.

"Come in, dear Roger." He waved me to the cushioned seat beside him and offered me a bowl of cherries. "They are ripe and fresh," he explained. "They clean the mouth and are good for the digestive system." He stared out through the half-open window, breathing in the fragrance from the rose garden. "You know, Roger," he began, "there's a point in time in every man's fortunes when there is a subtle change, like a ship at sea as the wind shifts and blows from another direction." He leaned over and patted my hand. "That is what is happening to me, Roger. The King wants a divorce. When he doesn't get it the King will blame me."

He took back the bowl of cherries and started popping them into his mouth.

"Isn't life strange?" he murmured as he chewed slowly. Do you remember when you first came to court, Roger, and I sent you to Scotland over that business of the White Rose? The court laughed at you then but now the King trusts and likes you. Anne Boleyn trusts and likes you.

Catherine of Aragon trusts and likes you. Cardinal de Medici trusts and likes you. Benjamin Daunbey trusts and likes you. Tom Wolsey trusts and likes you." He laughed.

"Don't you think it amusing? Shallot the villain trusted by all these great ones?"

"Fortune is fickle, your Grace," I murmured.

"Oh, I haven't brought you here to beg for your help." Wolsey put the bowl down and closed the window. "First, I thank you over this business of the Orb. You and Benjamin did well. Secondly, Roger my friend, when I fall, I'll fall like Lucifer, never to rise again. So look after Benjamin. Guard his back."

He extended his hand as a sign the meeting was over. I went down on one knee and kissed his ring. I was almost at the door when he called me back.

"Roger, this Poppleton business? Benjamin has told me about it." He raised one eyebrow. "Is there anything I can do to help?"

I paused. My eye caught a wall painting at the far end of the chamber, a dolphin leaping above a blue sea.

"Why yes, your Grace." I closed the door and came back.

★ ★ ★

By the end of that week we were back at our manor. I put flowers on Lucy's grave and paid a local mason to carve a stone. I gave Vicar Doggerel five pounds sterling to say Masses as surety for her soul. On the second Sunday back, I strolled down to the White Harte tavern and sat in a corner of the taproom, watching the hated Poppletons hold court. I was just in time. A short while later, the Cardinal's messengers, who had been staying at the manor overnight, came into the taproom. They were all officious, with their cloaks thrown over their shoulders, and their swords slapping against their thighs. Their leader, one of Agrippa's lovely boys, clapped his hands and stood in the centre of the taproom.

"Edmund and Robert Poppleton!" he declaimed.

My two enemies stepped forward. The 'lovely boy' thrust letters into their hands.

"The Cardinal's warrants," he declared. "The King has decided to show you great favour. He is sending his ship the *Peppercorn* down the west coast of Africa. Two gentlemen are needed to serve as officers. You have been chosen and, on your loyalty, must accept."

Oh riches! Oh sweet revenge! Oh darling Tom and his lovely boys! The Poppletons could not object. They were gone within the week. The *Peppercorn* left at the end of September and, I am sad to report, has never been seen since. So, Lucy now lies in her grave avenged. And Castor's brave spirit roams the fields of Heaven. Since then, the only dogs I have ever owned have been of the same breed. If you go into Burpham Church you will notice a carving on the wall. To one side is a very good likeness of Lucy Witherspoon and, on the other, the shaggy, massive head of brave Castor. Oh, my eyes weep, my heart breaks for, indeed, they have all gone into the darkness. Only old Shallot stays watching the sun dip behind the trees. A cold breeze has sprung up. My chaplain is getting tired and I need more claret to face the terrors of the night.

Author's Note

The Orb of Charlemagne may be just a legend but the English medieval kings did own (and keep hidden) just such secret and sacred relics. In his diary, Samuel Pepys makes reference to these and how they may have been destroyed by Cromwell under the Protectorate. However, Pepys and Shallot had much in common: in another part of his voluminous diaries, Pepys talks of such sacred, royal relics being hidden somewhere in the Tower, secreted in a pit — for all this author knows, they may include the Orb of Charlemagne and still be there!

Michael Clynes

McLEAN AT THE GOLDEN OWL
George Goodchild

Inspector McLean has resigned from Scotland Yard's CID and has opened an office in Wimpole Street. With the help of his able assistant, Tiny, he solves many crimes, including those of kidnapping, murder and poisoning.

KATE WEATHERBY
Anne Goring

Derbyshire, 1849: The Hunter family are the arrogant, powerful masters of Clough Grange. Their feuds are sparked by a generation of guilt, despair and ill-fortune. But their passions are awakened by the arrival of nineteen-year-old Kate Weatherby.

A VENETIAN RECKONING
Donna Leon

When the body of a prominent international lawyer is found in the carriage of an intercity train, Commissario Guido Brunetti begins to dig deeper into the secret lives of the once great and good.

A TASTE FOR DEATH
Peter O'Donnell

Modesty Blaise and Willie Garvin take on impossible odds in the shape of Simon Delicata, the man with a taste for death, and Swordmaster, Wenczel, in a terrifying duel. Finally, in the Sahara desert, the intrepid pair must summon every killing skill to survive.

SEVEN DAYS FROM MIDNIGHT
Rona Randall

In the Comet Theatre, London, seven people have good reason for wanting beautiful Maxine Culver out of the way. Each one has reason to fear her blackmail. But whose shadow is it that lurks in the wings, waiting to silence her once and for all?

QUEEN OF THE ELEPHANTS
Mark Shand

Mark Shand knows about the ways of elephants, but he is no match for the tiny Parbati Barua, the daughter of India's greatest expert on the Asian elephant, the late Prince of Gauripur, who taught her everything. Shand sought out Parbati to take part in a film about the plight of the wild herds today in north-east India.

THE DARKENING LEAF
Caroline Stickland

On storm-tossed Chesil Bank in 1847, the young lovers, Philobeth and Frederick, prevent wreckers mutilating the apparent corpse of a young woman. Discovering she is still alive, Frederick takes her to his grandmother's home. But the rescue is to have violent and far-reaching effects . . .

A WOMAN'S TOUCH
Emma Stirling

When Fenn went to stay on her uncle's farm in Africa, the lovely Helena Starr seemed to resent her — especially when Dr Jason Kemp agreed to Fenn helping in his bush hospital. Though it seemed Jason saw Fenn as little more than a child, her feelings for him were those of a woman.

A DEAD GIVEAWAY
Various Authors

This book offers the perfect opportunity to sample the skills of five of the finest writers of crime fiction — Clare Curzon, Gillian Linscott, Peter Lovesey, Dorothy Simpson and Margaret Yorke.

DOUBLE INDEMNITY — MURDER FOR INSURANCE
Jad Adams

This is a collection of true cases of murderers who insured their victims then killed them — or attempted to. Each tense, compelling account tells a story of cold-blooded plotting and elaborate deception.

THE PEARLS OF COROMANDEL
By Keron Bhattacharya

John Sugden, an ambitious young Oxford graduate, joins the Indian Civil Service in the early 1920s and goes to uphold the British Raj. But he falls in love with a young Hindu girl and finds his loyalties tragically divided.

WHITE HARVEST
Louis Charbonneau

Kathy McNeely, a marine biologist, sets out for Alaska to carry out important research. But when she stumbles upon an illegal ivory poaching operation that is threatening the world's walrus population, she soon realises that she will have to survive more than the harsh elements . . .

TO THE GARDEN ALONE
Eve Ebbett

Widow Frances Morley's short, happy marriage was childless, and in a succession of borders she attempts to build a substitute relationship for the husband and family she does not have. Over all hovers the shadow of the man who terrorized her childhood.

CONTRASTS
Rowan Edwards

Julia had her life beautifully planned — she was building a thriving pottery business as well as sharing her home with her friend Pippa, and having fun owning a goat. But the goat's problems brought the new local vet, Sebastian Trent, into their lives.

MY OLD MAN AND THE SEA
David and Daniel Hays

Some fathers and sons go fishing together. David and Daniel Hays decided to sail a tiny boat seventeen thousand miles to the bottom of the world and back. Together, they weave a story of travel, adventure, and difficult, sometimes terrifying, sailing.

SQUEAKY CLEAN
James Pattinson

An important attribute of a prospective candidate for the United States presidency is not to have any dirt in your background which an eager muckraker can dig up. Senator William S. Gallicauder appeared to fit the bill perfectly. But then a skeleton came rattling out of an English cupboard.

NIGHT MOVES
Alan Scholefield

It was the first case that Macrae and Silver had worked on together. Malcolm Underdown had brutally stabbed to death Edward Craig and had attempted to murder Craig's fiancée, Jane Harrison. He swore he would be back for her. Now, four years later, he has simply walked from the mental hospital. Macrae and Silver must get to him — before he gets to Jane.

GREATEST CAT STORIES
Various Authors

Each story in this collection is chosen to show the cat at its best. James Herriot relates a tale about two of his cats. Stella Whitelaw has written a very funny story about a lion. Other stories provide examples of courageous, clever and lucky cats.

THE HAND OF DEATH
Margaret Yorke

The woman had been raped and murdered. As the police pursue their relentless inquiries, decent, gentle George Fortescue, the typical man-next-door, finds himself accused. While the real killer serenely selects his third victim — and then his fourth . . .

VOW OF FIDELITY
Veronica Black

Sister Joan of the Daughters of Compassion is shocked to discover that three of her former fellow art college students have recently died violently. When another death occurs, Sister Joan realizes that she must pit her wits against a cunning and ruthless killer.

MARY'S CHILD
Irene Carr

Penniless and desperate, Chrissie struggles to support herself as the Victorian years give way to the First World War. Her childhood friends, Ted and Frank, fall hopelessly in love with her. But there is only one man Chrissie loves, and fate and one man bent on revenge are determined to prevent the match . . .

THE SWIFTEST EAGLE
Alice Dwyer-Joyce

This book moves from Scotland to Malaya — before British Raj and now — and then to war-torn Vietnam and Cambodia . . . Virginia meets Gareth casually in the Western Isles, with no inkling of the sacrifice he must make for her.

VICTORIA & ALBERT
Richard Hough

Victoria and Albert had nine children and the family became the archetype of the nineteenth century. But the relationship between the Queen and her Prince Consort was passionate and turbulent; thunderous rows threatened to tear them apart, but always reconciliation and love broke through.

BREEZE: WAIF OF THE WILD
Marie Kelly

Bernard and Marie Kelly swapped their lives in London for a remote farmhouse in Cumbria. But they were to undergo an even more drastic upheaval when a two-day-old fragile roe deer fawn arrived on their doorstep. The knowledge of how to care for her was learned through sleepless nights and anxiety-filled days.